"**What do the doctors say about your long-term** prognosis?"

She shrugged. "Too. Soon." After a moment she added, "They're being optimistic. So. I. Don't. Give. Up."

He couldn't imagine her doing that. Even now, looking like she'd gone twenty rounds with Mike Tyson, she acted ready to take on the world. "You've been through so much, angel. It just isn't fair."

She barked a laugh. "Haven't. You. Heard? Life. Not. Fair."

"But you've had more than your share of trouble."

"Everything happens—for a reason." She let out a breath. "Mrs. Brooks says, 'God doesn't. Give. More. Than. We. Can. Bear.'"

Never a particularly religious man, he especially didn't like when a person tried to shove their beliefs on to others. From what he knew about the formidable Mrs. Brooks, the woman from a privileged background hadn't had much in her life to put her theory to the test. "If that's true, then God must think you're a badass."

Mia covered her smile with one hand while she smacked him on the leg with the other. "You're. Naughty."

"No," he said, teasing back. "I'm just telling it like I see it. You've been through a helluva lot and you deserve a break."

"We both do." Her smile faded. "Both. Of. Us. Have. Why. You. Should. Date. Be happy."

She'd found her Prince Charming in Charles Brooks III. As much as he loathed the too-slick, *Gone with the Wind* throwback, he wouldn't stand in her way if Tripp made her happy.

Out of Sight

by

Melissa Klein

Out of Uniform Series, Book Two

Out of Sight

Cover Art by *Angela Anderson*

The Wild Rose Press, Inc.
PO Box 708
Adams Basin, NY 14410-0708
Visit us at www.thewildrosepress.com

Publishing History
First Champagne Rose Edition, 2017
Print ISBN 978-1-5092-1482-2
Digital ISBN 978-1-5092-1483-9

Out of Uniform Series, Book Two
Published in the United States of America

Dedication

I dedicate this book to Laura Klein,
whose perseverance and determination
are my daily inspiration,
and with gratitude to the doctors, nurses, and staff
of Legacy Emanuel Hospital in Portland, Oregon.

Chapter One

Mia Jones rinsed the last of the shampoo from her hair, wishing the spray coming out of the shower had more oomph behind it instead of the anemic dribble that barely got the job done. What she wouldn't give to be back at her condo with her rainfall showerhead—and her jetted tub. God, she'd kill to be up to her neck in bubbles instead of freezing her skinny behind off.

Holding onto the stainless steel grip bar, she shut off the water. A shiver racked her body. Her goose bumps grew goose bumps as she waited for the nurse to hand her a towel the size of a postcard. After scrubbing it over her closely cropped hair, she fastened it around her body.

Nurse Elise Watkins—a woman Mia took undergraduate classes with—offered her hand to help Mia step out of the tub. As she crossed to the white, plastic bench in the middle of the bathroom, the nurse kept her gaze averted. A surge of appreciation welled inside Mia. Not all the staff was as thoughtful. It might be commonplace for them to see naked patients, but she'd always tried to keep the number of people who saw her girly parts to a minimum.

"Here are your undies." Elise kept her gaze fixed on a spot over Mia's shoulder. Then came the T-shirt, sweatpants, and slippers.

"All. Done," Mia said, still seated on the bench.

Elise wrapped the gait belt around Mia's waist and hovered ready to catch her as she made tentative steps to the sink.

"Your balance is even better than it was when I saw you earlier in the week."

"Bathe. On. My. Own?"

"Baby steps," she replied. "You've come a long way in a short amount of time. Your speech is coming along and even your short-term memory is getting better."

The traumatic brain injury left her with aphasia, a disorder that made it difficult for her to verbally express her thoughts. Mia nodded as she reached for her toothbrush. Going from a coma to brushing her own teeth in as many weeks might seem like a warp speed recovery to the doctors and therapist, but she chafed against submitting to the will of others. It was too reminiscent of St. Anne's, the group home where she'd spent her teen years. At least she wouldn't have to spend her outpatient therapy living at Milestones, the residential home associated with LaGrange General's Rehabilitation Center. *See, there was always something to be thankful for.*

Then there was the fact her appearance would return to normal. Eventually. She avoided looking at herself in the mirror as she combed her hair, not needing a reminder of the damage her attacker had done. The plastic surgeon did an excellent job repairing her broken nose and crushed cheekbone, and the scar above her eyebrow would fade with time. So would the craniotomy incision still visible through her quarter-inch long hair.

Another benefit of her involuntary makeover, she

also no longer had to cope with long strands of her light brown hair all over the bathroom floor. And what was the point in makeup? It wasn't like she was going anywhere. "Toothbrush. Comb. Deodorant—all I need." She tucked her toiletries back into the pink tub provided by the hospital.

Elise grabbed the webbed nylon belt from behind, and guided Mia into her tiny hospital room. "Bed or chair?"

"Chair." For years as she worked her way through Wake Forest Law School, she'd longed for a weekend in bed. Several weeks confined to one cured her of that wish.

"Will you be having company?"

Mia settled into the faux-leather chair, reaching for the television remote. "Tripp and family later," she said, referring to her fiancé, his mother, and his younger sister. While in LaGrange General's ICU, they'd kept vigil at her bedside. They visited several times a week now that she'd moved to the inpatient rehabilitation floor.

She tried to muster up some level of anticipation for the visit. During his midweek drop-by, he'd badgered her again to let him pack up her home and put it on the market. Her two-bedroom condo represented the first place that had ever truly been home. She'd dug in her heels and he'd left in a huff. Mia reminded herself to be patient with his moodiness. The aftermath of her attack while biking on the Coastal Comet Trail had been difficult for both of them. Hopefully, Pamela and Dianne, his mother and sister, would help defuse the tension that permeated the room whenever she and Tripp were together.

"Go. To. Garden?"

"Sure," Elise said, tidying the room. "Your doctor wrote orders this morning so you can leave the floor with assistance."

"Good." Mia forced a smile to her lips. Perhaps in another week she could use the bathroom without calling for a nurse.

After Elise left, Mia clicked through the channels of mind-numbing programs, hoping for something to redirect the dark path her thoughts took her. *I'm getting better every day. I have a lot to be thankful for. This is temporary.* She found the last line in her mantra harder to believe than the others. Having seen the slow recovery of some of the other patients, she understood there was no guarantee she'd regain all she'd lost. As it was, it would be many months before she could return to her position as assistant district attorney for Polk County, North Carolina. At twenty-six, she was the youngest person ever to hold that position. She wanted to get back to the job she loved more than she wanted to pee without an audience.

Mia switched off the TV and reached for the Sunday edition of the *LaGrange Daily Journal*. She turned to an exposé on the rise of organized crime in the city. The words danced before her eyes as she pieced together each word. After struggling through a couple sentences, she ended up scanning the caption under the picture of Dillon O'Riley, a local businessman with possible ties to the Boston mafia. The aphasia made reading with any speed somewhere between very difficult and impossible. One more thing she had to relearn. Her stomach twisted—not because she was afraid of hard work. She fought for every accomplishment she'd achieved.

What would she do if she could no longer practice law?

From the time she was thirteen, her only career goal had been to protect people who weren't able to defend themselves and prosecuting criminals had been the perfect way to achieve that goal. *It's early days.* She repeated the phrase her therapist quoted, but impatience had her tossing the newspaper aside. What if this was the new normal? Reading was like breathing to her, to the point she couldn't remember when she'd learned to do it.

A knock on the door pulled her out of her head. "Come. In." She glanced at the clock on the wall. Too early for Tripp and his family, who usually didn't come until after church.

A nurses' aid stuck her head in the room. "Your brother wanted me to check to see that you were up and dressed before he came in."

The dark cloud hanging over her head evaporated. Until Tripp, his mother, and his sister came into her life, Hank Taggart had been her only family. "I'm. Dressed." She squirmed in her seat with anticipation.

Seconds later another tap came at the door, and then all six and a half feet of him filled the doorway. Though he had a good foot of height on her now, as kids they'd often been mistaken for siblings. Both had fair skin, green eyes, and now even their short, light brown hair matched.

She opened her arms to him, simultaneously wanting to laugh and cry. Her words became a tangle and all she could get out was, "Hug." Not nearly enough to express the emotions tightening her chest.

As his broad arms engulfed her, all seemed right with the world. His was the first face she remembered after coming out of the coma, and a visit from him would keep her spirits lifted for days.

His ready smile lit up her insides. "How's it going, angel?"

Mia squeezed his hand. "Good. Now. You. Here."

His brow furrowed as his gaze combed her from top to bottom. "You're looking better. I swear I can see the improvement from one time to the next."

She touched a finger to her healing tracheotomy scar. "Hard. To. Look. Worse." She laughed. Between the scars from her attacker and the marks left by the doctors' lifesaving efforts, she looked grizzly enough to scare small children. "I. Wasn't. Expecting…"

After returning a month ago from a tour in the Persian Gulf, he'd visited a couple times a week, but he'd already made the thirty-minute trip that week from the New River naval base near Wilmington to her home here in LaGrange.

"I had some free time, so I had to come see my best girl. I hope you don't mind that I didn't call first."

She shook her head. "Glad. You. Did."

Hank's gaze shifted toward the door. "When's the fiancé coming?"

"Later." She waved a hand. "Let's. Go. Garden."

He arched an eyebrow. "You can do that?" When he'd visited a few days ago, she'd still been using a walking frame.

She hooked a finger under the belt wrapped around her waist. "I've. Been. Upgraded."

Once the nurses briefed him on how to hold the belt, they were free to roam the grounds. They quickly settled in a shady spot under a huge live oak. Mia breathed in the fresh air. "What's. New?"

****

Staring down at Mia, Hank forced a lid on his impotent rage. Despite being thousands of miles out at sea when she was attacked, he couldn't help feeling he'd let her down. Again.

Her look of adoration burned in his gut. "Nothing worth talking about," he answered, trying not to beat himself up over something he couldn't have prevented from half a world away. But where was that asshole of a fiancé when all this went down?

"I'm going to Admiral Griffin's retirement ceremony Tuesday," he said, trying to redirect his thoughts to things that didn't make him want to punch a wall.

"Didn't. I. Meet. Him?" she asked.

"Yes, you did. He was my commanding officer when I first got my commission," Hank answered, half distracted. Maybe he *would* have a private convo with the fiancé about doing a better job looking after Mia. And keeping him abreast of her recovery.

He'd learned of her attack on the Coastal Comet Trail, a cycling path that ran from Wilmington to LaGrange, a week after the incident and only because he happened to read about it in the newspaper. He tried to see the positive in being grounded from flying his F/A 18 Super Hornet. At least now he could make up for lost time while he waited to hear from the Medical Evaluation Board.

"Dating. Anyone?" A mischievous smile teased the corners of her mouth. Every conversation they had, she somehow managed to work in the question of who he was dating. Even when she could barely string two words together, she was a nosey thing, never leaving well enough alone.

"Not much of an opportunity on board *The Eisenhower*." Although that didn't stop some people on the aircraft carrier from hooking up, he wasn't interested in a shipboard romance. Or one on land. Thanks to his ex-wife's infidelity, he was off the market permanently.

"Plenty. Of. Nurses. Here."

"Thanks, but no." He patted her arm. "Besides, you're reason enough to visit."

No woman could match the one sitting across from him. She hadn't given in or given up when life kept knocking her down. Her shorn hair and multitude of scars didn't diminish her beauty either. Those deep green eyes of hers were just as warm as her smile. They could also dance with mischief or pin a man to his seat when she trained them his way.

He'd been four years old when newborn Mia was brought to the foster home where he'd been placed. She was pink and wrinkly and screaming her head off. An immediate bond formed with her—another kid nobody wanted.

"Now *The Eisenhower* is back in port, I have some leave coming. I can visit again later in the week if you like."

If the navy's findings didn't go his way, he'd have more than a few days off. He shoved that worry aside. He refused to waste the few moments he had before The Fiancé arrived focusing on something he could worry about later.

Her smile brightened. "I'd. Like. That."

"When are you getting out of rehab?"

She wrinkled up her nose. "Hate. That. Word. Rehab. Sound. Like. Detox." She fiddled with her hospital bracelet. "Discharge. A couple weeks."

So soon? His gaze landed on the arching scar that covered the side of her head. Surely she wouldn't be capable of caring for herself in just a few days. "Where will you go afterward?" he asked, wishing he could be the one to care for her. The place he was renting was far from ideal, but he'd jump at the chance. Except that privilege now belonged to another man.

"Tripp's mother insisted." Her gaze turned to a two-story building just beyond the garden. "Otherwise, live. In. Milestones." Her expression darkened, her thoughts surely rushing to the same place as his. After being removed from the foster home, they'd been sent to separate group homes.

Oh, hell no. Not if he could help it would she ever spend a single night in another soulless institution. Hank's stomach knotted, and he managed a bit of gratitude toward the Brooks family. He still didn't like the arrogant jerk, but at least Tripp had seen to this. "Have you two set the date for the wedding?"

"Before the attack—May tenth."

"Have you postponed it?" he asked, hoping he didn't sound too eager. No man would ever be good enough for her and Charles Brooks III fell well below the mark.

Mia shifted in her seat. "Tripp. Doesn't. Want. Lose. Deposit. On. Reception."

Hank rolled his eyes. Even he knew the loss of a few hundred dollars wasn't the appropriate motivation for moving forward with a wedding—and he didn't have a romantic bone in his body. "Are you going to be up for that? What do the doctors say about your long-term prognosis?"

She shrugged. "Too. Soon." After a moment she added, "They're being optimistic. So. I. Don't. Give. Up."

He couldn't imagine her doing that. Even now, looking like she'd gone twenty rounds with Mike Tyson, she acted ready to take on the world. "You've been through so much, angel. It just isn't fair."

She barked a laugh. "Haven't. You. Heard? Life. Not. Fair."

"But you've had more than your share of trouble."

"Everything happens—for a reason." She let out a breath. "Mrs. Brooks says, 'God doesn't. Give. More. Than. We. Can. Bear.'"

Never a particularly religious man, he especially didn't like when a person tried to shove their beliefs on to others. From what he knew about the formidable Mrs. Brooks, the woman from a privileged background hadn't had much in her life to put her theory to the test. "If that's true, then God must think you're a badass."

Mia covered her smile with one hand while she smacked him on the leg with the other. "You're. Naughty."

"No," he said, teasing back. "I'm just telling it like I see it. You've been through a helluva lot and you deserve a break."

"We both do." Her smile faded. "Both. Of. Us. Have. Why. You. Should. Date. Be happy."

She'd found her Prince Charming in Charles Brooks III. As much as he loathed the too-slick, *Gone With the Wind* throwback, he wouldn't stand in her way if Tripp made her happy.

A few droplets of rain pelted them. "I guess we better head back inside."

Mia held up a hand. "Not yet. Maybe it won't get worse," she said, even as the sprinkles turned into full-on rain.

"Better not chance it. He scooped her into his arms. "Sugar melts."

Holding Mia in his arms felt more right than anything in a long while, which was why he needed to get gone. She belonged to another man—even though the fucker didn't deserve her. Hank let himself breathe in her scent and absorb the way her breath tickled his neck for the time it took to return her to her room.

Chapter Two

All too soon, Hank had Mia back inside the building, her excursion spoiled by a few drops of rain and an overprotective man. She resisted the urge to lace her fingers around his neck as he lowered her feet to the floor. They'd had fun together bantering back and forth despite her difficulty getting words out. The feel of his chest against her cheek hadn't been a hardship either. It had been a long time since she had physical contact that wasn't related to someone caring for her medical needs. The momentary affection soothed her soul like a balm.

"Race. You. Back," she joked, wondering where those errant thoughts came from. She was engaged to Tripp, and while he wasn't built along the same rugged frame as Hank, he was handsome in his own way. They were a good match, working in the same profession. His family cared about her. He was thoughtful. She continued the litany of Tripp's attributes as she and Hank navigated the hallways and elevator up the Acquired Brain Injury Unit.

He signed her into the patient log and handed the smiling nurse back her pen. "Brought her back in the same condition I found her in."

Having him check her back in irritated like sandpaper. It was, however, a necessary bit of protocol. TBI patients, herself included, got easily disoriented and could get hopelessly lost in LaGrange General's maze of floors and hallways.

With her squared away with the staff, they toddled toward her room, his hand gripping her ever-present accessory—the gait belt. "Movie?" she asked, determined not to let the rain or her loss of autonomy dampen her mood. All that mattered was she had Hank with her. Their time together was too precious to waste on a pity party.

He paused outside the door. "I have to get going as soon as I get you settled." He shifted his weight from foot to foot as he studied the tiled floor outside her room. "I'm sure you're worn out."

"But—"

As his gaze met hers, something intangible clouded his expression. "I'll come see you later in the week."

Don't go. It could be hours before Tripp and his family visited. The thoughts of returning to an empty room made her consider begging him to stay. More than easing her loneliness, his presence centered her. She couldn't get enough of his reluctant smiles or quick wit. Even before the attack, his infrequent visits outshone Christmas and her birthday.

After a lifetime of goodbyes, they should have gotten easier. She widened her eyes to keep the sudden onset of tears from trickling down her cheek. He was her touchstone and the only other person who understood what it was like to grow up the way she had.

He had his own life to live that didn't include playing nursemaid and counselor to her as she navigated her recovery. Mia wouldn't cause him to feel guilty for not spending more time with her. She wasn't his responsibility, nor would it be right for her to dump in his lap her truckload of issues. Besides, the shadows under his eyes hinted he had some crap of his own to deal with.

Keeping her voice light, she said, "Sure. Visit anytime." Willing her emotions under control, she pushed open the door.

Tripp bolted from his seat as she entered. "Where have you been?"

Mia froze, covering her mouth to hold back a startled yelp. "Hi," she said, trying to regroup from his emphatic question. *What had his undies in knots?*

Seeing him still dressed in one of his many dark suits, she guessed he must have come straight from church. Although when it came down to it, his version of casual was khakis and a golf shirt. That explained the way he was dressed, but not the reason for him jumping down her throat.

Alongside her, Hank's body vibrated tension. His hold on her tightened. Things could get testy in a New York minute. In the past, her two men had prowled around each other like mountain lions. She patted his arm, hoping to sooth him as she explained things to Tripp. Except her words became a tangle as they lost their way from her brain to her lips. "Visited the—" *What was the place they'd been called?* It started with the letter G. Doing as her speech therapist taught, Mia talked herself around the word that escaped her. *Damn. It has trees and flowers.* The more she tried to force the word, the more it eluded her.

"I took our girl for a walk in the garden. I thought she'd enjoy a little fresh air," Hank answered for her. It might have made her angry that he'd filled in the blanks, except she was too thankful for the tight rein he had on his temper to fuss over such a little thing. Then he took the next step, proving what a stand-up guy he was.

"By the way, it's good to see you, my man." Hank extended his hand.

Tripp's lips pressed together to form a straight line. "Thank you for keeping her company," he said, finally accepting the hand Hank offered. His icy-blue eyes trained on her. "I don't think it's a good idea for you to be roaming around."

Mia rolled her eyes, tired of people treating her like a child. "I needed sunshine. Besides, not on my own."

Less than six feet tall, his size and demeanor stood in contrast to Hank's—tight bundle of anxiety to calm giant. "I still don't like it." Tripp paced the room like a caged animal. "You're not as well as you think you are."

Her energy sagged. Maybe Hank was right and the walk had tired her out. She dropped to the bed and sighed. Pulling the blanket over her legs, she said, "Sorry you worried." The last thing she wanted was to cause anyone more grief. She leaned against the pillow and closed her eyes.

"I'm going to head out." Hank leaned over to press a kiss on her forehead.

She nodded, keeping her eyes shuttered so he wouldn't see her tears.

Once Hank left, Tripp finally sat down in the room's only chair. "Detective Price called. He's coming by in a few minutes."

Mia levered up in bed. "Something new?" So far, the Polk County police had few clues as to who'd tackled her off her bike and beaten her nearly to death. Perhaps they found some evidence at the scene or a witness had come forward. Nerves made her light-headed.

Tripp bolted from the seat like his butt was spring-loaded. "I don't know." He made laps around the room. "But I can tell you I'm more than a little ready to put this behind us."

She couldn't argue with him on that. Except moving forward would be a whole hell of a lot easier if her assailant wasn't still out there roaming free. "I know." The attack had been a strain on both of them individually and as a couple. Tension crackled in the air. She leaned back against her pillow and closed her eyes again. His pacing made her a little squirrely. Her fiancé had many fine attributes. Patience wasn't one of them. Thankfully for both her nerves and the hospital flooring, a rap on the door gave them some relief.

"Come," Tripp barked.

Detective Price eased into the room. Dressed in dark slacks and a white shirt, he looked as if he too had recently attended church. He also exuded an air of confidence she found reassuring. But, with every day that passed, the likelihood he'd find her attacker lessened.

"Hello, Detective." Mia prayed there'd been some developments in her case.

His shrewd eyes softened as their gazes met. He further won her approval by coming to her bedside to address her first. "You're looking well, Miss Jones." He took the hand she offered.

"Feeling better." Her thoughts become a jumble as a dozen questions whirled in her head. Had a witness come forward? Tripp was offering fifty thousand dollars as a reward for information about the attack—a handsome sum in that part of North Carolina. Perhaps the police found forensic evidence at the scene? She opened her mouth, but as it often did when it counted most, she couldn't get her questions from her brain to her lips. "What'ssss," she stammered. "New?"

Tripp blew out a breath and took over from there. "Tell me your people have made some progress on Mia's case," he demanded.

Frustration boiled inside her. Not just because he'd cut her off again, but for his impatience with the detective. It wasn't like the police were ignoring clues or failing to follow up on leads. Investigating a crime wasn't as linear as TV made it out to be. In her job as ADA, she worked closely with Polk County's finest, so she'd experienced firsthand the force's professionalism. While effective, CSI was a matter of meticulous investigation, it was often also a search down any number of dead ends.

"This is more a follow-up visit." Detective Price folded his arms across his chest and turning his attention toward Mia. "To recap what my team has done, immediately after your attack, we combed the area. We searched for physical evidence such as clothing, or disturbed brush as well as forensic material like blood, hair, or fibers."

Mia nodded. What he relayed to her was SOP for any criminal investigation.

"And so far they've found exactly nothing," Tripp said. "Not one goddamned shred."

"The samples my people gathered have all been attributed to you, Miss Jones," Detective Price continued, registering no outward appearance of Tripp's interruption or his continued impatience. "At the time of the attack, there were no tire tracks in the crushed gravel that we could identify as yours, nor was there evidence of where the perpetrator might have lain in wait for you. This week my team and I went back to the section of the trail where you were found, hoping to find something we'd missed."

"And," Tripp said, "did you do any better job the second go-round?"

Detective Price turned his attention to Tripp. "I assure you, Mr. Brooks, my team has made a thorough search of the area, extending our efforts for miles up and down the trail and yards into the brush along the trail." He cocked an eyebrow. "There is a distinct *lack* of evidence."

Mia's heart sank. With each day that passed, the likelihood they'd catch her attacker dwindled, especially with nothing to go on. Her insides twisted at the thought. Even if this was simply a case of her being in the wrong place at the right time, how could she ever lead a normal life looking over her shoulder?

"Witnesses?" Mia asked, unwilling to give up. Perhaps a biker or jogger noticed someone suspicious lingering on the trail.

Detective Price shook his head. "None so far. Which leads me to the reason for my visit. I was hoping you might have regained some of your memories of the time leading up to your attack."

When she'd first emerged from her coma, most of the last six months had been fuzzy. Though she'd never admit it, she hadn't even remembered who Tripp was until nearly a week later. When she confided that fact to one of her therapist, he assured her that memory loss was normal. Over the next few weeks, the details of her life returned—her job, buying the condo, and her whirlwind romance with Tripp. The events of that day were still elusive. She couldn't even remember getting dressed that morning. "I'm sorry." She shook her head.

Detective Price's penetrating gaze bore in to her. "I need you to try, Miss Jones. Do you remember anything about your attacker? Even a small detail might help."

Mia closed her eyes and tried to recall loading her bike on the back of her car, or even making the decision to go for a ride that Saturday morning. She came up empty on both. Then she tried envisioning the section of the trail closest to her condo—the spot where she'd been found. Something dark. A fleeting image flickered through her mind like a wisp of smoke. She grasped at the memory, trying to latch onto the details. "Dark. Haired. Man." Her head pounded with the effort of trying to get her once-sharp brain to work.

"Can you recall his race? Even what he was wearing or how tall he was would help."

She pressed the palms of her hands to her temples, as if she could squeeze the memory from its hiding spot. She could remember her first pair of high-heeled shoes and the name of the guy she went to the prom with. Hell, she could even remember a few things she'd like to forget. Nothing more came to mind—other than a deep-seated conviction her attacker wanted her dead. Bile burned her throat. "Nothing." She shook her head.

"I need you to try." The detective grasped her hand.

The sense of failure sat on her chest, making it hard to breathe. If solving the case rested on her memory, the detective might as well quit now. According to her neuropsychologist, Mia's brain hadn't had time to store the events leading up to the attack in long-term memory where she'd be more likely to recall them. Instead, they'd been recorded in short-term memory only—with the blows to the head acting like the computer equivalent of closing a Word file without saving it. Tapping into her damaged brain couldn't be their only option. Surely there was something they hadn't thought of before.

Mia chewed on her nails, a habit from childhood she'd tried for years to break. Tugging them free from her mouth, she asked, "Scratch. Him?"

"We checked underneath your nails and found nothing."

Tears blurred her vision then spilled down her face. She turned away, not wanting Tripp and the detective to see her cry. If only she could get her brain to work, but she was just in the last week getting to the place where she could remember what happened the day before.

"That's enough, Detective." Tripp came to sit on the edge of the bed and patted her head. He wrapped a protective arm around her shoulders. "I won't have you upsetting her. She's been through a lot, and her mental faculties aren't up to par yet."

She gnawed at her nails again, not caring that Tripp hated when she did so. Better that than taking a bite out of him. While what he said was true, she hated being treated like an addled child. She wanted to shout that there was nothing wrong with her, but the truth was the blows to her head had affected her mind. Her unknown assailant also broke a myriad of small bones and inflicted kidney damage with the blows he struck to her back.

"I'll keep trying." She thumbed away the tears. Not

that the effort guaranteed results. She busted her butt during her therapy sessions, especially with the speech pathologist who helped Mia with the arduous task of getting her thoughts from her brain to her lips. Though she made progress, he hadn't promised she'd regain everything she lost. The details of the attack might remain known only to her assailant.

Detective Price nodded, a sympathetic smile on his lips. "I'm sure you will. I'll leave you to rest. Please call me if you remember anything. Your fiancé has my contact information."

Tripp took her hand as the detective left. "I want you to lie down for a while. He urged her to lie back. "You've had enough activity for one day and need to rest." Pity colored his expression.

God, I hate that look.

Mia plastered a smile on her face, swallowed her tears. "Don't go," she pleaded not so much because she'd miss his company but because it was barely two in the afternoon and other than dinner, she had nothing to occupy her hours.

He kissed her forehead. "I'll try to get back out here this evening. I've got some work that needs my attention."

As a junior partner at Williams, Mims, and Gantry, he logged in as many hours as she had when working a case. If fact, during the week, it hadn't been unusual for them to only see each other once or twice. "I understand. Bring Traveler?" she asked, mentioning Tripp's German Shepard. "Miss him." He probably wondered where she'd gone.

Tripp rolled his eyes. "I'll try." He kissed her on the cheek.

After he left, Mia tried to remember something of her attack, rewinding to the last memory not filled in by others. Though her eyes grew heavy with sleep, one thought kept her awake. Why her? Was it as Detective Price thought—a random act of violence? Something in her gut told her there was more to the attack—a niggling worry that kept her mind churning.

The last thing she remembered with clarity was her lunch-hour trip on Friday to the office supply store. The urgency she'd felt as she returned with a package of flash drives reignited, though the reason behind the feeling eluded her. Mia trained her attention on the memory, trying to recall why she wanted flash drives when she backed up her files to the office server.

Chapter Three

Tuesday morning, Hank unlatched the gate that separated the hospital parking lot from the walled garden. Tension coiled every muscle in his body. He'd been summoned by The Fiancé. No details or assurances, just a directive, time, and place. *Asshole.* Hank took the bait, seeing the text for what it was—a dick-measuring contest in which the natty lawyer asserted his prominence in Mia's life. Since there wasn't anything Hank wouldn't do for her, he complied with the instructions even if his go-to response had been to shoot back a big—*fuck you.*

He pushed through the wrought iron arch that groaned on rusty hinges, slamming it shut with a little more force than necessary. The bang ricocheted through the morning air like a shotgun blast. *Damned satisfying.* It sated his stewing temper just enough that he might manage to get through the meeting without taking a chunk out of Tripp Brook's hide.

His feet ate up the bricked path as he made his way to the large live oak at the far side of the enclosed area, jonesing to get the meeting over. Besides finding the guy a pain in the ass, Hank was due at New River for the admiral's retirement ceremony in less than two hours.

Around a curve in the garden's brick pathway, he caught sight of a tableau so perfect his heart ached.

Mia, dressed in a light-blue tracksuit, sat flanked on either side by her future mother- and sister-in-law. Sunlight streamed through overhead branches, casting a glow on her close-cropped hair and highlighting the rosy color that was slowly returning to her too-pale skin. Lost in conversation and unaware of his arrival, she smiled in turn at her company as they chatted. To their right, Tripp lounged, one seersucker-clad leg stretched out in ease. A perfect family right down to the large dog resting at Mia's feet.

Her laughter carried across the open space, piercing his chest with an emotion too elusive and all-encompassing to identify. The only thing that would please him more than having her direct that laugh toward him was for him to stop wanting it. As the echo of her happiness faded, it left him with a reality too certain and too awful to be anything but the truth. It was time for him to let her go. They'd clung to each other in their makeshift family, but now she'd found the real thing. And he was ballast—a reminder of their awful past she didn't need.

His hands clenched at his side; he made a vow to her. He'd see her though her recovery and then begin fading into her history—a few emails or calls to keep tabs on her, but that was all he'd allow himself. The disappearing act would be easy enough to pull off regardless of the medical review board's decision. *The Eisenhower* was due to begin sea trials soon and would be underway by June. He could use that as an excuse. He swallowed hard against the knot in his chest. He'd always done what was best for Mia, and he wouldn't let his own selfish needs stop him now.

"Good morning, all," he called out when he'd

mastered his emotions.

"Hank." Mia's eyes lit up and her broad smile tested his resolve. "Why here?" She stood on still-wobbly legs and encompassed him in a hug.

"Good morning, Mrs. Brooks, Dianne." He acknowledged the two women and eased Mia back to her seat after pressing a kiss to the top of her head. The ladies nodded in return while she looked up at him expectantly.

"I got a message from Tripp that he needed to see me."

"I wanted to ask your brother a favor," he said to Mia as he gestured for Hank to take the vacant wooden seat across from him.

Wariness churned in Hank's gut. "All right." He wondered what he could do for a guy who had everything—even some things he didn't deserve.

As Tripp took his fiancée's hand in his, her brow furrowed. "It's about the wedding," he began. "We're going ahead with our original plans, despite Mia's reservations about her appearance."

She snatched her hand from Tripp's grasp, sending Hank's instincts into overdrive. What the fuck was this guy pulling? "Why—?"

Tripp tugged on the cuffs of his jacket and plowed on. "In the spirit of joining our families together, I'd like you to be my best man."

Anger gripped Hank so tightly, a moment passed before he could control the urge to throw a punch at the guy—or bolt from the garden. *Not no, but hell no.* Of all the things the fucker could ask for, why this? Hank narrowed his gaze at the man who probably didn't take a dump without a strategy. Regardless of the reason, the answer was still no.

He'd never planned to attend the wedding, much less be in the bridal party. Hank wanted Mia's happiness more than he wanted his next breath, but witnessing her marry a guy barely good enough to tie her shoes was more than he could manage. "That's quite an honor…"

As he mentally worded his decline, Mia interrupted his thoughts. "Tripp." Her expression brightened. "You. Do. For. Me?"

A slick smile curled his mouth as he brought her hand to his lips. "I'd do anything in the world to please you."

Hank's stomach sank. The exact reason he would say "yes" to the slick fucker. "I'd be happy to." He took to his feet and jutting out his hand.

Tripp took the offered palm, ratcheting down his grip until Hank's bones ground against each other. "Excellent. I'll be in touch with the list of responsibilities you'll need to perform," he said with a final take-that squeeze.

He refused to massage his hand despite the ache shooting up his arm. Only someone with a tentative hold on his world needed such a pissant display of strength. And those were the kind of men who needed watching most. "I'm your man." He winked at Mia. "I'll be the most thorough best man on the planet."

"Happy." Her green eyes sparked in a way he hadn't seen since before her attack.

Her beam reminded him of when he'd bought her a pair of tennis shoes popular back in the day. He'd worked a solid week at a hot, greasy burger joint by the beach to buy them for her because he wanted her to have just one thing like the other girls in school. Back then, she hadn't asked for her heart's desire, he'd known on instinct what would make her happy. It was the last thing he'd been able to do for her before they'd been separated and to this day one of his proudest achievements.

"I'll talk to you soon, angel." He kissed her cheek. "But, I've got to get going if I'm to make it back to Wilmington in time." He could never deny her anything, not even if it made him miserable. With a goodbye to Tripp's mother and sister, Hank made an about-face and got the hell away from there as quickly as his size thirteens could take him.

****

Two hours later, Hank sank into his chair as the ceremony began. He nodded a hello to Opie Collins and his wife, Stephanie, his thoughts still firmly back in LaGrange. How the hell was he going to manage to be Tripp's best man and not want to punch the guy in the face every minute or so? Doing the right thing ought to come with a little more job satisfaction.

After the presenting of the colors and the chaplain's invocation, Lieutenant Commander Avery Madigan stepped to the podium. A smile touched his lips as she began her speech. Now, there was someone who knew how to stand back up after she got knocked on her ass. Just like another woman in his life.

He and Mad Dog had more in common than a respect for Admiral Griffin and a love of the navy. Two years ago when their squadron returned from duty in the Gulf, they found their respective spouses having an affair. The news that greeted them on their return led Avery to the reserves and him to the bottom of a bottle.

He'd nearly wrecked his naval career with his drinking. Probably would have if Mia hadn't gotten ahold of him. His angel showed up at his pigsty of an apartment and put a boot so far up his ass she made his first flight instructor seem like a kindergarten teacher. He chuckled inside, recalling the idle threats she'd thrown at him as she shook her manicured finger in his direction. She was right. There was more to life than a faithless wife.

But what about a career that defined him? Or a woman who'd always been there for him?

As Avery spoke, his thoughts rewound to February. His stomach twisted as a mental image formed of Mia hooked up to a respirator with wires and tubes coming out of her in half a dozen places. Those memories and the knowledge he'd nearly lost her would give him nightmares for years to come. That day was the first time since childhood he'd asked the Almighty for something. His prayer had been answered moments later and was still being fulfilled as she continued to heal. The immediacy of His response to Hank's appeal still shocked the hell out of him, especially as until that time he wasn't a hundred percent sure he believed in God. As he'd leaned over her hospital bed, she opened her eyes for the first time. The bonus was that she knew him—he was certain he saw recognition flash in her warm green eyes.

The admiral took the podium, bringing Hank back to the present. Going by the large crowd filling the aircraft hangar, Hank's wasn't the only life the man had influenced. Back when he was a cocky lieutenant with a talent for getting into trouble, the Old Man had offered some sage advice. "Stop being a fuckup before you ruin your life." Even if the words of wisdom weren't offered up in a Father-Knows-Best way, they were sincere and worth listening to. He'd also seen something in Hank that others hadn't—not even himself. After that, becoming a Super Hornet pilot became his life's ambition and the navy his family.

While Hank had been reliving his seminal moment, the ceremony ended. He joined the dignitaries, elected officials from the area, and other navy personnel in line to speak to the admiral.

"Congratulations on your retirement, sir." He offered his hand to the admiral.

"Thank you, Taggart. What's the word on your flight status?"

Hank wasn't surprised the Old Man heard about the incident. News as dramatic as ditching his plane in the sea traveled as fast as the gale in which he'd been flying. "I'm grounded until the investigation wraps up."

"I'll put in a good word for you if that will help," the admiral said. "You're a skilled pilot, and the navy's lucky to have you." The man smiled sadly. "I'm not sure either one of us knows what to do with himself if we're not aboard ship."

Wasn't that the God's honest truth. His gut twisted. While in college, he'd worked construction, but he wouldn't be able to manage even that if the doctors' preliminary diagnosis proved correct. "Thank you, sir." He gripped Griffin's hand again. "I appreciate everything you've done for me."

After greeting Mrs. Griffin, he milled around with the others. He took a piece of cake he didn't particularly want just to have something to do with his hands. Across the hangar, he caught sight of Connor St.

James, or Titan as most still called him. Seeing people who been a part of his life during the height of his career set off a tug-of-war inside him. One part wanted to rehash every adventure they'd ever had together, while the other side wanted to run and hide.

Hank tossed the cake into the garbage and took a couple steps toward the front of the hangar. One thing was certain, once the review board's findings were published, and his medical diagnosis known, he'd never be able to stomach the look of pity in his friends' eyes. He wound through the crowd and was nearly home free when a hand clasped his shoulder.

"Tank," the jovial voice said. "Damn, but you're a hard one to chase down."

He tensed, but plastered on a smile despite having been pinned down by the person he most wanted to avoid. Besides being a top-notch pilot, Sebastian Baron had a skill set that made keeping up the bullshit nearly impossible. Bash read folks like he could tell what they were thinking or planning before they knew it themselves.

"My man," Hank began. "Good to see you. I heard some crazy ass rumor about what you were getting up to these days. Any of it true?" he asked, trying to deflect the attention.

Bash grinned. "I'm afraid to ask what you heard." He thumbed over his shoulder. "A bunch of the guys are getting together at Wayfarers later on. Do you know the place down Trade Street?"

He knew the place all right. After discovering his wife's infidelity, he spent more time than he cared to admit prowling that stretch of road.

"Come with, and we'll catch up," Bash urged.

"I'd love to, but…"

Typical of most military bases, the area surrounding the installation was peppered with tattoo parlors, pawnshops, and dives. The bar's reputation was hardly the issue. As far as places to find a drink or a little company went, Wayfarers was a paragon of virtue.

"Shoot some pool, drink a few beers, flirt with women—it'll be like old times. We can even reenact that scene from Top Gun."

Man, they'd had fun back in the day. The offer spoke to a part of him itching to hang onto the past. "One more" had always been his downfall: a mile farther from the aircraft carrier, another hand of poker, that last shot of tequila.

Hank couldn't fight the smile on his lips or ignore the lure of one more time with his crew. Wayfarers had the added bonus of being less than a mile from his apartment, so he could easily make it home when the time came.

"Sure. Why not? I haven't taken your money in a long time."

Even as they parted, Hank added another vow to the list of promises he'd been making recently. Soon he'd start distancing himself from the people who knew the old Hank, the ones who saw him as a fellow aviator, friend, and brother. For his own sanity, he had to start letting go. After one more.

****

Later that night, Hank slapped the twenty dollar bill down on the pool table. "Rack 'um up, Mad Dog. This time you're going down."

He tossed back another shot, slamming the empty glass onto the highboy table. The effects of Jose

Cuervo's finest were just beginning to put him in the right frame of mind.

Avery cocked a smile at him. "Whatever you say, Tank." She then proceeded to run the table, adding another twenty to the ones she'd won off Bash and Opie. Besides those two, Jester and Titan had joined them, making the bar's back room look like the ready room on *The Eisenhower*.

He shook his head with a laugh as the last ball sank. "This just isn't my lucky night."

The morning hadn't exactly been his either. The garden scene penetrated his glorious tequila haze. How in God's name was he going to pull off the bachelor party when he could barely stand being in the same room with the guy? His mind's eye conjured an image that made a reception toast seem a breeze. He'd have to stand alongside Tripp and watch Mia walk down the aisle—and out of his life. At least she was getting her life back, he reminded the selfish bastard at his core. She was healing and thriving after the attack that could have had them all attending church services of a different nature.

"Another one of these." He spun around to catch the waitress as she collected the four empties he'd already knocked back. The floor undulated like the deck of a ship, and he had to lean his pool cue against the wall and grab the table as he tried to get his sea legs beneath him.

"I need to give my wallet a break." Bash came up to him and put a steadying hand on Hank's shoulder. "What'd ya say we grab a couple burgers."

"Nah, I'm good," Hank countered, not at all ready to sober up. "We're supposed to be having fun."

Bash fixed him with a stare. "We are, my man. We are. I thought you might want to slow down on the agave juice. If I remember correctly, after about five or six you really become the life of the party."

Problem was the booze wasn't getting the job done like it used to. His gaze raked over the room, landing on another of his old standbys. He nodded toward a couple women sipping drinks at one of the bar's high-boy tables. "What say we try our luck at another sport?"

Bash looked over his shoulder then back at Hank, a smirk creasing his face. The only thing Sebastian Baron liked better than chasing insurgents out of the no-fly zone was chasing tail. "I'll be a gentleman since you're having such a crappy night at the tables." He punched Hank's shoulder. "You can have first pick."

He eyed the two who were dressed in jeans and tight-fitting tank tops, trying to decide between the blonde with pink streaks or the redhead. "Maybe I want them both."

Bash flashed a shit-eating grin. "Good to see you back in action. I was beginning to think your ex got your balls as well as your car."

Hank threw an elbow that caught his buddy in the ribs. "Man, that's low, even for you." He turned his attention to the women. Before he could head in their direction, Bash nodded at the two and flashed his trademark grin. Right on cue, the girls headed their way. He might as well have whistled like they were good little puppies the way they beat feet across the room.

"What are you two lovely ladies drinking?" Bash asked.

"Sex on the Beach." The blonde giggled.

"Well, what do you know, that's my favorite." Bash wrapped an arm around her shoulder.

"I'm Crystal and this is Lacy."

"Pleased to meet you. I'm Bash and this here is Tank."

Lacy giggled again, making Hank want to shove an ice pick in his ears so he wouldn't have to hear the grating noise. Getting back into the saddle was proving harder than he thought. But then again the woman he'd been spending most of his time with had a whole lot more going for her than a big rack and a perfected come-on walk.

"What kind of woman names her sons Bash and Tank?"

Bash threw back his head, laughing like she'd just fired off the joke of the decade. "That's my call sign. My mother stuck me with my old man's name, sorry rascal that he was."

"I can certainly see why they call you Tank." Crystal ran her hands across his chest. "Are you this well-built everywhere?" She inched them south to his hips.

He hardened in his jeans as his body anticipated what he'd gone without for so long. But something was off. He smiled down at her as he caught her hand. The fault certainly didn't lie with her. She was exactly his type—Tiffany 2.0. And he wasn't so wasted that he couldn't get the job done. With a few sweet words in her ear and a couple caresses, they could be out in the alley before her drink had time to get warm. He could lose himself and escape his misery for a little while. But—

Crystal's sultry expression faltered as his two

heads argued.

Opie—God bless him—provided a distraction. "Nothing to see here, folks. Return to your posts." He barred the doorway to keep Titan and Jester from entering the main bar area.

Hank caught sight of Opie's wife, Stephanie, and Mad singing. "Excuse me, ladies. I see my friend needs my help."

Relief washed over him as he extricated himself from Crystal's arms. Watching Mad throw herself into the rock anthem, he envied her ability to make the best out of a shitty situation. Would he be able to do the same if it turned out he could no longer fly? Who would fill his life once Mia recovered from her injuries and married her Prince Charming?

He called for another shot as he watched the two women on stage. The tequila burn brought him back to the level of numbness he needed to pretend he was having the time of his life.

The trio he'd left behind caught up to him. "I got us a booth up front so we can watch the floor show," Bash said.

Hank eyed the bar's front door, unable to stand the thought of getting trapped with Miss Handsy. The only thing alcohol made clear was that fucking Crystal, or any other woman for that matter, wasn't going to fix what was wrong with him. Catching up with his mate would have to wait for another opportunity. As Crystal nestled into the cradle of his hips, he braced her shoulders and put some space between their bodies. Rather than a turn on, the feel of her ass grinding into his crotch gave him the scratch.

"Look at that," he said, trying to distract her with

the chick flick—worthy scene playing out at the foot of the stage. Opie scooped his tipsy wife into his arms and carried her out of the bar.

Some people were destined to find their soulmate and live out their days in marital bliss. He cut his eyes to Bash, who was feeling up Lacy like he was fitting her for a new coat. Others were perfectly happy with whomever they were with at that moment. It seemed fate thought he worked best as a solo act.

"I'm going to head out," he said, gripping Bash on the shoulder. At the sight of Crystal's crestfallen expression, he cupped her cheek. "Thank you for your company. Be good to yourself." He turned then booked it outside, ignoring Bash's call for him to wait.

Hank stumbled into the parking lot then had to hit the brakes on his retreat. Between the lack of security lighting and the alcohol flowing through his system, he'd be lucky to make it to his truck without going ass over heels. He picked through the parked cars, using his memory of where he'd parked when his eyesight proved useless.

Feeling along the side of his truck, he clambered into the bed too trashed to drive. He'd sleep it off for a couple hours, and then drive home when it got light. As sleep and booze pulled him under, the familiar voices of Mad and Titan carried across the parking lot. Sounded like he wasn't the only one reliving old issues.

****

A metallic rumble and bang inches from his head jerked Hank from his unconscious state. He groaned and then threw his arm over his head in a feeble attempt to block the grating noise from stabbing his brain. For a few foggy moments, he couldn't remember where he was. Then there was that oh, yeah moment as the night before came back in living color.

Once the garbage truck moved on, he worked his way to a sitting position. Waking up in places other than his bed was beginning to be a habit with him—one he didn't see himself breaking anytime soon. He swiped the dew off his face then inched the along truck bed. What difference did it make how he treated his body? The end result would be the same. His feet hit the gravel, sending shockwaves of pain throughout his body.

Hank pulled his phone from his hip pocket to check the time as he climbed inside the cab. He had fifteen minutes to make it to the follow-up appointment with the specialist at the Veterans Administration hospital in Wilmington. Wasn't that going to be a treat, having some white-coat poke and prod him while little gremlins hammered away inside his skull?

As he worked up the energy to get going, his phone chimed announcing an incoming text. He unlocked the screen then winced at the three-inch-long missive. Guess Tripp wasn't kidding about Hank being the best man, he thought, reading through a laundry list of duties and a lunch meeting that afternoon to discuss places for the bachelor party. Suddenly, the doctor's appointment seemed like the highlight of his day. Surely, there was someone better suited to the job, or another role he could play in the wedding. Or maybe he could find a way to miss the event all together. He racked his brain, but nothing that didn't involve faking his death immediately came to mind.

Just as he set the phone in the truck's cup holder, another text came through. His pulse kicked up a notch at the trill he'd assigned to Mia's calls and texts.

—*Thanks for saying, "yes" to Tripp. Can't wait to see you dressed in a tux. This is the happiest I've been since the attack.*—

Just like that, the urge to chuck his phone out the window disappeared. If it made Mia happy, he'd walk across hot coals, so wearing a monkey suit for a few hours was no big deal.

—*I thought about asking you to give me away, but this is better. Now I get to see my two favorite men at the end of the aisle.*—

His chest tightened as an image of that scene played out in his imagination. Mia dressed in some white confection, gripping his arm as they walked toward an altar. Tears pricked the back of his eyes as that scenario played out. *Damn sunlight.* He reached for the sunglasses hooked to the sun visor.

—*Anything for you, angel.*—

He put the truck in gear, hoping come the May wedding date, he could keep that promise.

Chapter Four

In LaGrange General's rehab gym, Mia struggled against the elastic resistance band hooked to the bottom of her shoe. Her weak muscles burned with the effort of lowering her leg to the mat. She cheered internally as her heel touched the blue vinyl.

"That's good," the therapist encouraged. "I think that's enough."

"Five more," she countered, not ready to call it a day. How else was she going to get better if she didn't push herself?

Trisha shook her head. "Okay. But after that, you're done. I don't want you pushing too hard and being in pain all night."

Mia rolled her eyes. The two of them had this argument every session with the same result. She finished the reps then after unhooking her foot from the band, took a moment to shake out her fatigued muscles. "What's next?" she asked, swinging her legs over the mat's edge.

Trisha helped her off the table, but in a break from their usual routine, she didn't automatically take hold of Mia's gait belt. "Let's see how you do walking back to the room without my help."

Progress. Mia grinned all the way down the center's main hallway. Any step toward regaining her independence was one to celebrate, no matter how small. Or painful. By the time they made it back to her room, pain shot up her leg. Thank God, she'd completed all her therapy for the day. Her daily rehab schedule began at nine o'clock and usually didn't end until late afternoon. Her progress made the fatigue settling into her bones well worth it. Not only was she recovering her physical strength, her speech was more fluid than it had been just a week ago.

"Bed or chair?" the therapist asked.

Perspiration trickled down her back. "Bed," she said, glad for once to crawl onto the board-like surface.

"Get some rest before supper." Trisha raised the bedrails. Before leaving, she put the call button within reach and flipped off the lights.

The door had hardly closed before her eyelids grew heavy. She plumped the pillow. Perhaps if she took a quick nap she'd be more alert when Tripp made his scheduled visit. It would be nice to spend some time with someone other than the TV. Even better than a date night with her fiancé would be a date night back at her condo. They'd had some pleasant evenings cuddled together on her sofa. She turned over on her side searching for a comfortable position, and then drifted off thinking about the delicious way her own furnishings cradled her body.

Instead of dreaming of pillow-top mattresses and down comforters, her imagination took her to Tripp's townhouse. Anxiety bubbled inside as a silent film starring Tripp and her began. They were arguing, a real doozie of a fight. Both their arms were flailing about as they made their point—wordless in her dream. She wrestled against the nightmare.

She focused on their lips, trying to decipher the

words without any success. Their argument reached its zenith when she stripped the engagement ring off her finger, tossing it at him. Both her incarnations shrank back in fear as Tripp's face turned puce with rage. Her heart pounded, in anticipation of his reaction. Why was her brain cooking up this departure from their real-life relationship? They didn't fight. Of course, like any couple, they had a few disagreements—nothing like this one.

A noise jarred her from her nightmare. Mia shot upright in bed, momentarily disoriented and gasping for breath. Her gaze darted around the room.

"I'm sorry, dear." Pamela Brooks looked startled as well. "I didn't know you'd be sleeping."

Mia let out a breath, thankful for once to find herself back at LaGrange General. "That's okay, Mom." She rubbed her eyes. "If I sleep too long, I won't be able to later tonight." As the dream's shadow still lingered, she wondered if she'd be able to sleep at all. Goose bumps dotted her flesh, and she shivered at the chill the nightmare left behind.

"I brought you clean clothes." The formidable matron placed a wicker basket atop the dresser and tucked Mia's things into drawers.

"Thank you." Still shaken, she clung to the woman's efficient movements as she tidied the room.

Her future mother-in-law altered Mia's notions of how the wealthy spent their time. Rather than lazing her days away shopping and lunching with other women in her social circle, Mrs. Brooks ran her family's estate like a business—right down to her adult children's lives. She extended her sphere of influence to include Mia, taking time to help with wedding plans and choosing the home she and Tripp would eventually share. She'd also graciously volunteered to see to it Mia no longer had to wear hospital gowns, although it was likely her maid who did the actual washing.

"Is Tripp coming?" Mia half hoped he wasn't, even if she hadn't seen him since the morning he asked Hank to be his best man. Tripp could be a bit of a grump if he was feeling the pressures of a case. Besides, if he stayed at the office, she and her future mother-in-law could watch this chick flick they'd both been anxious to see.

It should have bothered her more that she enjoyed Mrs. Brooks' company as much as she did Tripp's. Weren't brides-to-be anxious to spend every waking moment with their fiancés? What did she know about romance? She'd only ever had one other serious relationship, and when it ended, she hadn't shed the first tear. Maybe she was wired wrong.

"I've got him running an errand." Mrs. Brooks took the bedside chair.

A twinge of anxiety danced up her spine. That nightmare had really knocked her off kilter. Mia pushed a button to raise her head, thinking if she stirred a bit, she could chase the remnants of the dream away. It was then she noticed the new bouquet of flowers on the window sill. "Are those from your garden?"

"They are." The woman beamed with pride. "I know you like the color yellow, so I had the gardener select these especially for you."

Gratitude warmed her heart. "They're magnificent. Tell Mr. Rodrigues thank you."

Mrs. Brooks pulled a booklet from her purse. "Speaking of favorite colors, I brought you some swatches to look at." She fanned through the pallet of pastel satins, landing on a lovely buttery-yellow. "This would make an ideal color for the bridesmaids' dresses."

"That is pretty." Mia took the booklet from Mrs. Brooks and thumbed through the swatches. None cried, "I'm the one." But not because they lacked beauty. Any one of the array of colors would do as far as she was concerned. Since the attack, the only thing that excited her about the wedding was Hank's role as best man. "I'm not sure..." She stalled while she conjured up an excuse. May seemed so close, and she had so much recovery still to make. What was the rush anyway?

Tripp's entrance saved her from having to explain her hesitance to make any wedding decisions. He burst through the door with a determined stride. "God, I hate the parking at this place." Dressed in a dark gray three-piece suit, his only concession to afterhours was he'd loosened his navy tie. He crossed the room, kissing his mother first before coming to sit on the edge of Mia's bed. "What were you two talking about?"

"Wedding plans," Mrs. Brooks said. "There are dozens of decisions Mia still needs to make."

"Don't overwhelm her with too many choices," he said, taking the swatch book from Mia's hand and passing it to his mother. She bristled at his remark. Although she moved with all the grace of a drunken toddler, she wasn't a two-year-old who couldn't make up her own mind. And what was up with talking like she wasn't even in the room?

"She may look better than she did a few weeks ago, but she's far from recovered," he said, leaning into her as if he meant to kiss her.

Mia turned her face so the kiss landed on her

cheek. The petty act pricked her conscience, but after the nightmare she'd so recently left, the thought of his lips on hers was more than she could bear.

His brow furrowed, but he quickly recovered his breezy affect. "How was therapy today? Did you talk to the doctor about ordering another CT scan? I also want a date on the neuropsych testing. We need to get a bead on your prognosis," he said, referring to a battery of psychological and cognitive tests she'd undergo before being discharged from inpatient care, then again as she reached the conclusion of outpatient therapy.

"Saw Dr. Cowboy," she began, referring to one of the residents who made rounds in the inpatient ward. She'd dubbed him with the nickname because of his boots and because she couldn't remember his name. "He said it would be the week of my discharge."

Tripp began pacing, stopping to make adjustments to her personal items scattered around the room. "I've scheduled movers to pack up your condo on Friday."

Anger sparked inside her, and suddenly she couldn't wait for him to leave. So much for a pleasant evening of dinner down in the hospital's cafeteria and a stroll in the garden. When did he get to be so domineering? He certainly hadn't been that way before the attack. She missed the suave southern gentleman who'd wooed her with his charm. He seemed determined to push all her buttons tonight.

She wasn't ready to give up the first place that had ever truly been hers even if it was likely she'd never return there full time. "Not yet." She released her frustration at his taking the decision out of her hands. One argument per day was all she could manage, even if the one they'd had was only in her dreams. "When I get discharged."

"I don't see the point in waiting." Tripp planted his fists on his hips. "By the time you're able to get around on your own, the wedding will be here. Besides, I want to put your place on the market. Maintaining two residences is a waste of money."

But it was her money. And she wasn't going to be bullied into a decision she didn't want to make. She opened her mouth, meaning to let him know just how tired she was of him treating her like she didn't have sense to come in out of the rain. The words wouldn't come. She closed her eyes and willed them to her lips. Dammit, why couldn't she just get the words out? All she got for her efforts was more frustration.

"Mine," she finally managed after giving up on plucking a more articulate word from her jumbled vocabulary. The right words swirled in her mind just out of reach. "No movers." She met his gaze and held it.

Her mouth might not work the way she wanted, but she could still give a damned good death stare. His mouth formed a thin line.

Mrs. Brooks broke the stalemate, fluttering out of the chair and crossing the room to take her son by the hand. "Let's not have a lovers' quarrel. We should talk about something happy?" She turned to Mia, an overly-bright smile turning her sweet features into a mask. "Have you made a choice which pieces of my jewelry you'd like to borrow for the wedding?"

"I have," she began, thankful to leave the sore subject, even if it was for another issue Mia wasn't totally comfortable with. Having left many of the decisions to Mrs. Brooks, the nuptials were quickly moving into the land of British royalty. The costs boggled her middle-class mind.

Then there was the jewelry. Who actually wore stuff like that? She thought back to the winter day when her future mother-in-law took Mia to the family's safety deposit box. Some of Pamela Brooks' precious stones rivaled Elizabeth Taylor's or perhaps even the Queen of England.

While Mia had stuck to her guns on the number of bridesmaids, she conceded the jewelry battle. Every girl wanted to look like a princess on her wedding day. "If it's all right," she said, the words flowing again as her anger subsided. "I'd like to use the Cartier parure." She'd chosen one of the more modest suites consisting of a small diamond pendant, bracelet, and teardrop earrings that matched her engagement ring.

She touched her bare left hand. The conversation prompted a memory of her dream. "Where is my ring?" Had she been wearing it while she'd been riding on the trail? Perhaps the four carat stone prompted the attack.

Tripp smiled indulgently and patted her hand. "Don't you remember? I've told you the same thing every time you ask. The staff gave it to me in the emergency room, and I've put it in the wall safe back at my place."

Her cheeks heated. God, she hated it when her short-term memory proved exceedingly short. She covered her face. "Oh, that's right." She murmured, "I don't know why I keep forgetting." Early in her recovery, her family and staff used a small notebook to help her recall events that kept slipping from her memory. Perhaps she needed to dig it back out.

Mrs. Brooks patted her shoulder. "We have tired

you out too much."

Mia nodded, tears choking off her words. She pressed a hand to her mouth. God, she hated feeling stupid. For someone who'd come from nothing, her intelligence had been a ticket out of poverty. She graduated with honors from Duke at nineteen and passed the bar at twenty-two. Her analytical mind was a point of pride. Something she'd always believed no one could take away from her.

"Okay." She swallowed past the lump in her throat. "I. Am. Tired."

Tripp pressed a kiss to her temple. "I'll be back in tomorrow evening, and we can revisit the plans for the condo then."

Back to that again? His persistence only made her dig in her heels. Along with her high I.Q., she had stubbornness in spades. It had gotten her through school when no one believed a sixteen-year-old could manage college on her own. She wasn't going to be railroaded into giving up her condo. But my-way-or-the-highway was no way to have a successful relationship. She could sidestep the issue. "There's no rush."

His brow furrowed, something he seemed to be doing a lot with her lately. He leaned in, kissing her hard. "I'll let you know if I can't make it."

After he left, she brushed her fingers over her mouth, scrubbing away the feel of his lips on hers. She might need to be reminded about her engagement ring and if asked she'd be hard pressed to recall what she'd eaten for breakfast. She did, however, remember experiencing the rush of emotions when Tripp proposed. She recalled days prior to the attack when she couldn't wait to leave the office so they could spend a few hours together.

Dr. Cowboy explained head injuries such as hers could cause changes in personality. Was this the reason for the change in her feelings toward him? Mia rubbed her temples as if the massage would solve the puzzle. Were her feelings for Tripp changing?

Chapter Five

Mia chewed on her fingernail, waiting for Trish, her physical therapist, to tally up the results of her latest balance test. "How'd I do?" she asked, anxious to learn if she'd finally be allowed to walk without someone holding onto her gait belt like she was a wobbly colt. "Much better than last time, right?"

In the last two weeks, it seemed as though someone had pushed the "restart" button on her brain. Not only was her balance better, her short-term memory had improved. When she first transferred to LaGrange General's rehabilitation center, she couldn't remember how to get back to her room from the gym, although she made the trip at least three or four times each day. She hadn't gotten lost once this week.

"You did it. I can take you off Fall Risk Status," Trish said with a broad smile.

Mia performed a modified version of a happy dance—safely seated on the therapy table. No sense blowing her freedom by falling. Her fingers couldn't unbuckle the gait belt quickly enough. "Woohoo." She rolled it up neatly. "Free at last, free at last."

"Not so fast." Trish touched her shoulder. "You can't leave the floor on your own, and you still need help getting in and out of the shower."

Mia rolled her eyes, but her therapist was right. After the job her attacker did to her head, she didn't have any brain cells to spare. Even a small bump on the head could have catastrophic consequences. "When will I be able to shower on my own?"

"Not for a while yet."

Of the many indignities she suffered since her attack, the lack of privacy bothered her the most. "I'm tired of the wrong people seeing me naked."

A shock of realization ringed through her. Since the accident, Tripp hadn't helped her shower or dress once. With one exception, he'd also kept his displays of affection to chaste kisses to her cheek or forehead that wouldn't even make a nun blush. The situation was unlikely to change when she moved in with his mother. She thought back to the discussion the three of them had regarding where she'd live once she got out of inpatient care. Initially, she wanted to move in with Tripp, but he persuaded her to accept his mother's generous offer.

Had her brain injury, along with the myriad of scars marking her body, changed how he saw her? Worry niggled at the back of her thoughts. What if he broke up with her?

Mia had been having her own doubts about the state of their relationship, so she could hardly fault him for entertaining his. She put those concerns away to explore at a later time. Nothing was going to dampen her mood, not even a fiancé who may be falling out of love with her. Leaving the PT room, she made her way to the small cafeteria where the patients took their meals.

Mia drew a breath before pushing open the door. Mealtime was her least favorite event of the day—and that was saying something considering how torturous she found occupational therapy. Facing her fellow patients—some of whom had been here far longer than she—riddled her with guilt. Her gaze caught on Livi, a young mother who'd been in a car accident and now had the mind of a two-year-old. Mia learned from speaking with the other woman's husband that she'd been there for six months—and likely would never return home.

One day soon, Mia would leave this place behind. While she wouldn't be one hundred percent, and the doctors hadn't made any promises she'd be capable of returning to her job as ADA, she'd be able to live independently eventually.

Between bites of food, she texted her good news to Tripp and his sister—and of course, Hank. She got a congratulatory response from Dianne, who said she'd forward the message on to her mother. It wasn't until she was digging into her vanilla pudding that Tripp responded—*Excellent.*—

She immediately pinged him back. Maybe he was waiting for her to make the first move toward resuming their life as a couple.

—*Let's celebrate. Bring takeout when you come tonight, and we'll have a quiet dinner together. It's been a while since we've had a date.*—

—*Sorry. I've got to work on the Watkins case.*—

She deflated like a balloon with a slow leak. Well, darn. As an attorney herself, she understood how many hours it took to prepare for a trial. Since he wouldn't expect a response, she tucked the phone in the pocket of her sweatpants and finished her meal.

It wasn't until several hours later she realized Hank hadn't returned her text. Since her attack, he'd checked on her every day. "It looks like it's me and the remote."

The prospect gave her pause. Was this her future? Sadness settled on her shoulders like a blanket of despair. Not allowing the indulgence of self-pity, she cautiously walked back to her room. At least if she needed to go to the bathroom, she didn't have to buzz for the nurse. And if TV became too monotonous, she'd sit in the day room for a while.

She pushed open her door and all thoughts of having to spend the evening watching *Real House Wives* evaporated.

Hank came to his feet. "Congratulations." He thrust a bouquet of flowers toward her. "Next year, you'll be back to running circles around us."

"You're here!" She squealed.

"I was headed to the gym when I got your text. So I turned my truck around and came here."

Mia walked into his embrace as quickly as her still-wobbly legs would take her. His arms came around her in an all-encompassing embrace. She pressed her cheek against his chest. The sound of his heart beating hard against her ear brought her comfort, and for a moment, all was right with the world.

Too soon, Hank pulled away. He cleared his throat. "I'll just put these in some water." He snagged a vase containing the wilted flowers he'd brought earlier in the week and headed to the bathroom.

"I feel like celebrating. What should we do?"

After stepping back into her room, he placed the flowers on the windowsill, taking an unusually long time fidgeting with the blooms. "Let's go down to the cafeteria for dinner."

"It's a date," she said, keen to celebrate her

milestone. "Let me freshen up a bit, and I'll be ready to go." She took a moment to dab on some lip-gloss and a touch of mascara. Dianne had been thoughtful enough to bring some toiletries from Mia's condo, but until now she hadn't felt the need to do more than the basics.

When she returned from the bathroom, Hank's mouth spread into a smile. "You look great, angel." He fingered the barrette she'd clipped to the tuft of dark blonde hair that was beginning to curl. "Your hair's growing back."

"Thanks for noticing." She ducked her chin. As she went about her day in the rehab facility, she tried not to feel self-conscious about her half-inch-long locks that made her look more like a preadolescent boy than a twenty-six-year-old woman. His praise warmed her.

He grabbed the door handle before she could reach for it. "Ladies first."

As they trekked down the hall, his hand went to the small of her back. The contact felt more like tender affection than the clinical way Tripp and the staff guided her around like she was spun glass. Though her legs felt strong and her equilibrium balanced as they toddled toward the nurses' desk, his touch was what truly grounded her. He'd always had the ability to make her feel secure. As a small girl, she'd been afraid of thunderstorms. During those times, she'd often sneak across the hall to the boys' bedroom. Using a flashlight, he'd read or make up stories for her until the storm passed.

"I can't believe how much you've improved in just the past few days," he said as they entered the facility's cafeteria. He snagged a couple of plastic serving trays, placing them on the rail attached to the serving line.

The odor of overcooked cabbage and fish didn't exactly whet her appetite. "I'm feeling better every day." She took the least offensive entrée, broiled chicken.

Besides being her protector, he'd been a one-man cheering section. But his leave would be up soon, and she couldn't let herself become too dependent on his presence. "When does *The Eisenhower* begin sea trials?"

Hank shrugged. "Not for a while." He paid acute attention to the desserts at the end of the line. "Pudding or gelatin."

A shudder ran through her. "Neither."

She redirected her distaste from both so-called desserts. His less-than-straightforward answer piqued her curiosity. What wasn't he telling her? She eyed him as he led them to the far corner of the cafeteria. "Thank you," she said as he held out her chair.

There wasn't much the two of them didn't share, and the last time he'd been this evasive, his marriage to Tiffany was falling apart. She took a sip of her iced tea biding her time. He'd share when he was ready, or if he took too long, she'd needle the information out of him. "I'm going to miss you when you leave again."

His eyes darkened as his gaze darted to hers. "You're going to be so busy getting well and adjusting to married life that you won't have time to think of anything but redecorating Tripp's townhouse and getting back to work."

"Not true." She picked at her food. "I already told Tripp I want to have you over for dinner before you're deployed again. You're going to be our first guest when we return from our honeymoon." Tucked into the pocket of her sweat pants, her phone vibrated against her leg. She pulled it out. "Speaking of fiancés, it's Tripp. I better get this." She pressed the button to begin the call. "How's the case coming?"

"It's fine." He sounded tired and distracted. "Listen, I'm sorry about canceling on you. If you're too bored, I can see if Dianne or Mother can keep you company."

While she appreciated his efforts, she didn't want to be babysat. She wanted a fiancé who desired spending time with her and not someone who saw her as another obligation.

"No. I'm good." She worked to keep her aggravation from her voice. "Hank surprised me with a visit. We're having dinner in the cafeteria."

A couple seconds passed. "How nice," he bit back. "What's your brother been up to lately?"

His word choice pinged around in her head. When she and Tripp first began dating, he'd had a hard time seeing Hank as her brother. Now it seemed he emphasized it at every turn. "I'm not sure." She tried reading between the lines. Was Tripp jealous? Was that the reason he'd asked Hank to be his best man—a keep-your-enemy-close tactic?

"Listen," he began, sounding more upbeat. "If I shift some things around tomorrow, I can probably squeeze in a quick lunch date. I'll get my secretary to pick up some sandwiches for us, and we'll have a picnic in the garden. Just the two of us. Would you like that?"

No. What she wanted was to be a priority, not another appointment penciled in between a deposition and a conference call. "That would be nice." She struggled to appreciate his efforts.

Mia also had the urge to say that Hank wasn't her brother. *Where did that come from?* The shift in the way she viewed him caught her off guard. Her gaze darted to the man across from her who was studiously not listening in to her conversation. That Hank was sinfully handsome was as obvious as the scar creasing her skull. He was also kind, and she dreaded the time when his squadron would be deployed again.

"If you can't get away, I'll understand."

"You're a peach. It's one of the things I like best about you, Mia. You're not one of those demanding women."

His words—meant as praise—sounded discordant in her ears. Like a well-written tune played by unskilled hands. Was keeping her company such a hardship?

"Sleep well, dear," he said then disconnected the call.

Mia stowed her phone in her pocket and let out a breath. She picked up her fork, returning to her dinner that even when piping hot had been only marginally appetizing. After a bite of cold, tough chicken, she pushed her plate away.

"Everything okay?" Hank asked. "Did he say something to upset you?"

"No, not at all." The reflexive white lie passed her lips without effort. It wasn't so much what Tripp said that had worry tangling her insides. It's what he hadn't said. He used the three little words early and often in their courtship. His demonstrative affection took some getting used to at first, but after a while, she learned to enjoy being told she was loved.

He gestured to their dinner. "If you're finished,

why don't we head back to your room?"

The Acquired Brain Injury Unit suddenly seemed miles from the cafeteria instead of two floors above. Leaning into Hank for support, they returned to her room. She looked longingly at her bed where most days she loathed returning to the hard mattress. With a brain that struggled to remember directions and piece together words, trying to process the conversation with Tripp taxed her to the point of fatigue.

"I should get going. You look done in."

As tired as she was, she didn't want him to leave. Not because she didn't want to be alone. In a world that seemed to be shifting underneath her feet, Hank was her constant. "Not yet." She grasped his hand. "I'll just lie here on the bed, and we can watch TV for a while."

He tensed, his gaze shooting to the room's window. "Sure. I can stay for a bit longer." He held back the covers for her while she slipped underneath them. "Are you comfortable?" He leaned over her to fluff her pillow.

The crack of the door slamming against the wall had them both jumping. Tripp's brow furrowed for a split second before he smoothed out the expression. Smiling, he crossed the room in a couple quick strides. "I said to hell with it. The work will keep until tomorrow." He waved his arms dramatically.

Tripp edged Hank out of the way to sit on the side of the bed. Then he brought his mouth to hers in a hard kiss—one that lingered, growing more demanding as she struggled to respond. His fingers dug into her shoulders as his tongue thrust between her lips. Rather than igniting any long-buried passion, his attempt at romance angered her. This wasn't about missing her.

Mia shoved against him. "What brought that on?" She wiped at lips that felt bruised.

Now that he'd marked his territory, he was back to his cool, suave self. He jerked the sleeves of his jacket back in place. "Can't a guy miss his fiancée?"

She took several deep breaths, not trusting herself to answer. Four-letter words along with a couple well-worded directives about where he could go and what to do when he got there came to mind. Hank's presence played a major role in keeping those thoughts to herself. His narrowed gaze darted between her and Tripp, and he seemed to be struggling with how to respond to the aggressive display of affection.

Mia held up her hand, letting him know things were okay. The last thing she needed at that moment was for Hank to feel the need to defend her.

His jaw clenched. "I guess I should get going." He held his arms stiffly by his side.

"Good to see you again." Tripp turned and extended his hand. "Thanks for keeping my girl company," he said a little too politely.

Hank ignored Tripp, moving to the far side of the bed. He took her hand and drew it to his lips. His soothing touch radiated throughout her. "Talk to you tomorrow, angel. I'm damn proud of you."

The door had barely closed when Tripp asked, "When did you say he was getting deployed again?"

Chapter Six

Mia plucked a spent bloom from one of the bouquets Tripp had sent during the past week. Her room smelled of roses and lilies, with vases covering every flat surface. As she moved to attend a dozen crimson roses, intuition told her they represented further attempts to stake his territory and were not displays of affection.

As she refilled the water in the cut crystal vase, a memory niggled at the back of her brain. The surreal sensation of *déjà vu* unbalanced her. This wasn't the first time her fiancé had made the same over-the-top gesture. She closed her eyes in thought. *Roses.* There'd been dozens and dozens of pink, red, and white roses filling not only her apartment but her office. Those had definitely been of the "don't break up with me" variety. *But why?*

She stared at the red blooms in her hand, a sudden inexplicable rage filling her. She crushed the flowers in her fist as the memory trickled back. They'd had an argument right before the attack. Tripp's ghost-like face, twisted in anger, danced in her mind's eye though the source of their argument remained out of grasp.

"I brought your favorite, sweetheart," Tripp said, breezing into the room.

Jerked from her thoughts, she turned her attention to the corporeal version of her fiancé in front of her, the one who smiled sweetly as he presented her with a Styrofoam box of chicken enchiladas. Ever since the night Hank had visited, Tripp faithfully stopped by every evening after work. He lavished her with food from her favorite restaurants and bought her expensive track suits to wear to her last week of therapy.

After placing the takeout container on the rolling tray, he crossed the room, tipped her chin with his fingers, and kissed her. She pressed her lips together, denying him entrance. Not noticing her lack of response, he continued playing the part of loving fiancé to the hilt. "I missed you today. How was therapy?"

Memories, blurred in a gray fog, swirled in her mind. *Why had they fought?* When he pulled her in for a hug, a cloyingly sweet scent filled her nose. Perfume. And not hers. As if someone had flipped on a light switch, it all came back. She shoved out of his embrace as tears pricked the back of her eyes.

His jaw ticked. "What's wrong?"

She waved him away, covering her mouth as a wave of nausea washed over her.

"My God, Mia." His eyes widened. "You look like you've seen a ghost."

She let him guide her to the nearby chair. His use of the cliché fit perfectly. A specter had lingered in the corners of her brain for weeks, whispering unease in her ear. "I just remembered something about the morning of my attack."

His face darkened. "I've told you that you shouldn't be wasting your energy trying to recall things."

She gazed up at the man she now saw in a new light, the master manipulator working his charm on her.

"You sent me flowers trying to make up with me."

"I sent you flowers that day because I love you," he countered, his lips upturned in a smile that didn't reach his eyes. A lie if she'd ever heard one. He didn't love her now. And maybe not even then.

With her memory of that morning returning she began questioning everything she thought was true. Her head swam with the onslaught of images. She'd been so angry with him that she'd stormed over to his townhouse to confront him. The exact cause of her anger still eluded her. It did, however, explain so much of the unease she felt around him. "Why were we fighting?"

He dismissed her question with a wave of the hand. "We had a little misunderstanding. In the end we worked it out." He knelt beside her, taking her hand. His forced smile sent anxiety dancing over her skin.

She bolted out of her seat, putting as much distance between them as the small room would allow. "No, we didn't." Women's intuition, prosecuting attorney's instinct, whatever it was, she knew to her marrow he was lying to her.

Tripp let out a breath. "If you promise to hear me out, I'll tell you everything that happened that morning."

Mia sank to her bed. "Of course." Anything to lessen the pounding in her head.

"A couple days before your attack, you found lipstick on my collar. It was nothing—either Mother's or Dianne's," he said, with a flick of his wrist. "You blew it all out of proportion, and I tried to smooth things over with flowers."

She narrowed her eyes, instinct now screaming. "If

we worked it out, then why did I show up at your townhouse gunning for a fight? I remember being really furious with you."

"You were being irrational." He shook his head and shrugged. "I guess it was PMS or something."

Her breath quickened as her pulse surged. His dismissal wasn't the only thing igniting her temper. The dream she'd had weeks ago had been her brain's way for handling the painful fight. "I took off my engagement ring and threw it at you," she said, the true story coming into focus.

He nodded, looking away. "Then you stormed out. I guess when you got back to your apartment, you decided to ride your bike to clear your head. The police found you on the trail several hours later."

He'd kept all this from her. She dashed angry tears from her eyes. "Why didn't you fill in the blanks for me? You knew I was struggling to put the pieces of that day together."

Tripp sat on the bed next to her. "It broke my heart that you thought I'd been unfaithful. When you woke up from your coma and didn't remember the fight, I seized the chance to start over with a clean slate."

Her brain might not have remembered until now, but her heart knew the truth. He had been cheating on her. That certainty led her to push him further. "Have you told the police that we fought?"

His jaw ticked. "I didn't see the point. Our quarrel has no bearing on the case. You were attacked on the trail by a random person acting on an opportunity. During that time, I was in the office. My secretary corroborated my whereabouts." He shot her a glare. "Mother's and Dianne's movements are also accounted for, in case you were wondering."

Given the evidence the police had in hand, that scenario was likely true. But so was the fact their relationship—and her future—lay in the balance. Could she ignore that he'd lied to her repeatedly, keeping information from her to ease his own conscience? Was she willing to look past the unfaithfulness for the sake of maintaining the status quo and ensuring she had a place to go while she further recovered? The answers were no and hell no.

This wasn't the first time she'd made the decision not to hide from the truth when maintaining a lie would be the easier route. Years ago in the last place she and Hank lived together, their foster father had been abusive. Fred Gilbert hit all the kids, but Hank seemed to be a particular favorite. He'd pleaded with her to keep the abuse under wraps, saying he could handle what the man dished out. Then came the time she discovered cigarette burns on his back. Mia told the school counselor knowing the end result, both good and bad. It nearly killed her when they separated her and Hank. Back then, she couldn't stand by and wait for things to get worse, any more than she could stand by and listen to Tripp's lies or wait for him to cheat again. Resolve steeled her spine as she stood. "I want you to leave."

Tripp's mouth opened. "But-"

"Consider the engagement broken." She held up her bare left hand. "I've already returned the ring."

"Mia, sweetheart, this is just the brain injury talking." He took her hand, which she snatched out of reach. "You forgave me."

She swallowed past the lump in her throat. "Please

leave and don't come back."

He bolted to his feet, planting his fists on his hips. "Who do you think is going to take care of you when you get out? If you do this, you'll have no one. Mother won't let you in her house, much less wait on you while you recover." His eyes narrowed. "If you ever recover. You could stay the invalid that you are. How are you going to look after yourself if you can't go back to your precious job in the district attorney's office?"

She levered her chin to meet his gaze. "I'll continue to do as I always have—take care of myself."

"How are you going to get to your therapy?" he asked, taking the reasonable tack. "Who's going to help you bathe and dress?"

A vision of her alone and helpless tempered her anger. Fear pricked her skull, sending a chill across her skin. Mia locked her worst nightmares behind a steel door. "That's none of your concern," she said in a calm voice that strangled her true emotions. "I'm sure I'm not the first person to be in this predicament, and I'll work out my problems on my own."

He stabbed a finger in her direction. "Mark my words. If I leave here, there will be no going back. No fancy dinners out. No vacations. No big house on Country Club Drive."

"Promise," she retorted, using sarcasm as a shield. Those things had never mattered. She'd only wanted someone to love and a sense of belonging. She thought she'd found it in Tripp and his family.

He took a step toward her, his nostrils flared and his face a bright red. For two seconds, she thought he might strike her. Her gaze darted to the nurses' call button just out of reach. Instead, he turned on his heels and bolted. The door slammed, the echo reverberating around the room.

Mia collapsed back on the bed, covering her eyes with her arm. Though he'd brought up the issue of her care as a way to frighten her into staying, he made a valid point. She'd never be able to manage the tub in her condo, and she wouldn't be medically cleared to drive for several months.

She'd been in worse predicaments and managed. Tomorrow she'd make an appointment with her caseworker to sort out a visiting nurse for her baths and transportation to and from the outpatient facility.

Thank God, she hadn't let Tripp talk her into giving up her condo—otherwise she'd be forced to live in the resident home attached to Milestones. For all she'd been through in the last hour, at least that knowledge comforted her.

****

Later that week, Hank entered through the double doors of LaGrange General's Acquired Brain Injury Unit and stifled a shudder. The place gave him the creeps and not just because he had to be buzzed onto the floor or from the line of orthopedic equipment that looked a lot like torture devices. The staff did their best to create a safe, happy environment, but no amount of artwork hung on the walls could hide the fact it was an institution—something he and Mia knew well through firsthand experience.

"I'm here to see Mia Jones," he told the nurse sitting at the flower-lined desk. A particularly exotic vase of lilies caught his attention. Hadn't he seen some just like that in Mia's room when he took her lunch earlier in the week?

"I remember you." She smiled broadly as she passed him the visitor sign-in sheet. "You're her handsome big brother." The early-twenties nurse preened, leaning over the counter, and patted his hand.

"I am." He quickly scribbling his name and handing back the clipboard. "Is she in her room?"

"She was asleep when I checked on her a little while ago. She's had a rough couple days, what with her break up and all."

His brows hit his hairline, the woman's words capturing his attention the way her augmented breasts hadn't. "What?"

The nurse covered her mouth. "She didn't tell you?"

"No," he growled. A dozen questions scrambled to his lips, none of which he was going to ask this nurse. She had no business discussing Mia's personal matters.

As he turned to go, the nurse touched his hand. "Don't tell her I said anything. I thought you knew."

"I won't." Not for Nurse Nosey but because it would embarrass Mia to be the topic of conversation.

Moments later, he eased open her door and slipped inside the room. Late afternoon sun streamed in from the tiny window. He had about an hour before he had to hit the road back to Wilmington.

Her tiny frame barely lifted the covers, the lightweight blanket hiding most of her scars. His gaze traveled to the incision that began at her temple, arched over her ear, and ended at her nape. God, he'd almost lost her—his worst fear realized. It made being discharged from the navy about as worrisome as losing his car keys.

Mia rolled over in her sleep, turning her face

toward him. Her full lips tempted him. His imagination took him to the place where he was free to find out if they were as soft as they looked, to where she'd return his feelings toward her. Loosening the reins on his self-control, he leaned over her, pressing a kiss to her temple. The scent of strawberry shampoo filled his nostrils. He'd loved her longer and deeper than anyone else who'd entered his life, including his ex-wife. Yet she remained out of reach.

Her eyes popped open.

He jerked back. "Hi, Rip Van Winkle." He laughed to cover the intensity of his feelings for her. "Did you sleep the day away?"

She sat up, looking warm and comfortable as she yawned and stretched. "No. I meant to only close my eyes for a few minutes. I haven't slept well lately."

His mood shifted from the clawing hunger he felt for her to frustration. He wanted to light into her for not telling him about the breakup. She shouldn't be trying to carry those burdens on her own. But the thing that made him want to punch a wall—or a face—was her ass-wipe fiancé. What kind of man broke up with his girl while she was in the hospital? If he discovered Tripp had called off the wedding because of her lingering disabilities, Hank would probably show up at the guy's house.

Even as the idea took root, he cast aside that idea. She didn't need anyone adding to her grief. Smothering his anger, he asked, "Care to explain why all your flowers are sitting at the nurses' station?"

The corner of her mouth turned up. "Not all of them." She pointed to a vase of orange and yellow Gerber daisies he'd picked up at the grocery store on his last visit.

He arched an eyebrow. "Why didn't you tell me Tripp broke up with you?"

She jutted out her chin. "He didn't. I broke up with him."

Hank suppressed the urge to fist pump the air in celebration. Something about the way Mr. Perfect had swept in and took over Mia's life never set well with him—not that she didn't deserve a guy who could buy her all the things he could never give. The whole love-at-first-sight thing was like Tripp himself—just a little too perfect to be real.

"Tell me." He drew up a chair.

"It was the flowers that started it." She shook her head as if still trying to get her head around what happened. "I'd been feeling like I was supposed to be mad at Tripp about something, but I couldn't remember why. I kept chalking it up to the brain injury until I smelled the roses he brought and a memory of me throwing my engagement ring at him returned." She let out a breath. "He filled in the blanks for me. Evidently, the morning of the attack I found out he'd been cheating on me. We broke up, and after I left his townhouse, I went for a ride on the Coastal Comet Trail to clear my head."

"I'll—" On instinct Hank bolted for his seat. He'd pound Tripp into oblivion and hide the body. What man would cheat when he had Mia in his life?

The touch of her hand reined in his anger. "That's why I didn't tell you. I don't want you trying to fix all my problems."

"But..."

"It's over, and I'm fine," she said, her voice as

level as glass.

He cocked his head, examining her closely. The dark circles below her eyes gave her away. "Really?"

"Okay," she conceded. "I'll be fine after some time's passed." She smiled up at him. "You know this is partly your fault."

His eyes widened. "How's that?"

"You've set the bar pretty high. Not many men measure up to you. You're thoughtful, kind, funny, and very easy on the eyes."

He was so far from perfect that he wasn't even in the same hemisphere. But he'd always treated the women in his life with respect. "Then there's your low tolerance for crap."

"There's that." She laughed. "Funny thing though, I'm more upset about losing his mom and sister." A few tears shown in her eyes.

His heart ached for her. "They didn't understand?" What kind of family turned away someone when they needed them most? The same type that left a newborn in a gas station bathroom or beat a four-year-old nearly to death—those incapable of love.

"You could hardly expect them to choose me over him." She shrugged. "Anyway, I won't be staying with Mrs. Brooks for outpatient therapy, so I've made arrangements to return to my condo."

"You can't take care of yourself." Visions of her falling sprang to his mind.

Mia met his gaze, her voice steady. "The alternative is to go to Milestones. I wouldn't have to worry about transportation or getting the little bit of nursing help I need, but I'd have even less privacy than I do here. Unlike this place, all their rooms are semiprivate."

Oh, hell no! They'd both been there and done that whole communal living thing. Sharing quarters aboard *the Eisenhower* didn't have the same institutionalized feel that an orphanage or a group home did. Perhaps the difference lay with one being voluntary and the other a situation completely out of his control. Either way, every fiber of his being screamed that it was he who should be taking care of her.

One issue lay in the way. If he offered for her to stay at his place, it wouldn't take many days before she began to wonder why he wasn't participating in sea trials, which were part of the run-up to *The Eisenhower's* next deployment. Now wasn't the time for her to learn he'd been discharged—or the reason why. She had enough on her plate without worrying about his issues. Helplessness twisted in his gut. "What can I do to help?"

"Not a thing." Mia shook her head. "My condo's on the first floor, so there are no steps for me to negotiate. The facilities manager installed grab bars in the bathroom, and Veronica from the DA's office wants to fill my freezer with meals I can microwave."

"How are you going to get back and forth?"

"My caseworker at Milestones arranged for transport, so I'm all set."

The all too familiar sense of failure weighed on him. If only he'd shared with Mia his concerns about Tripp, but he'd wanted to believe at least one of them would finally have a family to love them. "I'm so sorry," he said, wishing he could take away some of her pain.

"The good news is that I remembered something

about the day of my attack. Maybe with time, I'll remember more."

"Yeah, but what a thing to remember. Did you tell Detective Price what you remembered?"

"I haven't since it doesn't really change anything."

"I still think you should. I'll remind you, when I come by your place to check on you tomorrow."

She shook her head. "About that. Give me a couple days to settle in. I just want some solitude for a while. Besides, I have tons of laundry to do and hospital bills to look over. Once I get some housekeeping done, I'll be ready to play hostess."

"Monday then." He fought the urge to argue. He wanted nothing more than to tackle her problems and smooth out all life's little wrinkles until all she had to do was concentrate on getting well.

"That would be great. We can go see a movie, and afterward you can take me to the Creamery. I've been dying for some of their fudge ripple."

"I can definitely make that happen," he said, wishing he could do more, be more, spend every moment with her. His gaze shot to the window. He was already cutting it close. "I better go." He leaned over to kiss the top of her head. He lingered, stroking her curls as the urge to take her into his arms nearly overwhelmed him. He couldn't recall when exactly his feelings for her began to change. Rather than a seismic shift that resulted in an earthquake, the change came subtly like spring slipping slowly into summer. Finally, he worked up the will to pull himself away.

As he did, Mia tugged him back. "Stay," she pleaded. "Now I've had that power nap, it will be hours before I'm sleepy again."

His chest tightened. She asked for so little, and yet he couldn't manage to even pull off that. "Visiting hours are nearly over."

"The nurses don't care."

He brought her hand to his lips to ease the sting of his rejection. "I can't."

Pain flashed on her face before she plastered on a smile. "I understand. See you in a couple days."

"I'll be all yours then."

Chapter Seven

Mia tucked her cosmetics inside her duffle bag, zipped it closed, and placed it on the floor next to her hospital bed. Then she gathered the magazines visitors brought so she could leave them with the nurses on her way out. Her deliberate movements belied the nervous energy thrumming through her body. She paced the small room, her steps still cautious, while on the inside she did the happy dance. In less than an hour, she'd be back in her condo where her decadently-soft bed, jetted tub, and round-the-clock privacy awaited her.

Thanks to a fever, her discharge had been pushed back a day. She woke that morning feeling perfectly well and more than ready to be set free fom the rehab center's confines. She looked around the room that had been both prison cell and home for the past several weeks. With its nondescript walls and simple furnishings, one would never guess the battle she'd waged in these four walls. Each increment of independence she regained counted as a win. Feeding and dressing herself, talking and walking—all small steps toward regaining what her attacker had taken.

As she stood on somewhat-steady legs, the war wasn't over by a long shot. Ahead lay the real work of relearning to read and write and hopefully regaining her memories. More than anything, the black hole of amnesia influenced her life going forward. Moving on with her life without Tripp and his family was hard enough without the shadow of the unsolved attack. The man, who'd lain in wait for the perfect victim, had beaten her unconscious and left her to die in the ditch along the trail. Until he was caught, prosecuted, and jailed, she wouldn't be fully healed.

Mia's favorite nurse, Elise, entered the room, drawing her thoughts to the present. "You ready to do this?" She grinned broadly and held up a pair of scissors.

"You have no idea." Mia extended her wrist.

Elise snipped through the plastic identification bracelet. "I declare this Mia open for business."

Unexpected tears pricked the back of her eyes. "Thanks for everything." Despite the wall she erected around her emotions, several of the staff became more than caregivers. Along with Hank, they were cheerleaders.

Warmth infused Elise's smile. "Come back and see us sometime." She patted Mia's arm. "We'd love to see how you're doing."

She nodded. "Absolutely." It would be some time before she could muster the courage to return. "I'll have plenty follow-up appointments with the doctors in the months to come, so I'll come say hello."

"The transport company will be here in a few minutes to take you home. I'll send him in." Elise opened the door then turned to look back over her shoulder. "You got this."

Later that morning, Mia's gaze absorbed the scene passing outside the transport van window. Other than visits to the garden, she hadn't left the confines of the hospital in months. A whole season had passed while she'd been cloistered away. Winter had turned into spring, during which she'd missed the town's annual Easter parade as well as Founders' Day.

After months of slow motion, the rush of traffic outside the van window made her dizzy and she would have shut her eyes to stop her head spinning if it wouldn't prevent her from taking it all in. Tall palm trees swayed in the breeze, and every block or so she caught a glimpse of the gray-green water of the Atlantic.

Cars with out-of-state license plates clogged the streets, making the cross-town trip take longer than it did for nine months of the year. From Labor Day to Easter, LaGrange was little more than a hamlet midway between Wilmington to the south and Norfolk to the north. With the tourist season in full swing, the sidewalks were dotted with folks who vacationed at the town's many seaside resorts.

A dark thought penetrated her happy ride home. What if the man who'd attacked her wasn't a resident? Bile burned the back of her throat as she considered the prospect as well as the alternative. Which would be worse, her attacker being a tourist who could be hundreds of miles off police radar or a resident who still walked the streets where she lived?

Her driver's erratic lane change kept her from dwelling on the issue for long. Once she settled in, she'd reach out to Detective Price and put the question to him. Perhaps they'd already considered that avenue. She'd been so focused on her recovery, letting Tripp handle the investigation; she had little idea what angles the police were following.

Mia let out a breath, remembering she promised

Hank she'd bring Price up to speed on her breakup with Tripp, along with the reason. Embarrassment twisted her stomach. She hated airing her personal business, wishing she could avoid the tawdry details of her love life. Hopefully, the detective wouldn't read more into the situation than was there. While their relationship hadn't worked out in the long run, Tripp and his family had seen her through the worst of her injuries. She'd always be grateful for that and didn't want the police wasting time investigating dead-end avenues.

As they turned off Palmetto Street and crossed the railroad tracks, her pulse kicked up a notch. Built in the late eighties, the development of modest apartments, condos, and single family houses, was as old as she. While it wasn't as posh as Tripp's upscale neighborhood that boasted other lawyers, doctors, and IT professionals as residents, she wouldn't trade her working-class neighbors or her down-at-the-heels home. Mia couldn't wait to sit on Mrs. Brewster's stoop and catch up on the latest gossip. She could almost taste the sweet iced tea the elderly woman was known for.

The driver slammed on the breaks, jerking her out of her thoughts. "Look at that." He pointed skyward to a column of gray smoke. "Looks like there's a fire."

Her heart went out to the unknown neighbor. "Can you tell which building it's coming from?"

The driver tilted his head to gaze skyward. "Not from this far away."

"My place is at the end of the complex," she said, worrying about Mr. Willoughby who was eighty and lived alone and Manuela Vasquez who sometimes had to leave her kids without a sitter. "Hopefully they won't have my street blocked."

As they wound their way deeper into the condo complex, the smoke not only blocked the sun, it curled along the sidewalks and hugged the ground. Her stomach twisted with worry. Whose life had been turned upside down? Her heart went out to them. Then, seeing a fire truck blocking the street leading to her building, her pulse began to race. She rolled down the window and craned her neck in time to see firefighters dragging hoses out of her building.

God, please don't let it be... Mia bolted from the van, racing toward her home. "No, no, no." Her stumbling feet brought her closer to the nightmare. Billows of smoke poured out of every window, and the exterior had bubbled and warped from the heat.

"Hey, lady, wait," the driver said.

Ignoring his command, she rushed forward only to be stopped by one of the firefighters. She struggled against his hold, needing to see if there was anything left. Individually, her possessions meant little. Collectively, they represented everything she'd worked so hard to achieve.

"Hold on." He grabbed her by the shoulders. "You can't go in there."

As he blocked her path, the acrid stench from his bunker gear filled her nose. Everything not burned would carry that odor, she realized as tears began rolling down her cheeks. "That's my home," she managed through a throat choked with smoke and emotion.

The firefighter took her by the elbow and led her to the one of the department's cars. "Wait right here, and I'll get the chief. He'll want to talk with you." He touched her shoulder, sympathy infusing his expression.

"Don't go back over there. I know you want to see what's left, but it's not safe."

It's just stuff. She repeated the mantra as she mentally inventoried her belongings. All that mattered was that no one had been hurt. The alternative outcome hit her hard. She would have been inside her home had it not been for her fever. At the time, she'd been frustrated with Dr. Cowboy for refusing to discharge her. Looking at the charred remains of her home, she sent him mental thanks. What would have happened to her if she'd been at home when the fire started?

"Miss Jones."

Mia turned her attention to the familiar voice. "Detective Price, why are you here?"

"I heard the nine-one-one dispatcher call your address over the scanner."

He'd been thorough in investigating her case, but this seemed out of his jurisdiction. "What made you come?" She dashed tears from her eyes.

He met her gaze. "I hadn't planned on it until the fire chief called for the arson investigator."

"Oh God." Her vision narrowed as blood rushed to her head. She slumped to the rear bumper.

Price placed a steadying hand on her. "Put your head between your legs," he coached as she fought to keep her breakfast down. In the end, she lost the battle with her stomach and stumbled to the grassy area on the other side of the car to vomit.

When she was finished, he helped her to her feet. "Let's come over here where we can talk." He led her to a nearby bench.

"Who would do such a thing?" She accepted a bottle of water he handed her.

A shadow passed over his grim face. "My money's on the same person who attacked you on the trail."

Confusion swirled in her head. "How can that be? It was a random act."

He steepled his fingers together. "Maybe not. I've been following a new theory. Your attacker could be someone you prosecuted. Or their family looking for revenge."

Her eyes widened. She'd had a couple people make threats in the courtroom, but nothing that made her worry. Having people hate her came with the territory of someone who went up against criminals for a living.

"I hadn't planned to say anything to you until I had more evidence." He jerked his chin in the direction of her burnt out home. "I think I have it."

"I guess at this point, anything's possible," she said, feeling like she'd fallen down a very dark hole.

"I'm waiting on a preliminary from the arson investigator. If he says what I think he will, I'm going to assign a protection detail for you. I'd also like a list of people you think may want to get back at you."

Where would she even begin? She tried scores of cases in her two years as ADA. "That could be a very long list, detective, given my job description." It could also take days if not weeks, considering the speed at which she now digested the written word. She could call Veronica, one of her fellow prosecutors. "I'll get working on a list for you, but first things first."

She glanced at what had once been a very cute home. "I've got to find a place to spend the night."

"I understand. I'll touch base with you in a couple days when you've had a moment to get your bearings."

She barked a laugh. "It might take me more than a

few days, detective."

"I know. I'm sorry. Seems like you've had more than your fair share of troubles." Detective Price stood and placed his hand on her shoulder for a moment, then gave her a quick squeeze and pat before leaving her on the bench.

Thankfully, before she had time to give into despair, the fire chief came up to her. "I've been in touch with the Red Cross, and they've found places for you and your neighbors."

"Wonderful," she said, glad that one issue had been taken care of. "Where?"

"There are a few empty units on the third floor of building ten."

Her spirits sank as quickly as they'd lifted. That would never work. Perhaps she could hobble up the steps, but then she was stuck. She'd never be able to negotiate the three flights on a daily basis. She looked at the burnt shell of her former home. If the arsonist tried again, she'd never be able to get out of the building in time. Tears welled. "That's not going to work. I guess I'll have to figure out something on my own."

"I'll talk to the Red Cross folks and let them know," he said, leaving her alone.

She needed to get her suitcase from the transport van, and then she'd have to call a taxi to take her to a hotel. Details swirled in her brain when all she wanted to do was curl up on the bench and have a good cry. Later when she had a roof over her head.

Moments after the chief left, a hand touched her elbow, drawing her back to the here and now. "Mia, oh thank God." Tripp hauled her to her feet and hugged her tightly. "I came right over the second I heard the news. I can't believe this happened to you after everything else you've been through. I'm here now, and I'll take care of everything."

She pulled out of his embrace. "Why *are* you here? We broke up, remember."

"Now don't be that way." He pouted through a smile. "I screwed up. I admit."

"Yes, you did," Her temper spiked. "I believe I told you that I never wanted to see you again."

His expression darkened. "Let's put this all behind us and begin again. You can move in to Mother's. It'll be like we never broke up."

Perhaps pride clouded her judgment, but she deserved better than a man who cheated. "The problem with that is it did happen. You were unfaithful, and I can't get past that. Please leave." When he opened his mouth, she held up a hand to ward off whatever crap he was about to feed her. "I have enough on my plate without dealing with your nonsense."

He grabbed her hand. "Stop being pigheaded. You've got nowhere to go, and no one to help you. You need me."

An old fear nearly had her giving in. After aging out of the foster care system, she'd been entirely on her own. Sink or swim, the only one who'd cared what happened to her was Hank. Since he'd been aboard ship for many years, even he couldn't have offered help. But she'd managed back then without a safety net and she'd do the same now. She tilted her chin. "No, I don't."

"You're a fool." He jabbed a finger in her direction. "And your stubbornness will earn you nothing but trouble." Then he turned on his heels and stormed off.

Mia sagged back to the bench, tired to the bone. And yet, the confrontation with Tripp had put a bit of starch in her spine. As long as his was the last difficult conversation she had to hold with someone, she'd muster through. One more shock might send her over the edge.

When the transport driver approached, Mia pulled herself together. "Miss Jones. Is there some other place I can take you?" he asked, his voice full of compassion.

She wanted to hug the man, not only for hanging around but for having the sense she'd had just about as much of this day as she could stand. She nodded. Mia knew where she needed to go, if they'd take her. "I need to make some arrangements," she said, pulling out her phone. It looked like she'd be moving into the group home after all. Better there than the streets.

After leaving the hospital hours earlier, Mia found herself yards from where she'd begun her morning. She trailed alongside a matron as she gave Mia the fifty-cent tour. "Here is the kitchen," said the woman in her late forties who was built like a linebacker and was about as feminine. She gestured to the industrial kitchen. "You'll be making your own meals every day."

Mia eyed the stove with suspicion. "I don't cook. Is there another option."

"There isn't," the woman said briskly. "It's part of Milestone's plan to get you back to normal."

Mia bit back the urge to tell her normal was only a setting on the dryer. "I guess I'll be learning a new skill," she said instead.

Taking an elevator, they eventually made their way to the residence floor. Mia lumbered behind the nurse, every muscle screaming. Her head throbbed and her clothes stunk of smoke.

"You'll be sharing a room with another woman."

Her heart sank seeing the cramped room that was smaller than her college dorm room. "Wow, this is tight. You don't think my roomie would be interested in bunking the beds?" she said, trying to make light of a situation that made her feel less human by the hour.

The nurse seemed to be lacking a sense of humor as well as eyebrow tweezers. "You're very lucky we had a place for you, Miss Jones."

Mia leveled a glare at the woman, having reached the end of her patience with humanity. "I got out of the rehab center this morning to come home to a place that burned over night." She pointed to her suitcase. "I've lost everything with the exception of the things in this bag. You'll forgive me if I'm feeling less than lucky at the moment."

Mia's tirade failed to pierce the matron's hide. She bobbed her head in acknowledgment. "I'll leave you to settle in."

Tears fell as she sank to the bed. The sense of loss and abandonment was all too much and cuttingly familiar. She recalled as clearly as if it had happened yesterday. At age five, a couple had taken her out of the foster home with the intent to adopt her. One glorious month later, they'd learned they were pregnant and returned her to child protective services. The same sense of hopelessness settled on her shoulders. Maybe it would have been better if the attacker… The situation was temporary. She'd only lost her furnishings. Monday morning she'd get on the phone with the insurance agent and begin processing a claim.

At the moment what she needed was a hug. Someone to tell her everything would be okay, even if it wouldn't be so for a very long time. She longed to call Hank, to feel his massive arms around her. Just hearing his voice would help. But once he found out, he'd be over as fast as his truck could take him. She'd relied on him so much in the days after her breakup with Tripp, coming to crave the way he made her laugh, the way his aftershave lingered on her clothes after he left, the feel of his lips against her cheek.

As much as he pretended all was well with him, she sensed he was dealing with some issues of his own. He'd been vague when she asked him about his last tour or when his squadron would be deployed again.

She'd call him first thing Monday morning before he had a chance to head to her condo like they'd scheduled. Then she'd make the call to the insurance company. Thinking of the mounds of paperwork ahead triggered a realization. All her vital records were inside her burned condo. She smiled for the first time since she'd left the hospital that morning. In the midst of loss, she recalled one pinpoint of hope. She'd stored her photos, important papers, and the few mementoes she had from childhood inside a firebox bolted to the bottom of her closet.

It wasn't much, but for now it was enough. She'd collect the box as soon as the fire department deemed it safe to venture in. Grasping that shred of hope, she lay down and turned her back to the door.

Chapter Eight

Hank jolted awake, his sudden movement sending him over the edge of the sofa and onto the floor. "Fuck." He groaned, levering upright as the ringtone continued its little ditty. He pressed his palms to the side of his head as if he could stop the impending explosion. "Shut up." It didn't, of course. Instead, the chipper tune continued to pierce his eardrums like jolly gremlins with ice picks. Blindly reaching out, his hand knocked against the shot glass and mostly empty bottle of tequila before it made contact with his phone. He palmed the thing, giving serious consideration to chunking the offending object across the room. He'd worked damned hard to achieve the inebriated state that would allow him a few hours' sleep. Hank cracked an eyelid and saw Bash's number on the screen. Pressing the key to activate the call, he growled, "This better be important."

"Tank, my man, what the hell are you still doing asleep? It's a bright and beautiful day out."

"It is?" Hank looked across the darkened living room to the sliding glass doors. Light peeked out from the gaps in the blinds. "I'll have to take your word for it," he said with absolutely no enthusiasm for the weather.

"I have a favor to ask," Bash continued in his typical boisterous way. "I'll buy you lunch if you'll help me out for a couple hours."

"Sure," Hank said without a second thought. What else did he have to do to pass the time? "Do I need to bring a shovel and duct tape for this expedition?" Not that it mattered. Despite the guy's obnoxious *joie de vivre* and craptastic timing, there wasn't anything Hank wouldn't do for him.

Bash laughed. "No. That's not the type of help I need. Just bring yourself. I'll meet you at Wrightsville Beach Marina at noon."

After ending the call, Hank staggered to the kitchen and started the coffee pot. For once, the upcoming appointment at the VA hospital wasn't the motivating force behind the need for self-medication. Despite Mia's assurances she could take care of herself once she left the hospital, worst-case scenarios flooded his thoughts. A slip in the shower, a loss of balance, a trip over an uneven curb. To say nothing of the fact her attacker hadn't been caught. His girl was smart, cautious, and had been on her own since she was sixteen, he told himself over and over. She didn't need him in the fucked up state he was in. And certainly not if the doctor he'd seen a few weeks back was correct. Yet, he couldn't stop the potential disasters his imagination conjured up. Thus the need for Jose Cuervo. While he waited for his second favorite addiction, he reached for a couple aspirin and swallowed the pills dry.

Showered, shaved, and sober, he pulled into the parking lot right on time. He hadn't been down to the beach since the day of the admiral's retirement. Stepping out of his truck, he shielded his eyes from the sun and once again regretted his method of attaining sleep. He slipped on his shades and headed toward the dock. Midway down, he spotted Bash.

"Thanks for coming with, my man." He slapped Hank on the back. Dressed in a tank top and long shorts, his feet shoved bareback into deck shoes, there wasn't much navy showing on this guy. Until a couple years ago, he'd been Opie Collins's NFO, which stood for Naval Flight Officer. The saying went the initials also stood for No Future Occupation, and it seemed Bash agreed. He'd been out a couple years, having decided to take a different career path—an author of all things, writing military thrillers. Hank learned of his friend's pursuit, and the four books he'd written, over drinks during their last time at Wayfarers.

"No problem," he said, though truth be told, once he hit the highway that connected Wilmington to LaGrange, he'd nearly ditched his friend in favor of heading to the hospital. He glanced at his watch. Mia should be headed home in the next hour. "What am I supposed to be doing?" he asked, needing a distraction.

"I sold the movie rights to one of my books." The corner of Bash's mouth crooking up. He'd endured some ribbing from the squad when he first announced his post-navy career.

Hank hadn't joined in with the others who threatened to take Bash's man card for his less than macho-man pursuit, and his respect grew after he read the guy's first book. "That's awesome," he said only the tiniest bit envious of his friend's successful transition into civilian life. He tamped down on the green-eyed monster. More power to him. "Congrats." He patted Bash on the back.

"Thanks." He dropped his gaze to the deck. "I

never dreamed this would happen to me."

"Which book? I really like that one about the pilot shot down over Russia. That one would be great on the big screen."

"It wasn't that one." His smile faded. "Anyway, I'm thinking about buying a boat, and I wanted to get your opinion."

Hank looked to the line of yachts, sport fishing vessels, and family cabin cruisers. "I'm glad to take a look, but I'm no more of an expert on boats than you are." Ask him about any type of aircraft, civilian or military and he'd be able to give an intelligent opinion. To him, ships were simply things to be launched from.

"I'm not expecting you to give me an inspection." Bash walked farther down the dock. They stopped in front of a twenty-foot cruiser. "I just want your thoughts."

"Isn't this Titan's?" he asked, recalling the weekend he'd spent with the guy a few years back before he too left the navy.

Bash stepped across the gap and onto the boat. "It is. He mentioned he might need to sell her to help with some financial issues." Looking around, he asked, "What do you think?"

"It's a good looking yacht." Hank eyed the highly polished decking. "Why do you want her? It's not like you haven't had enough time aboard a ship."

Bash sat in the captain's chair. "I'm having trouble with my latest book, and I thought getting away might help."

Hank followed Bash's lead and dropped onto the cushioned bench that ran along the sides and stern of the boat. "Like writer's block?" he said, wondering how a change of location would make a difference. But what did he know about writing?

"It's more like the opposite. I've just got so much going on in my head. I thought a few less distractions might help."

"I say go for it." He shrugged. "If Titan decides not to sell, buy one of the others."

Bash's grin returned. "I might just do that." He leaned back in the chair, jutting his feet out in front of him. "Have you ever wondered if we're destined for a certain fate?"

Hank arched an eyebrow. "Not especially, no. What brings this on?"

He leaned forward. "If I tell you something, will you promise not to blab to the others?"

"Have you ever known me to run my mouth?" Hank crossed his arms.

"No. But if this gets out, I'll never hear the end of it."

Hank made a circle with his hand, giving the "get on with it" signal.

"The book that's getting made into a movie is one I wrote under a different name." He paused, biting his lip. "It's not my usual military thriller."

"So what's it about?"

"*Times of Turmoil* is the story of how my parents met and fell in love."

"You wrote a romance?" Hank worked to keep a smile off his lips. "It's a good thing you extracted a promise from me before you let that little cat out of the bag."

"I'm no dummy," Bash said, his own lips stretched into a grin.

"It's great that your story is being made into a movie. What does this have to do with fate?"

Bash shrugged. "While I was writing, I realized if Dad hadn't gotten hurt, he and Mom would have never met."

"So you believe everything happens for a reason—that good can come from terrible circumstances," he said, skepticism bleeding through his words. He preferred thinking the catastrophes that happened to both Mia and him were bad luck or chance rather than cosmic design.

"I guess I do. Especially since if they hadn't met, I would never have been born."

His parents' story struck close to home. Only instead of a happy ending, his story would likely have a much darker ending. Bitterness soured his stomach. "I didn't know you were religious."

"I'm not really." He shrugged. "I think in the end, things work out the way they're supposed to."

"Not me, man," Hank said. He was still waiting for the other shoe to drop. If he looked hard enough for the good in that clusterfuck, it was possible that his situation allowed him to spend more time with Mia. But there was nothing beneficial about her attack. The memory of her hooked up to the respirator, with tubes coming out of her body flooded his mind. He'd come so Goddamned close to losing her.

"Hey. I didn't mean to get all philosophical on you. I know things haven't exactly been fantastic for you lately."

Hank waved away his buddy's concern. "It's all good. I'm glad you can see the glass half full."

"It'll work out for you. Trust me. And speaking of

half-full glasses, let's head to Wayfarers for a couple beers." He wagged his eyebrows. "Perhaps fate will smile on you in the female department. I think you're about due."

With his headache finally beginning to ease, the last thing he needed was any hair of the dog, and the thoughts of hooking up with some bar honey held no appeal. Not when he could spend time with Mia. "Thanks anyway, I need to head home," he said, though his intentions would take him in the opposite direction up the coast. He stood and extended his hand to Bash. "Good luck with the movie and the writer's block thing," he said, planting his hand on the gunwales and leaping across to the dock. Hank took a couple steps then called a parting shot over his shoulder, "Your secret's still safe with me, as long as you score me a couple tickets to the premier."

"You got it," Bash called with a laugh.

All that philosophy mumbo-jumbo had Hank's thoughts in a tangle. Despite promising Mia he'd give her a couple days to settle in, he turned his truck north toward LaGrange. He pushed his truck up the highway, keeping his fingers crossed he wouldn't get caught in some cop's radar.

For once darkness wasn't the driving force urging him forward. He needed to lay eyes on Mia, see for himself she'd made it to her condo, and she had everything she needed. He'd made a vow to himself to begin pulling away. Of all the things he'd likely face in the next few months and years, seeing pity in her eyes ranked right near the top of things to avoid. "One more time," he said, repeating the promise. "That's all I need, and then I'll start pulling away."

Seeing the burnt out shell of her condo null and voided that vow. "Holy mother of..." He reached for his phone. A dozen questions swarmed in his mind as his imagination once again painted a vivid worst-case-scenario. "Please God, let her be okay," he pleaded as he punched in her number. To hell with Bash's kumbaya philosophy—nothing good could come of this.

"Hello." Her husky voice ghosted across the airwaves and eased his fears.

"Are you okay? Where are you? I'm at your condo." His words tripped over each other.

"Oh, crap. I was going to call you. I didn't want you to see. I'm sorry that I worried you. I'm okay. I'm staying at Milestones."

"Be packed when I get there."

****

Mia reached for the F-150's armrest as the force of acceleration knocked her off kilter. "Jeez, Hank, slow down," she said as they sped underneath a yellow traffic light.

She cut her eyes at him. Man, it had been years since she'd seen him this worked up. His jaw ticked, and he looked like he wanted to throttle the steering wheel he had a white-knuckle grip on. Back at Milestones, she tried to explain she had every intention of letting him know about the fire. He'd been beyond reasoning with. "I feel like we're fleeing the scene of a crime," she said, trying to add levity to the heavy air inside the truck.

Given Hank's reactions so far, she'd made the right call not telling him what Detective Price suspected. When he asked, she'd said the cause was under investigation. That was enough information for now. He'd probably stroke-out if he knew the fire wasn't an accident. Hell, she was having a hard time processing the theory one of the low-level thugs she'd prosecuted had sought revenge by torching her home.

Hank cringed. "Sorry." He eased off the gas. "I just had to get you out of that place. It makes my skin crawl."

No need for him to explain his reaction to the residential home. The institutional feel of its linoleum floors and the puke green walls evoked memories they both wanted to forget. "Thanks again for coming to get me," she said as gratitude washed over her. While she'd been thankful Milestones had a place for her, even the few hours there had her in the same dark, lonely place she'd spent her teen years. While the home for girls had been an improvement over their foster home, especially since it got Hank away from the man abusing him, it wasn't a particularly nurturing place to grow up.

"No thanks necessary." He released the death grip he had on the steering wheel to grasp her hand. "That's what family does for each other."

Mia nodded, tears stinging the backs of her eyes. She turned to stare out the window so he wouldn't see how close she was to breaking down. Comparing her day to a roller coaster seemed too mild. With her nerves on edge and her emotions raw, a wood chipper was more like it.

Pine trees lined both sides of the four-lane highway they were traveling, giving her little to distract her thoughts. How would she have coped if Hank had been at sea? She'd have put on her big girl panties and dealt with the crappy situation the best she could. But, thank

God, she didn't have to travel this dark time in her life on her own.

In the time they'd been on the road, the sun drifted below the tree line. Just a few hours more and this God-awful day would be over. Surely tomorrow would be better—or at least less eventful. With all the drama, her thoughts kept returning to Tripp. While not the most dramatic event—the fire had that billing—Tripp's attempt to reconcile with her made the least amount of sense. What was his angle? As proud a man as he was, she'd never expected he'd speak to her again much less plead for a second chance. She'd made the right call both times. All the same, the loss ached in her chest, especially the sense of security she'd experience with his family. Poor Traveler. Would the dog think she'd abandoned him? A tear trickled down her cheek.

Neither of them spoke as they rode the last few miles toward Wilmington, but his hand atop hers said more than all the platitudes in the world. He was all she had now that she'd broken up with Tripp. Her heart ached with the loss of Mrs. Brooks and Dianne as much as it did with her fiancé's betrayal. His mother rescinded her offer to let Mia live with her during her outpatient therapy, and Dianne wouldn't return her phone calls. She could hardly blame them for siding with Tripp. He was their blood, and they'd only tolerated her on his behalf. She rubbed at the ache in her chest. For a while though, it felt like she'd had a real family.

She gazed at Hank from the corner of her eye. With his attention trained on the road ahead, he looked as if he expected an ambush at any moment. But that was the way he'd always been—vigilant, protective and single-minded. What more could she ask for? Better to have one person who truly loved and cared for her than a multitude who'd tossed her aside without a second thought.

Her thoughts wound back to her earliest memories of her tagging along behind Hank and the older kids at the foster home. He'd never made her feel less than and insisted the other kids include her in their games. In a world of uncertainty, she had one constant. She twisted her hand, lacing Hank's fingers with hers.

He glanced down at their clasped hands. "You okay, there, angel?"

With her emotions awhirl—one moment thankful, the next nostalgic—she had to swallow hard before she could answer. "Just feeling a tad overwhelmed."

"It's been kind of a craptastic day for you hasn't it?"

"That's one way of putting it." She smiled for the first time in hours.

Tires rubbing against the shoulder cut off her laugh. "Crap." He jerked his gaze back to the road ahead. "Sorry about that." Hank gripped the steering wheel the rest of the way home, but that was the extent of his cautious driving. He drove his truck like it was a sports car, making her wonder why he was rushing. It wasn't until they pulled into his apartment complex that he eased off the accelerator.

He slid into a spot in front of a three-story building showing the hallmarks of 1970's design. "That's mine." He pointed to one of the first-floor units. "There's a couple steps leading from the parking lot to the sidewalk, but that's all."

"I can do a couple steps," she said, not wanting

him to worry. Since he spent most of his time aboard *The Eisenhower*, she understood why he hadn't chosen a more upscale place to live, but the place needed some serious upkeep. The exterior needed a good coat of paint, and the barely there landscape needed attention. All the same, it was better than Milestones even on its best day.

He scrambled out of the cab and around to her side. When she reached back for her bag, he stopped her. "I got it." Too tired to argue, she let him take it. They'd have a discussion about not treating her like an invalid when she didn't feel so much like one.

As he guided her up the two steps, his hand moved to the small of her back. Thoughts of a decidedly different nature replaced the lecture she'd been formulating in her head. Heat from his palm radiated through her thin T-shirt, sending licks of awareness dancing across her skin. The mental image of him taking her into his arms and kissing her softly bloomed in her mind. He'd draw her close and let his hands roam over her body.

Mia stumbled as her imagination's strong and unexpected creation flooded her brain—and planted a seedling notion of what it would be like to have him turn his considerable charm on her.

"You all right there?" Hank drew her closer to his side, sending her already overactive imagination whirling.

His gaze drew her in and she had to turn her attention to the path ahead in order to get her mouth to work. Damn, her emotions really were pinging off the walls. "I wasn't paying attention where I was going." While any woman with two eyes could see his physical appeal—and over the years she'd witnessed him dazzle more than a few women—until that moment, she'd never wanted that attention trained on her. Chalking it up to the emotional day she'd had, she pointed to the door ahead. "Home sweet home?"

Hank opened the door for her. "Such as it is." He flipped on the lights as he moved farther inside the space.

"I rented the place a few months ago. I looked all over town, but there weren't any one-bedroom units, so I ended up getting a two bedroom. Problem is I only have one bed."

"That's fine. I don't mind sleeping on the sofa."

"No way." He shook his head. "Not after the day you've had. I'll take the sofa."

She rolled her eyes. "That makes no sense. You won't be able to sleep with your knees up around your ears."

He arched an eyebrow at her. "I won't be able to sleep either if I'm worried about you rolling onto the floor." He tilted her chin to gaze into her eyes. "It's just for one night. While you were filling out the discharge papers, I called a friend who is bringing over a spare bed in the morning."

He carried her bag into his room and placed it on the floor next to an oak dresser. A neatly made queen size bed and nightstand completed the room. "I only have one set of sheets, but they were washed yesterday."

Suddenly, the events of the day caught up to her. "I'm so tired I could probably sleep on a bare mattress." She followed him back into the hall.

In the snug hallway, he opened the middle of three

doors. "We'll have to share the bathroom, but there are clean towels in the closet."

While the place was certainly Spartan, it was clean. "No toothpaste spatter on the mirror, and the toilet seat is even down. And you're single because?"

He laughed. "If that was all it took." He backed out of the room. "If you need anything, don't hesitate to ask." He seemed to sense her fatigue. "I'll grab a blanket out of my closet and then leave you to rest."

"You take such good care of me." She closed the distance between them and wrapped her arms around him. "I don't know what I'd do without you." Though they'd hugged countless times over the years, this time she was keenly aware of the hardness of his muscles beneath her cheek.

He stiffened before relaxing into her embrace. "And you're never going to have to find out. That's a promise." He kissed the top of her head as he pulled back.

She resisted the urge to cling to him. "Good night." She let him go. God, she wanted to nestle into his chest, to be held in a way that had nothing to do with familial affection. Mia shook loose those thoughts and after a quick trip to the bathroom, she climbed under the covers. She let out a sigh at the softness of the mattress, and then scooted to the middle of the bed where she stretched out like she hadn't been able to do since the attack.

As tired as she was, the myriad of thoughts racing through her head kept her from the sleep she so desperately needed. The fire, Tripp's appearance, and especially her new awareness of Hank kept sleep at bay. The scent of his aftershave clung to the sheets and filled her nose. Traces of sandalwood further awakened desires she'd never experienced for him.

Turning on her side, she hugged the pillow, imagining him at her side. With all she'd been through in the past several months, especially with the lingering effects of her head injury, she didn't trust the desires her brain conjured up. But even as she reminded herself of that, the images kept coming. And she let them.

Chapter Nine

Hours after the sun came up Mia strained her ears, listening for sounds of movement from the other room. She'd been awake most of the night, too many thoughts swirling in her head. More than processing the events of yesterday, her evolving feelings for Hank took up the most headspace. She couldn't remember a time when he hadn't been the most important person in her life. If she'd ever had any doubts he felt the same, that he'd taken her in was proof enough. The sound of the coffee pot gurgling let her know Hank was up. She dressed quickly and padded into the living room.

"Good morning, sunshine," he said. "How'd you sleep?"

"I tossed and turned all night, but not because of the mattress." She stretched the soreness from her stiff muscles. "It was a little slice of heaven to spread out like I did."

After taking a sip from the enormous mug in his hand, he said, "I know you don't drink coffee, but I've got some orange juice if you want."

"Sounds wonderful." She moved toward the fridge.

He touched her hand. "I got it. Have a seat."

She arched an eyebrow. "Do we need to have a conversation about your babying me? I can take care of myself."

Hank raised his hands in surrender. "Got it." He

smiled.

"Sorry." Guilt pricked her conscience. "I'm tired of being the invalid."

"You don't have to explain yourself to me." He took a sip of coffee. "Make yourself at home. My friends will be here in a few minutes, so I'm going to grab a quick shower."

"Sure."

She used his absence to explore. Over the years, they'd fallen into the habit of him visiting at her condo when he was on leave. She'd imagined what his place was like, and while she'd been correct that it would be tidy, she hadn't expected it would be this bare. She opened cabinet after cabinet finding them mostly empty—until she opened the one next to the sink. It looked like a liquor store with all the bottles.

Her heart sank at the sight of neat rows of tequila bottles. From his teens, he'd been a social drinker, but after his divorce from Tiffany he'd amped up his alcohol intake. She'd been a newly minted ADA at the time and worried what a DUI would do to his navy career—to say nothing of what the alcohol was doing to his body. After they had a heart-to-heart conversation, he'd promised to cut back on the drinking. So what had triggered renewed romance with the bottle? Guilt lanced through her as she wondered if her attack played a role. Surely that wasn't an issue now that she was on her way to recovery. She recalled the number of times he'd arrived at the hospital with dark circles under his eyes and his always-evasive answers when she asked about his next deployment. Perhaps it was time for her to needle him for information. When the shower cut off, she eased out of the kitchen. She'd give them both a couple days to settle into the new living arrangement before she put her cross-examination skills to work.

Last night, she'd been too exhausted from the day's drama to really take note of the room. With only a sofa, end tables, and giant flat screen, the room screamed bachelor, but what little he had was new and pristine.

Her attention gravitated to the framed photo resting on the fireplace mantel. Crossing the room, she picked up the decade-old picture of them at her high school graduation. Hank, wearing his dress white uniform, was all smiles as he draped an arm over her shoulder. She had the same photo on her mantel at home. *Had*. Her heart twisted. Moving around as much as she did growing up, she didn't have much in tangible reminders of her childhood. As she recalled the stuffed animals and souvenirs Hank sent from his travels around the world, she realized all the important mementos were gifts from him. Her heart ached with the loss.

She sensed rather than heard him approach from behind, and her thoughts shifted gears. His nearness lit up her insides, and she couldn't help wishing he'd wrap his arms around her again as he did last night.

"I can make copies of my pictures if you like." He hovered so near behind her that she could feel his breath against her neck.

"I might not need you to." His scent made it difficult to string a thought together. "I'm hoping the fire chief will let me take a look around my condo later today. I stored the negatives of the older photos and thumb drives of the digital ones in a little safe."

"After we get your furniture situation squared away, we can drive over to the site and have a look."

Driven by urges that were still too foreign to

identify, she replaced the picture on the mantel and slipped into his arms.

****

Hank jolted at the unexpected embrace. This wasn't the first time in as many days Mia caught him off guard with an uncharacteristic burst of emotion. He could hardly fault her for needing a shoulder to lean on with all the curve balls life kept throwing at her. What about him? What reason could he give for wanting to hold her tight? For the erection straining the front of his jeans? He'd always been protective of her, but the desire surging through his veins had nothing to do with keeping her from harm. He wanted to tilt her chin and kiss her generous mouth. Would she taste like strawberries—the color of her lips, or peaches—the scent of her body wash?

A rap on the door cut through his thoughts. "That's Avery." He extricated himself from Mia. And not a moment too soon. He was about two seconds from acting on his imagination's urging.

He raced to snatch open the door. "Hey there," he said, thankful for the interruption. He could no more justify kissing someone who only saw him as a brother than he could explain the origins of his desires. He did know kissing Mia would be a catastrophe on par with ditching his plane in the ocean. He'd already lost a career he loved. He couldn't risk losing the most important person in his life because he acted on an impulse—one he wouldn't allow himself to entertain again.

"Here, let me get that for you." He took the armload of sheets from her and placed them on the sofa. "Let me introduce you guys before we start unloading the bed. Avery, I'd like you to meet Mia Jones." He placed a hand against her back. "My angel is the closest thing I have to a sister," he said as a reminder she was off limits.

"Pleasure to meet you," Avery said. "I'm glad to hear you're out of the hospital." She nodded in Hank's direction. "I've been following your progress through Hank's updates."

Mia smiled. "Thank you for sharing your furniture." She pointed toward the front door. "I'll go outside and bring in the rest of the bedding."

"I'm right behind you," he said to her as she exited the room. "Don't try to lift anything heavy." He understood Mia's need to do things for herself. Hell, if he'd been reliant on others for everything the way she had, he'd be bat shit crazy by now. Trying to lift a heavy mattress wasn't the way for her to assert her independence. Before he could follow Mia to the parking lot, Avery snagged him by the arm.

"Hold up a second." Her brow furrowed. His former shipmate had been going through her own period of upheaval. Not only had she recently lost her job and was working for Titan, a man she competed against for years, her ex-husband was suing for custody of their son.

"Sure." He cast an eye to the door, hoping Mia would wait while he heard Avery out. "What's up?"

"What did the medical review board say?"

He let out a breath. This was so not a conversation he wanted to have, especially with Mia nearby. She had enough to worry about without taking on his issues. "Can we talk about this later?"

She crossed her arms over her chest. "No. You'll

just side step me like the last time I asked."

"The MRB ruled me unfit for duty." The words became more real as he said them aloud for the first time. "I'm being given a medical discharge."

Avery's eyes darkened with sympathy. "I'm so sorry, Tank." She patted his arm. "It just stinks."

Wasn't that just the understatement of the decade? All he'd ever wanted to do was fly Super Hornets, but a genetic mutation from the father who never wanted him put an end to that. "Well, you can hardly blame the navy. I did ditch a twenty-million-dollar plane in the drink."

He was lucky. Not only had he not killed himself or his NFO, the review board cleared him of any wrongdoing. Until that night, he'd never had an issue seeing the deck. He'd always ranked in the top five percent of pilots in his squadron on carrier landings.

"I'll be fine, though." He hoped Avery didn't want to delve into more details about his medical condition. Never one to share personal problems, the last thing he wanted to do was to open up about how that made him feel. "I'll figure something out."

Avery nodded. "I don't doubt that you will." She caught his gaze. "But are you sure you can take care of Mia at the same time? Do you even know how long she's going to need help?"

It wouldn't matter if she needed someone to care for her the rest of her life, he would never turn his back on her. "You don't understand. I have to." As soon as the words were past his lips, a new reality hit him full force. As his condition progressed, would he still be able to keep that vow? He'd find a way, he promised himself. As a teen, he hadn't been strong enough to endure the beatings from his foster dad without coming to Mia for comfort. He was older, stronger, and more determined fifteen years later. He wouldn't fail her again.

"She's my everything."

Avery's eyebrows shot to her hairline.

He waved away her misunderstanding. She was still as off limits as she'd ever been, but in the past few weeks, he'd come to see her in a different, inconvenient light. He noticed the delicate structure of her cheeks as well as the gentle curves of her breasts and hips.

"It's not like that." He tried forgetting how much he'd wanted to kiss her just moments ago.

But there was a growing part of him that wished it was.

****

Though she probably could have managed to carry more, Mia decided she'd pushed enough of Hank's buttons. If he wanted to look after her, she'd let him. She returned to the apartment with the rest of the bedding. "I got all the small stuff. I'm leaving the rest like you asked," Mia said, coming inside. At the sound of muffled voices coming from the kitchen, she let the rest of her sentence trail off.

Reality hit her squarely in the chest. So that's why he'd brushed aside her matchmaking attempts at the hospital—he already had someone. Her chest tightened with the surge of some unidentifiable emotion. The irrational urge to barge into the other room nearly overwhelmed her.

Instead, she eased a few steps closer. With each step, her conscience scolded her. How did the saying go about eavesdroppers? Something about how they never liked what they overheard. But she still couldn't rein in the urge to find out more about Hank's friend. She certainly didn't want to cause issues with his lover. They'd had enough of that when he was married to Tiffany. She couldn't make out the words they were exchanging, but it was clear by Avery's insistent tone and Hank's short replies, that the conversation was important. Was she having difficulty accepting Hank's decision to take Mia in? What if he changed his mind and asked her to return to Milestones?

Fear tangled her insides, sending tendrils of anxiety twining through her body. Hank was all she had left. She wiped her sweaty palms against her jeans. She took two steps, formulating the words ahead of time so she could get them out. As she worked out what she would say, a singular word popped into her head. *Jealousy.* Not that Avery was jealous of Mia's relationship with Hank—although that might be how the woman felt. The green-eyed monster had ahold of Mia. With both hands apparently. She sank to the sofa as the realization took root. Sure she'd begun seeing Hank differently in the past few weeks, but between rehab and her break up with Tripp, she hadn't fully explored her newfound feelings. When she noticed how nicely he filled out his jeans and anticipated each touch he gave her, she hadn't been looking at him as a brother or even as a friend. She'd been looking at him as a woman does a man she's romantically interested in.

Man, her timing really sucked. How was she going to hide that from Hank? The last thing she wanted to do was make him uncomfortable. He'd made his choice, and if Avery made him forget Tiffany, brought joy to his life, she'd just have to be happy for him. That's what family did.

Mia retreated to her bedroom to put away the bedding and wait until Hank and Avery worked things out. She closed the door to prevent their conversation drifting from the kitchen. While she certainly didn't want to be a source of strife between the lovers, paying witness to them kissing ranked top on the to-be-avoided list.

She didn't have long to hide out in the nearly empty room. A few moments later, a knock came on the door. She opened it to find Hank in the hallway with the mattress in tow. Avery followed with the other piece, and over the next half hour, they unloaded and assembled the bed and small dresser Avery was also loaning. Going by the easy atmosphere the two had, whatever they'd discussed in the kitchen must have been settled.

With the room complete, Mia surveyed the end product. The queen-sized bed took up most of the room. There was just enough space for a small dresser and nightstand. "Very cozy. Thank you for your generosity," she said, finding it hard to dislike Avery. She and Hank got on well together, working with ease to assemble the furniture. She'd coaxed several laughs out of Hank, something Mia hadn't been able to do in quite some time.

"You're very welcome," Avery said. "I'm sorry you're going through a tough time."

Mia nodded, the swirl of conflicting emotions and not her speech issues cutting off her words.

"I have a great idea," Hank said.

"What's up?" she asked, plastering a smile on her face.

"I'm taking you two ladies out to lunch."

Mia cut her eyes at Avery, trying to decipher how the woman might feel about her tagging along.

"I could eat." Avery shrugged.

Her stomach had been talking to her as well, but not enough to make her willing to be the third wheel. "You two go ahead." She waved him off. "I need a nap."

Hank's brow furrowed. "Are you feeling okay?" He drew close enough for her to catch the scent of his aftershave.

Her pulse raced. If he touched her now, there'd be no way she could hide the emotions surging through her. "I'm fine." She stepped backward. "Just a little tired from all the excitement. Go, have fun." She waved him away with a smile she hoped would alleviate his worries. And allow her to keep her secret. Even if she had a grasp on the newly found emotions, she'd never willingly do anything to cause problems with Hank and Avery.

"Okay, if that's what you want," he said, not sounding convinced. "What would you like me to bring back?"

"Nothing. I don't have much of an appetite. But if I do get hungry, I can scrounge around in your fridge."

"Rest up." He closed the distance between them to cup her cheek. "When I get back, we'll go over to your condo and look for your lockbox."

Her eyelids closed. Great. Another unpleasant task. She didn't know which was worse. Sifting through the rubble of her life, or having to pretend she wasn't falling for the man she'd always seen as her brother.

Chapter Ten

After Hank and Avery left for their lunch date, Mia put away the few clothes she had from the hospital. She warmed a can of soup and tidied after herself. Then she did a little more snooping, counting ten bottles of liquor, almost all of them tequila—Hank's drink of choice. She prayed the reason for the stash was a future party.

Eventually the fib she'd told him to excuse herself from being the third wheel became the truth. Fatigue settled over her in a way she hadn't experienced since the early days of her recovery. With a book in hand, she curled up on the sofa, intending to read while she waited for Hank to return. A thud of furniture hitting a wall woke her. She opened her eyes just as Hank switched on a lamp at her head.

"Oh, sorry. I didn't know you were in here." He adjusted the end table to its original position.

She shielded her eyes. "What time is it?" She sat up. Squinting past the ultra-bright lightbulb, she gazed at the French doors leading to the apartment's small patio. Sunlight flooded the room, making her wonder why he'd turned on the light.

"It's around three." He lowered himself to the sofa. "Avery had to head back to her place, but she wanted me to tell you she enjoyed meeting you."

She found herself reluctantly admiring Avery in

return—and caught off guard by her quick acceptance of the relationship Mia and Hank shared. She'd endured Tiffany's acrimony and hadn't expected Hank's latest love interest to understand his unique relationship with his foster sister. "She did?"

"Sure, I bet you two will hit it off once you get to know each other more."

Under different circumstances, she'd have looked forward to making friends with Avery. Mia curled her lips to form the smile she knew he expected. "I can't wait."

Hank turned to face her. "While Avery and I were out, we drove up to LaGrange and stopped at your place." His smile softened as he spoke. "I figured you didn't need to see the mess again. It was just a pile of burned out lumber and furniture. I hope you don't mind."

"No, of course not." In fact, if it weren't for the safe, she wouldn't bother going back.

"I sifted through the rubble and located the safe. It's all covered in soot, so I left it in my truck until I can get it cleaned up."

"Thanks for doing that, but I can get some cleaning supplies and have a go at the box." Eventually, she was going to have to put a stop to him solving problems for her, for both their sakes. She couldn't grow reliant on him, because it didn't take a lot of intuition to know eventually Avery wouldn't be as patient with sharing Hank's attention. Today, she'd simply enjoy having someone smooth over the rough spots for her.

Hank leaned back on the sofa and propped his feet against the coffee table. "So what should we do this evening? Card game, a movie, I'm all yours."

If only that were true.

"How about a Schwarzenegger marathon?"

****

Sometime after the second movie began, Mia woke as Hank lifted her from the sofa. "I can walk," she muttered, more asleep than awake.

"I know you can, angel." Humor colored the deep timbre of his voice.

Mia nestled into his embrace, letting him carry her to bed. She'd pick something less enjoyable to assert her independence over.

"Sleep tight." He pressed a kiss to her forehead. "Holler if you need anything."

"I will." Mia drifted off, thoughts of Hank kissing her on the lips running through her mind instead of the brotherly one he'd given. She guessed a person really couldn't choose who they fell in love with because if she did have control, she sure as heck wouldn't have done something as inconvenient as falling in love with a man who was already in a relationship. Especially one who only saw her as the little sister to protect.

At the first crack of thunder, Mia's eyelids sprang open. Instantly, she was on high alert, every nerve ending humming with anticipation of when the next strike would occur. She'd earned her fear of thunderstorms honestly, having been caught out in one as a child. She witnessed what ten-thousand volts of electricity could do to a hundred-year-old oak and lived with the indelible experience ever since.

As she'd grown up, she'd learned to control the fear. Mia called to mind the beach near her condo. Envisioning the gentle outgoing tide and the sand beneath her bare feet, she concentrated on breathing in through her nose and out through her mouth. She could almost smell the briny air and the warm breeze against her face.

A strike hit dangerously close, jolting Mia upright. The hair on her back of her neck stood up as fear danced along her skin. Mostly she'd conquered her phobia. She drew her knees to her chest and tried to return to her happy place. "Gentle breeze, sunny sky, salty air," she chanted to herself as she concentrated on her breathing.

A loud thump rattled from the living room, then her bedroom door opened. "You okay?" Hank whispered.

"Yeah." Her voice came out thin and reedy.

He stumbled across the floor, coming to sit on the edge of her bed. "I didn't know if storms still frightened you the way they did when you were little."

"Not as much." Another lightning strike hit nearby, and she jumped into Hank's lap. Perspiration trickled down her brow and panic took root. This was the first storm since her attack. Perhaps having recently experienced an act of violence, her brain was still in fight-or-flight mode. At the moment, the instinct to flee had her by the throat. "I have a favor to ask," she drawled, uncertain how he'd react but unable to resist asking. "Will you lie down with me?"

He stiffened.

"Never mind." Mia scooted off his lap. What an inappropriate thing to ask. She flipped on the bedside lamp. "I'll be fine." Mia retreated to the far side of the bed. She tugged the covers over her shoulders. These summer storms usually blew themselves out in a few minutes. She only had to get through the worst of the lightning.

Hank tugged her hand from underneath the covers. "No, Mia, I told you there wasn't anything I wouldn't do for you and I meant that." He kicked his feet up on the bed and settled himself atop the covers. "Lie down."

She scooted down on the bed, her heart thudding in her chest. "Just till the storm passes."

"I'm here as long as you need me." He crossed his legs at the ankles and used his hands as a pillow. "Lights on or off?"

Her gaze raked over his long and lean body, the urge to touch almost more than she could resist. She craved to trace his shadowed jaw as she molded her body against his. Guilt pricked her for entertaining the idea. Even if he wasn't involved with another woman, their feelings were nowhere near being in sync. "Off, please." She hoped darkness would put a strangle hold on her imagination.

Another strike had her cringing. She trembled even as embarrassment heated her cheeks. "I'm sorry for being such a baby."

"Anyone who's been through what you have in the past few months is entitled to a little fear."

The steadiness of his voice and the heat radiating off his body eased some of her tension. No one had ever accepted her, flaws and all, the way he did. It had been that way as long as she could remember. "It's been a minute since we did this," she said, to remind herself the nature of their relationship. "Remember when I used to slip into the boys' room back when we lived with Mrs. Gilbert? You used to tell me myths different cultures had about the origins of thunder and lightning. I liked the one from Greek mythology best, and I'd make you tell me that every time."

Hank's chuckle traveled through the dark, further easing her anxiety. "That's right. I'd forgotten about that. It feels like a lifetime ago."

"A lot's changed in those fifteen years." Especially her feelings for him. Even as she longed to return to the simplicity of their early days together, she also yearned to give into the new desires that had her wound as tightly as the thunderstorm did.

"And some things haven't changed at all, angel. We've always been there for each other, haven't we?"

The memory, while comforting as the storm raged outside, also served as a reminder he would never see her as anything other than a little sister. Even the nickname he'd chosen for her spoke of his feelings for her.

To distract her thoughts from what could never be, she shifted her focus to her place of comfort. In her mind's eye, the waves lapped at the shore and seagulls fussed at each other along her favorite section of shoreline. "Let's go to the beach tomorrow." It had been months since she'd dug her toes into the sand. Perhaps that's what she needed to center her emotions and gird up her strength for her outpatient therapy beginning on Monday. "I think some sand and surf will put me right."

****

"Why the beach?" He shifted in the dark, turning first on his side and then his back, anything to give his erection a break. He'd been hard as steel from the moment Mia asked him to lie down next to her. Even as he hated himself for the carnal thoughts flooding his brain, he had to admit he couldn't keep from falling for

Mia. The only control he had was over how he acted on those feelings. At the moment, those urges were stretching him to the breaking point.

"I just want to do something fun. I feel like the last few months have been nothing but hard work laced with tragedy."

If only Mia's request to climb into her bed was for a different reason. As his mind spooled out of control, a shit-ton of if-onlys clouded his brain. He should have stayed in his own room. The saying, so near and yet so far, had never been truer. But at the first notes of the summer storm, his feet had been on the floor and heading to Mia's room before his brain could catch up. Protecting her was ingrained in his soul—coming to her was instinct, ignoring a need she might have unthinkable.

"Anything you want," he said, meaning it to the bottom of his soul. There wasn't one thing he wouldn't give her. "But it's liable to be a mess after this storm."

"If it is, we can do something else. Any place will do as long as it's not LaGrange General." She took his hand, lacing their fingers together. "And you're there." Her words slurred.

Hank lay atop the covers, listening to her breaths slow and her grip on his hand loosen. He'd stay another moment to be sure the storm had passed then return to his room where he belonged. But even as her body relaxed into sleep, he couldn't bring himself to leave her. Since her attack, he'd endured many hours at her bedside, a sense of helplessness twisting his gut. Despite urging from his baser desires, he managed to keep a grip on his imagination. Just barely. He tensed as her hand shifted across his chest. God, what he wouldn't give for her to be awake and for her touch to mean more than what it did. Pride sated some of his sexual frustration. Despite his barely leashed lust, and his less than honorable thoughts, he'd been the one to offer comfort.

Certain facts kept him in check. Between her struggles to recover from her injuries and her recent break up, she had enough emotional upheaval in her life. The last thing she needed was for him to change the nature of their relationship. Besides, even if circumstances were different, divulging his newly discovered feelings for her, much less acting on them was too great a risk. He couldn't chance losing the one person who meant the world to him.

Just a moment more, he promised the honorable half of his nature that had been screaming predictions of doom since he left his bedroom. The rumbles of thunder echoed in the distance. Soon. He drew in a breath laced with the sweet smell of her shampoo.

He closed his eyes listening to her steady breathing. Every time he tried to put some space between them, she closed the distance. Her tiny body radiated heat. His last thought was of taking her to Wrightsville Beach where they'd lay in the sand and watch the waves roll in.

Once his unconscious mind had control of the yolk, all G-rated plans were quickly shoved in the corner for Hank's better half to ponder later. For now, his less heroic side had control.

The first thing naughty Hank would do was strip Mia out of that sheer tank top so he could suckle her breast. He'd take those turgid nipples into his mouth and tease them into tight buds. While his mouth was

117

busy, his hands would slide down her flat stomach to her mound. He'd delve beneath her panties to her hot center where he'd find that bundle of nerves at her cleft. He'd use her wetness, sliding along her secret folds while he drove her over pleasure's cliff.

Not until she'd found her release would he seek his own, but once she'd come down from that orgasmic high, he'd ease himself between her thighs and slide his cock inside her. She'd be slick and tight. And so damned hot that he'd lose himself inside her. He'd thrust inside her, coming with her name on his lips.

****

"Yes."

The word plucked Mia from her dream. Always a light sleeper, even six weeks in the hospital hadn't changed the habits of a lifetime. Was a nurse coming in to check her vitals? Being awake didn't preclude her from disorientation, especially as a heavy leg flopped across her waist. Tripp? She trailed her hand across the body lying next to her, coming in contact with a well-muscled chest covered in a cotton T-shirt. Hank! In bed next to her.

The past few hours came rushing back. He came in to check on her during the thunderstorm, and she asked him to keep her company. He must have fallen asleep. She listened to his steady breaths and wondered if she should wake him so he could return to his own bed. She quickly cast that notion aside, but not for any noble reason like letting him get some much needed sleep. She wanted the warmth his body provided. The comfort his presence lent. The feel of his hard body next to hers even if it would come to nothing.

He stirred again, muttering something

unintelligible as he drew closer. His erection prodded her hip, sending a surge of desire through her body. Quick on the heels of excitement, her conscience pricked her. Taking what he would not freely give her if awake was wrong. She scooted to the far side of the bed, but she couldn't bring herself to leave, despite knowing it was the right thing to do.

Hank followed her, draping first an arm then his leg across her body. "So warm," he groaned in his sleep. A thrill shot through her as he fused his body to hers. *Get up. Leave the room.* Even staying as long as she had felt like stealing. She pushed against his shoulder so that she could move away.

Before she could escape his grasp, his hand slipped between her legs, eviscerating her resolve. "Yes, baby, that's it," he said, working his hand against her mound. A single finger tunneled beneath her panties and eased through her folds.

"Ohhh." She groaned as pleasure shot through her body. Mia opened her legs, granting full access to her core. Desire washed over her, as he found her clit. "More." His touch making her greedy.

Just as quickly as he'd ignited lust, reality extinguished it. An ached bloomed in her chest. This passion wasn't for her. She pushed away his hand and closed herself to him. As much as she wanted him, she still had a little pride.

"Mia, let me make love to you, baby."

She froze. He said *her* name, not Avery's! As he rolled on top of her, she gave up wondering why and threw herself into the sensation of his body pressing her deliciously into the mattress. He ground his hips into hers as he made love to her through their clothes.

Unable to resist the feel of his cock notched into her cleft, she wrapped her legs around him. It was everything she'd dreamed it would be. Mia brought his mouth down to hers, reveling in their first sensual kiss. "Yes, make love to me."

Hank's eyes sprang open at her words. "Fuck." He rolled off her so fast that he tumbled off the bed. "Oh, my God, I'm so sorry." Fighting against the tangle of covers, he scrambled to his feet and moved to the far side of the room. "I didn't mean to do that," he said, his voice rough with anguish.

Mia ignored the lie. It had been her name on his lips. "It's okay." She flipped on the bedside lamp.

Was it guilt torturing his handsome face?

"But I'm your—" His gaze met hers for a moment before darting away.

"No, you're not." She cut off the sentiment that no longer held true. "That's not how I see you. Not for a very long time."

His eyes widened. "You don't?"

She ducked her chin but couldn't resist the smile teasing her lips. "While I would have preferred for you to be awake during our first kiss, I'm not sorry it happened." Did she dare tell him everything? The decision took only a moment to ponder. They'd always been honest with each other, and though she knew in her gut he was keeping things from her, she couldn't be anything but honest with him. "I've loved you my whole life, but in the last few weeks my feelings have shifted." Her gaze darted to his. "I've fallen in love with you, Hank."

He raked his fingers through his hair, turning the dark blond strands into spikes. "This can't happen."

Her heart sank into her stomach. Of course he'd say that. He was dating Avery. "I know. I'm sorry." She swallowed the lump in her throat. "It was a weak moment. I won't say a thing to Avery."

"What?" His brow narrowed. "No, she and I aren't together. We're just friends."

It was her turn to look confused. "If that's the case, then there's no reason for us not to make love," she said, daring to hope his feelings matched her own. His expression darkened, crushing her joy. Had she read him wrong?

"It isn't right." He shook his head and backing away farther. "You have a brain injury. Your thinking is off."

His words lit a fire in her belly. She bolted upright in bed. "Don't you dare use that argument." She stabbed a finger in his direction. "This has nothing to do with my injuries. I know how I feel about you." Pressing her hand to her chest, the truth came pouring out. "I love you more than I've ever loved another person."

Hank drew in a sharp breath. "You can't mean that," he bit out, his body vibrating in agitation.

But she did. She'd never uttered truer words. She craved the contact she'd enjoyed moments ago, like a newly born addict. One taste and she was hooked. Every muscle screamed for her to reach for him. The blatant fear in his eyes kept her from acting on her body's urging. She crossed her arms over her chest, reining herself in. "I don't think I could ever love anyone more than I love you. I think that's why my relationship with Tripp was doomed." She drew in a breath. "I'm in love with you, Hank."

"Don't say that," he shot back.

Her declaration made her bold. "I think you love me, too. You do, don't you?"

"God." He raked his fingers through his hair. "There ought to be a better word to use, something bigger, better to describe how I feel for you." His gaze pleaded with her to understand. "Your love is vital to me, as much as the air I breathe. But it's too important to risk ruining it with something that might not work out." He drew closer, lowering to the edge of the bed and taking her hands in his. "You're all I've got in this world, and I almost lost you once at the hands of another. I can't risk losing you because of my own stupidity. I haven't got a clue how to be in a relationship with a woman, and I'm certain somehow I'd mess things up."

At that moment, Mia wanted nothing more than to hunt down Tiffany for the pain she'd caused Hank. They both deserved better, a second chance at love. "I wouldn't let you. We could try," she said, convinced they could make it work. After all, they already had so much history together. They'd been each other's champion. The progression from loved one to lover seemed the next logical step.

"No way." He took to his feet and shook his head. "I can't risk it. Do you understand this is how it has to be?"

"No. I don't accept that."

"You have to," he barked back. "You're going to have to trust that I know what I'm talking about." His voice gentled. "Maybe not now, but in a few months things will be clearer."

His rejection didn't just sting, it burned, nearly

consuming her. Her whole life was filled with people who tossed her aside, beginning at birth. Her mother. The one family who'd taken her in at age four only to return her when they learned they were pregnant with their own child. And then Tripp.

Why had she not seen Hank would be no different, especially as she backed him into a corner? That was what she always did, never knowing when to leave well enough alone. She drew in a breath, marshalling her emotions. "Give me until the end of the week to find an apartment. Until then, I'll stay out of your way." Mia took to her feet, looking for her purse where she kept a small notebook. Her mind raced with the details she'd have to manage. Housing, furniture, transportation to and from the outpatient therapy she was due to begin on Monday. She needed to make a list.

"For the love of..." Hank took her by the shoulders. "That's not what I meant." He tilted her chin. "I promised I'd take care of you, and I will for as long as it takes for you to get back on your feet."

She jerked her face away as bitterness burned in her chest. "I'm done being everyone's charity case. I don't want your pity." She was sick to her soul of people doing things for her out of some noble sense of obligation. "You might not have noticed, but I can take care of myself." She stepped to the closet where she'd stored the duffle bag she'd brought from the hospital. Snatching it up, she moved to the dresser where she began shoving in her clothes. Perhaps, if she was lucky, Milestones would take her back.

"God, Mia," Hank took the bag from her and tossed it on the bed. "You're the most frustrating woman I've ever known." He captured her face with his palms. "You are no burden. I want you here. You'll just have to believe me when I say there can't be any more between us." He caught her in his gaze. "One day you'll be glad I stopped this from happening." He released her and fled the room.

Chapter Eleven

The next morning, Mia drew the sliding glass door closed behind her as she stepped out onto the apartment's small porch. In the wake of the storm, beautiful azure skies greeted her. A breeze caressed her cheek. Too bad the tears she'd shed last night hadn't eased the ache in her chest the same way rain washed away dust and grime from the air. She closed her eyes, tilting her face to the mid-morning sun.

After Hank bolted from her room the night before, the pain of rejection overwhelmed her. She'd cried for hours as if his words had broken the dam of her emotions. She dropped into the plastic seat, drawing her legs onto the chair. Overnight, her thoughts returned to one phrase in particular. *One day you'll be glad I stopped this from happening.*

She gripped the arm of the chair. No. Nothing could stop her from wanting to be with him, from loving him. Not even his rejection. Dawn found her still picking apart their conversation, analyzing each of his arguments. What future event would cause her to see him in a different light? Other than months of outpatient therapy and him returning to his squadron when the time came, nothing significant loomed in their future. His behavior must have something to do with his changing the subject every time she brought up his deployment.

Putting aside the unknown, she focused on the facts. First, Hank loved her, and on some level—even if he wasn't ready to admit it—he also wanted her as a lover. Second, he was definitely keeping something from her. Her instincts screamed the two were tied together in knots that would need to be untangled one strand at a time. Steeling her resolve, she began working the easier of the two issues—uncovering his secret. With luck, solving that mystery would also aid in convincing Hank to give their feelings for each other a chance.

Her go-to tactic was to ask Hank straight out—a come-to-Jesus meeting where she refused to be deflected from the truth. Even as she imagined the scenario, she realized it wouldn't work. Hank had built skyscraper-sized walls around himself not even a barrage of questions could blast through. Mia tapped her finger to her lips. Whatever he was withholding must be life altering for him to guard it with such vehemence. Which made it all the more important that she root it out.

Switching gears, she considered another tack. She could do the opposite, play it cool and ferret out the mystery. Perhaps she'd find the answer among the pile of papers atop the desk in his bedroom. Any issue as important as this one would have written evidence, especially if it involved his career as she suspected.

A twinge of guilt pricked her for even considering plundering through his things. She'd always prided herself on her integrity. Moral dilemmas were few and far between—things were black or white. Perhaps this time the ends justified the means.

She jolted at the sound of the slider opening. As if

Hank could read her thoughts, unease danced up her spine as he stepped through the door.

"There you are." He leaned his long body against the porch railing. Dark circles shadowed his eyes, proving he'd slept as poorly as she. "I was looking for you," he said, although he trained his gaze on everything but her.

The suppressed pain in her chest flared. More than anything—even recovering from her injuries and returning to work—she wanted Hank to love her the way she loved him. She'd let nothing stand in the way of her achieving that goal. "I thought I'd enjoy the sun a bit," she said working to keep emotion from her voice.

"Don't sit out here too long. You'll burn."

She clung to his concern for her like an emotional lifeline. "I won't. I have a long list of things I need to do before my outpatient therapy starts tomorrow."

He jerked his face toward her. "Looking for an apartment isn't one of those things, is it?"

"If the offer is still good, I'd like to stay."

"Good. I'm glad." His small smile failed to reach his eyes. The slump of his shoulders proved more than just last night's drama weighed on him.

She longed to soothe away the dark circles beneath his eyes, to make better whatever burden he kept from her. "I know we talked about going to the beach today, but I think I need to do something more practical." She hoped he wouldn't mind playing chauffeur while she readied herself for the first day of outpatient therapy. "Could you take me shopping? I'd like to have something besides T-shirts and sweats to wear."

"I came out to tell you I have an errand in Wilmington this morning." The corners of his mouth turned up. "I'd be glad to take you this afternoon."

"I can tag along." She took to her feet. Joy infused her soul at the prospect of spending time with him. "Give me fifteen minutes to get changed."

He pressed his lips together. "That's not going to work for me. I'm already running behind." He stepped inside, calling to her over his shoulder, "I'll be back by two o'clock, and I'll take you to the mall then."

She sagged in her seat. So much for pretending last night hadn't happened. "Okay," she called through the open door. "I'll be ready when you get back." One of Hank's objections to altering their relationship was the possibility of ruining their friendship. At the sound of the front door closing, she realized she already had.

Mia reexamined her decision to root out Hank's secret as she retreated from the porch. First, she tidied the kitchen, ran the vacuum, and then made her bed—any chore to keep her from dwelling on Hank's harsh and cold behavior. When she ran out of petty distractions, she turned to a task she'd anticipated doing on her own. She stripped out of her shorts and T-shirt and turned on the hot water. Gingerly, she stepped under the spray, letting the water cascade over her body. She took her time bathing, enjoying the soft texture of Hank's oversized washcloth. After weeks of relying on a nurse when she bathed, showering on her own should have brought her more pleasure. With her thoughts torn into two camps, joy eluded her. All the same, she appreciated the step toward independence—one she'd need if things continued to deteriorate between her and Hank.

Drying off and redressing, she ticked off all the ways snooping through Hank's personal papers could go south on her. On the other hand, the prospect of enduring the distance between them had her rationalizing the alternative. In the end, she caved to temptation. What did she have to lose since she'd already torn their relationship from its moorings?

The rule follower inside her shrieked as she stood at the threshold to his room. Snooping was a betrayal of his trust. That truth didn't stop her from easing open the door. A large L-shaped desk took up one corner. Beneath it lay her safe, washed clean of soot from the fire. God, he was so good to her. Sparing her the pain of seeing her home burnt, he'd combed through the rubble to retrieve her belongings. She longed to search the box, needing to reconnect with the remains of her old life.

Instead, she turned to the task at hand, sifting through the receipts, bills, and back issues of *Sports Illustrated*. The need to understand Hank's motivation spurred her on. Something more than an abundance of caution lay at the root of his desire to keep her at arm's length. In the end, she found only evidence that he bought groceries at Walmart, paid his bills on time, and liked women in bikinis.

Once she'd finished searching the desk, she looked to the filing cabinet. She eased open the top drawer with a hand that shook from guilt. Thumbing through the files, she found one labeled, "Navy papers." Opening it, her gaze caught on the first document. Still struggling to piece single words into sentences, she traced her finger along the page of text. In the second paragraph, two words leapt from the page—Medical Discharge. She sucked in a sharp breath. He'd left the navy? Not possible. He loved his job as a pilot. As she read further, looking for the medical issue behind the discharge, tears welled in her eyes. Pinpricks of anxiety dotted her skin, and fear overtook guilt as her dominate emotion. He looked so heathy with no outward signs of illness. Yet, any number of diseases could silently steal his health, his career, and his life. No wonder he'd been behaving like he had the weight of the world on his shoulders.

"What the fuck are you doing?"

Mia jolted in her seat. She turned to find Hank standing in the doorway. He gripped the frame, looking as if he were about to tear it from the wall.

****

Anger narrowed Hank's field of vision until all he could see was the open file where he'd stored his discharge documents. They spread out before him like dirty laundry. "Give that to me," he said, snatching the papers from Mia. "You had no right." His heart beat out a tattoo in his chest as he crumpled the pages in his fist.

She shuttered her eyes. "I know, and I'm sorry," she murmured. Her bottom lip trembled as she closed the distance between them, taking his hand. "I knew you were keeping something from me, and I had to find out what it was." Tears shimmered in her deep green eyes. "Talk to me. Please, let me help."

With her plea, time rewound to the last days they'd lived together. She'd found the cigarette burns on his back and wanted to tell the school counselor. Hank begged her to keep quiet. He assured her Mr. Gilbert had only done it that once, despite it being a lie. The man used Hank as a whipping boy, punishing him not only for his infractions but for the other boys'—a tactic that worked well for keeping the rowdy bunch in line.

He'd managed to prevent her from learning of the abuse—until one time when it became too much to bear. All these years later, he could still see the glowing end of his foster father's cigarette and feel the insidious pain as it seared his skin.

If only he'd been stronger back then. Or better able to keep the always perceptive Mia from ferreting out his shameful weakness—that he considered killing himself rather than continue to face the abuse. Only the need to protect her and the other kids kept him from taking action.

Some days, caring for her was all that kept him from ending it all now. The tender look in her eyes was more than he could bear. She knew his thoughts and intentions better than he knew them himself. Hank looked away so as to not see the fear-laced pity expressed on her face.

"Why can't you ever leave well enough alone?" Back then she'd gone against his wishes with disastrous results for them all. They were separated, Child Protective Services sending them to different group homes.

"Because I love you, that's why." Tears trickled down her cheeks. "Is it serious? Please tell me." Her words were a whispered plea that shot straight to his heart.

While the revelation of this secret might not result in physical separation, nothing between them would be the same. She'd downplay her own issues in favor of mother henning him. He could see it now. She'd make sure he took his prescribed vitamins on time and got to his doctor appointments, while keeping things tidy at home so he wouldn't trip over things.

Perhaps some men were content to have their lives managed, but he'd already lost the career that defined him. More than anything right now, as he clung to his identity by his fingertips, what he really wanted was for Mia to see him as someone *she* could lean on.

He cut the air with his hand. "I'm not having this conversation with you."

All she'd gathered from plundering was he'd been given a medical discharge. She'd learn no more if he refused to discuss it with her. He could offer the lie of a more manageable illness like high blood pressure. He'd just have to keep up the ruse until she could resume her life. It wouldn't take long before another upwardly mobile guy caught her attention. Even in theory the idea of her with another man made him crazed with jealousy. He tossed aside the papers, needing to escape. "I'm out of here."

He hadn't counted on warrior woman making an appearance. Like a shot, she darted between him and the open doorway, blocking his retreat with her tiny body. "The hell you are." She jerked up her chin, daring him to push her aside. Her gaze caught his in a tether he couldn't break. "If you get to know about my TBI and watch while I relearn everything like a toddler," she said, stabbing her finger at his chest, "you don't get to keep this from me."

Hank loved her tenacity. If only she'd trained it on a worthy cause. "But that's the exact reason I kept this from you." He cupped her cheek, no longer able to resist touching her. Only the need to make her understand kept him from lowering his mouth to hers. "You've got enough troubles without worrying about my shit."

Mia shook her head. "It doesn't work that way." She took his hands, pressing kisses to his palms. "Not when you love a person."

And love her he did, with every cell in his body, down to his very soul. "God, you're killing me." He groaned, as the heat from her lips went straight to his cock.

"Let me help you the way you've helped me."

"I see there's no getting around you." He led her to the edge of his bed. His body screamed for him to join her, to distract them both at least for a few moments. Instead, he pulled up the desk chair and sat across from her. "Back in the spring, I crashed my jet into the drink."

Mia drew in a breath. "Why?"

"I was flying at night, something that had never been any more of an issue than trying to put a Super Hornet going one-hundred-twenty knots on a spot the size of a couple football fields. Except this time, I couldn't see the deck. There was this halo around my peripheral vision as I approached." Adrenalin spiked in his system as he recalled the sensation of helplessness. "I completely missed all the traps and shot off the end of the carrier."

She covered her mouth with her hand. "It's a wonder you weren't killed."

He let out a breath. "Believe me. I know."

She inched forward, narrowing her gaze on him. "What have the doctors told you about the halos?"

His heart tried to pound its way out of his chest as the truth stood poised on his lips. Once she learned he'd soon be as helpless as a newborn pup, there'd be no sucking back that knowledge. He rubbed his palms against his jeans. "I was at the VA clinic down in Wilmington earlier for a follow up. The docs put me on vitamin A supplements in hopes that would help the problem with my eyes."

He met her gaze, the cruel irony not lost on him as he took in the emerald color. Tears clung to her lashes. "They should have a diagnosis hammered out in a few weeks, but for now they're thinking it's retinitis pigmentosa. If that's the case, over the next few years I will lose my sight."

Hank gripped the armrests, bracing for her reaction. Closing his eyes, he prayed for strength if she changed her mind—that standing by him as he slowly went blind was more than she wanted to take on.

He jolted as Mia slipped into his lap. She twined her arms around his shoulders and buried her face in his neck. He breathed in the floral scent of her shampoo, a longing he could never sate joining the ache solidifying his chest like concrete. "Don't cry," he said, when her warm tears touched his skin. "It'll be fine." He recited the platitude, hoping if he said it often enough he'd come to believe it himself. "Once the doctors nail down my diagnosis, I'll be able to make some plans." Visions of canes, service dogs, and suffocating darkness formed in his imagination.

Mia pressed a kiss to the underside of his jaw. "You don't have to put on a brave face for me. I know exactly what it's like to lose a part of your identity."

Hank acknowledged her words with a nod. "You sure do, angel." She'd coped with her memory loss and impaired speech with grace that still amazed him. His very soul screamed to reach out to her for help, to seek comfort not only in her body but in the brave heart at her core.

She thumbed away at her tears then drew in a breath. "I have an idea, but you must first promise to hear me out."

He arched an eyebrow. "Okay," he said, curious what solution she'd come up with.

"I had a classmate back in middle school who had the disease. So did several other members of his family. What if you—"

"Not a chance in hell." He realized the path her thoughts were taking. "I don't want anything to do with my birth family. Not only did my mother dump me into the system without a backward glance, her people knew where I ended up, and not one of them wanted me."

"What about your father? Have you considered looking for him?"

Hank fed the anger bubbling inside him, using it as fuel to get him through this revelation. "When I turned eighteen, I looked up my father." Resentment settled over him as he recounted the event he'd shared with no one. "Turns out he knew all about me. Even knew that I'd been turned over to Child Protective Services. He signed away his parental rights, washing his hands of the bastard kid he fathered while screwing one of his employees. Turns out he had a wife and kids who knew nothing of the old man's shenanigans. He didn't want to mess things up by springing me on them."

Mia rested her cheek against his chest. "I'm so sorry. I guess the only thing worse than not having a family was having one that didn't want you."

"I heard that."

They clung to each other for several moments before Mia spoke. "This is what you meant last night when you said that one day I'd be glad we kept things the same between us."

He swallowed the knot in his throat. "Yeah."

"You're wrong. I'm not going anywhere. I'm here for you whether we ever become more to each other or not."

The smallest part of him dared to believe—to hope if he had her at his side, he could stare down decades of darkness. But as much as he wanted everything she so willingly offered, cold reality blocked the path to making her his. Look what a cock-up he'd made of his marriage to Tiffany. Sure, she'd cheated on him with half the fleet, but he too bore a share of the responsibility. He'd never been able to give her all of his heart. Fear that he'd do the same to Mia held him back.

"It's your turn to listen." He took her by the shoulders. "Even if I wasn't losing my sight, I couldn't risk what we have for the chance of something more. Perhaps someday I'll change my mind, but I doubt it." He held her gaze. "In the meantime, it's not right for you to hope any of this will be different."

Mia's eyes sparked and a small smile played at her lips. "I'm a very patient person when I need to be. I'm not going to let a little thing like doubt discourage me."

Her promise thrilled and terrified him in equal measure. How hard would this determined woman work to prove her point?

Chapter Twelve

Mia tucked her pajamas under her pillow then smoothed her bedspread. She glanced around the sparse room looking for another task to put off facing Hank. With the nightstand clear except for her lamp and her dirty clothes in the hamper in the corner, the room was Sister Marie-Theresa tidy. Yesterday's confrontation left her raw. His rejection cast her adrift. Guilt twisted in her stomach. In the end, she still didn't regret what she'd done—any of it. Only that it widened the gap between them.

She padded into the kitchen to find Hank with his back to her. "Good morning," she said when he failed to acknowledge her entry. Were his thoughts as tangled as hers?

He turned then jerked a nod. Today, he varied from his usual uniform of T-shirt and jeans, dressing in tank top, long shorts, and flip-flops. Over the summer, the sun had lightened his dark blond hair, making her think he needed a surfboard to complete his ensemble.

"I'm ready to go when you are." She took a couple steps in his direction.

"We have a few minutes." He turned his attention to the coffee cup and bowl in the kitchen sink. "You need to eat before we go."

She pressed a hand to her stomach, weighted down with sadness but also aflutter with nervousness over beginning her therapy at Milestones. "I couldn't possibly eat."

He placed the cup in the rack beside the sink then turned. His expression softened from the impassive mask he'd worn moments before. "First day jitters?"

"Something like that." She returned his smile.

"Then it's good I made us a big lunch." He pointed over his shoulder to two brown paper bags. "The rehab place said you'd need a lunch every day. I wasn't sure what you'd want, so I packed a smorgasbord."

"Thanks. After today, you can just drop me off. I can manage on my own, and I know you have better things you could be doing with your time."

Milestones' policy was for new patients to bring someone with them the first day, so Hank would be following her as she got into the routine of classes.

A shadow of emotion crossed his face. "I'm here for whatever you need." He grabbed his cell phone, keys, and the bags.

She shuttered her eyes, as tears threatened. If only that were true.

Mia followed Hank out to his truck, shaking her head at him as he waited by the passenger door. "I can do that myself, you know." She hoisted herself into the elevated cab.

"Yep." He closed the door and crossed to the other side.

By the time they hit the highway, the silence filling the cab was so thick it was like trying to breathe under water. She opened her mouth to say something—anything to cut the tension. What was there to say that hadn't already been gone over or that would extinguish his anger?

Finally, they reached LaGrange General's campus. Instead of turning into the parking garage that served the main hospital, Hank steered them to the three-story glass structure that housed Milestones' out-patient clinic as well as resident housing. He killed the engine and was around the side of the truck while she was still gathering her things.

"Thank you," she said, conceding to the chivalrous gesture. With so much wrong between them, it seemed petty to make a fuss over a simple act.

Once they were inside, she approached the receptionist. Mia waited until the woman behind the desk finished her phone call. "Good morning." She forced a smile to her lips. Months of therapy lay before her like a mountain of misery. While she wanted to regain what her attacker had taken from her, and no one was less afraid of hard work, at that moment the task felt insurmountable. But what was the alternative? She drew in a breath, steeling her resolve. "I'm Mia Jones. I'm supposed to begin out-patient therapy today."

The receptionist, an African-American woman in her late fifties, returned Mia's smile. "Did a family member bring you this morning, dear," she said, speaking with the same patient tone one usually reserved for children—or the addled. "They need to fill out some paperwork before your therapy sessions begin."

Mia gestured over her shoulder. "I brought my..." What were they to each other? Their relationship had never been in question before a few days ago. She turned and craned her neck to take in his dark green eyes, strong jaw, and cleft chin. His steady gaze warmed her and eased some of the anxiety over beginning this segment of her recovery.

She loved him, always had, and always would. But, she saw him differently than she had just a short time ago. Not as a brother or protector, but as a man she wanted to build her life with. Make love to. A fissure of pain sliced through her. One thing was certain. He didn't see her that way. And likely never would. "He's my—"

"We're family," Hank finished for her, inching closer to the desk.

The receptionist consulted a list. "Yes, I see her schedule here." She gazed up at Hank as she passed over a clipboard. "There's some paperwork for you fill out. She'll be on the blue team."

Mia tugged the clipboard from Hank's grasp. Car doors were one thing, but this much she'd do on her own or at least give it her best shot. How else was she going to change his perception of her if she took his help with the simplest of tasks? She crossed the lobby to the nearest chair.

After flipping through the sheaves, she understood why the staff had her arrive an hour before the start of classes. Clicking her pen, she tackled the first sheet. "Name," she began.

Mia shot a glance at Hank who pretended to ignore her by thumbing through last month's issue of *Sports Illustrated.* She did all right filling in the forms until she arrived at the last page. A solid sheet of text confronted her. She began with the first paragraph, using her finger to guide her. Two lines in, and the document lost all meaning as she struggled to decode each word. Prior to the attack, she'd have breezed through this in a matter of minutes. Legalese was her bread and butter.

Her thoughts rewound to a phone call she'd gotten last week from one of her colleagues at the district attorney's office. On the surface, Veronica's call had been a friendly check-in to see when Mia would be released from the hospital. The staff wanted to stock her freezer with meals she could reheat as needed. The generous offer was classic southern hospitality—with dual purposes. Mia's gut told her that her coworker had been sent as a scout to assess Mia's progress.

She let out a breath and reread the first paragraph of the insurance liability form. Again she struggled to make sense of the words. At the rate she was going, it would be next year sometime before she'd be able to return to work.

Her pay was secure, having gone on long-term disability. But, what would she do once that ended? Anxiety twisted her stomach at a worry more significant than money. What if she could no longer practice law?

It's early days.

Except it wasn't. The attack happened months ago, and her recovery had begun leveling off. Tears pricked the back of her eyes as she continued her attempts to read the words before her. She had months of daily therapy ahead. While she'd improved enough that she could dress herself, and her short-term memory had gotten better, she was light years away from where she needed to be. She dabbed at the corner of her eye, hoping Hank didn't notice.

He squeezed her free hand.

"Don't mind me." She smiled up at him. "I'm out of sorts today."

"I'm here if you need me."

She passed him the clipboard, his words ringing in her ears. "Read this to me, if you would. Otherwise we'll both be drawing Social Security by the time I finish."

Soon after, her new physical therapist escorted her and Hank to the PT room. Mia glanced around, finding the space almost exactly the same as the one in the hospital. A woman with *Beverly* stitched on her shirt pointed to a mat that was raised on legs a couple feet off the floor. "Let's begin with some stretching exercises so I can see where you are with your range of motion."

Mia did as instructed, concentrating on extending her muscles as far as she could, while not toppling over. From the corner of her eye, movement caught her attention.

Hank's leg was drawn out in a pose that mirrored hers. "What are you doing?" A laugh bubbled up.

"Practicing with you." He made an adjustment until his pose matched hers.

She straightened up, a smile tugged at her lips. "You don't need to practice, you goof. I don't know anyone more physically fit."

He shrugged. "I said that I'd be with you every step of the way."

And he meant it, following her through all her sessions that day. During the third week of therapy, she finally convinced him that he didn't have to wait in the lobby all day. The first month of daily classes passed with incremental improvements in her ability to comprehend short passages of text, but none when it came to her relationship with Hank.

Chapter Thirteen

Over the next several weeks, Hank and Mia settled into a routine centered on her therapy, doctors' visits, and the mundane tasks of life. Tonight, it was Hank's turn to handle dinner, and pizza from D'Angelo's waited on the kitchen counter. Despite the warm, spicy scent of sausage, onions, and peppers wafting from the box next to him, he couldn't muster much enthusiasm for the meal.

He gathered a fistful of napkins and a couple paper plates, placing them atop the pizza box. "Water or soda?" he called over his shoulder. Since leaving Milestones hours before, they hadn't exchanged more than a handful of words. His body hummed with tension. He hated the silence that often stretched between them as they retreated behind their emotional barricades. For once, it wasn't the twin clusterfucks from their first week together that had the atmosphere in the apartment heavy with regret.

Hank snagged a bottle from the cabinet by the refrigerator and threw a few ice cubes into his glass. "Your friend's still picking you up in the morning?" he asked Mia while he poured a generous amount of tequila and topped it off with a splash of Sprite.

He'd scheduled his own appointment with the VA's ophthalmologist to coincide with one of her routine checkups at the hospital. Though she'd pleaded for him to change the appointment so she could go, he'd stuck to his guns. This was something he had to face without an audience. He took a big swig off his fourth drink of the evening. Come tomorrow, he'd learn for certain if he had retinitis pigmentosa. God, how was he going to handle going blind and still be of any use to Mia? With another sip to maintain his buzz, he managed to shove his issues to the corner in favor of hers.

"Did you hear me? Is Veronica still picking you up?" When Mia didn't answer, he looked to the living room behind him. Seated on the sofa, she stared out the sliding glass doors to the darkened patio beyond, lost in her thoughts. Ever since learning the results of her neuropsych test earlier in the week, she'd retreated to a place he couldn't reach. Who could blame her? He didn't know squat about neurology, but even he recognized the results weren't great.

Hank balanced drinks and plates on top of the pizza box and brought their dinner to the coffee table. Then he opened the lid, hoping the scent would draw her attention. Still watching her, he slid a couple slices on each of the plates, and then cracked open her diet cola. After setting it down in front of her, he took a seat on the sofa. None of his movements managed to draw her out of her head.

His chest ached as he watched her, not just because of the bad news she was still struggling to process, but with a burning desire for her. She'd dressed in her usual nighttime wear of a tiny tank top and cotton shorts. How had he never noticed the delicate blush of her cheeks or how long her legs were? Her creamy skin begged to be touched.

It was as if the dream he'd had weeks ago awakened a hunger inside him. His gaze raked over her still-short hair, down the slender column of her neck, to the gentle curves of her body. He took a long draw of his tequila concoction, hoping it would cool his need. Or at least give him a case of liquor dick. No such luck. He subtly adjusted the erection that tented his shorts.

Despite her assurance that her desires matched his own, now was the worst possible time for the two of them to alter their relationship. Even under ideal circumstances, he wouldn't have risked losing her because sure as shit he'd find a way to fuck things up. As it was, between her attack, the TBI, and the fire at her condo—not to mention his vision problems—they had enough problems without adding sex to the mix.

Regardless of their issues, he could no more stand by and watch her suffer and struggle than he could take wing and fly. He put down his drink. Twining their fingers, he asked, "Do you want to talk about what's bothering you?"

Mia looked to the ceiling, dabbing the corners of her eyes with her free hand. "What is there to say?" She turned to face him. "I have an IQ of eighty-five. That's thirty-five points from where it was when I was in high school." Her lip quivered. "It's not even in normal range."

He gathered her into his arms. "Oh, angel, it's going to be okay. I promise." Anger boiled inside him as he held her. The tears dripping onto his neck fueled his impotent rage like drops of gasoline on a flame. He'd gladly face a darkened future for the chance to hunt down the person who'd attacked her and beat more than IQ points out of the bastard. As a result of that animal's actions, Mia lost not just her ability to express herself or process the written word but a career she loved.

While he won his ticket out of the foster care system through an ROTC scholarship, Mia earned her way with her smarts. After flying through high school, she'd gotten her undergraduate degree and been accepted to Wake Forest's law school before turning twenty. For her, education and academic success was more than a way out of poverty. She'd lost a vital part of her identity.

Hank combed his fingers through her hair. "It's not that much below average, and the doc said you'd still be getting better for years to come." He continued the gentle strokes, praying his touch soothed her pain as much as it fanned the flames of his desire. He longed to kiss away her tears but couldn't trust his will power to that much temptation.

She pulled back, looking up at him with red-rimmed eyes. "I'm not going to improve enough to get me back where I need to be. I'll never be able to argue a case again. I couldn't even convince you to let me go to the doctor with you."

He cupped her cheek. "My decision has nothing to do with your abilities to make your point." Their close proximity made focusing on anything other than getting her underneath him impossible. He pulled away, turning her so they faced each other knee-to-knee. "Listen." He needed her to understand.

When she refused to make eye contact, he tilted her chin. "Can I be straight with you?" She nodded, still keeping her eyes lowered. "I don't want you going with me because if I get the news I'm expecting, I might not take it very well."

Her gaze darted to his. "All the more reason why I should go with. No one should face that alone."

He drew in a breath. "I just can't, angel," he said, struggling with how to express his deep-seeded fear of seeing her look on him with pity. He wasn't too keen on her witnessing him lose his shit either, which was a distinct possibility. "It's not up for discussion." He reached for the remote. "You never did answer my question. Is Veronica taking you to your doctor's appointment tomorrow?"

She nodded. "After that, I have some business to take care of at the courthouse. Then she's going to take me to the hair salon and to buy a dress for Avery and Connor's wedding Saturday."

"Great. Sounds like a fun day for you." he said, forcing excitement into his words. "But if you don't feel up to attending the wedding, I know they'll understand."

He couldn't have been more surprised when the invitation came in the mail. Those two had been bitter rivals for years, and now they were getting married.

She shook her head. "No, you're a groomsman. You have to go. Besides, it'll be good to be with people who won't be asking after my health." She scooted closer and leaned on his shoulder. "I'd also like to go with you to your doctor's appointment."

The contact sent his alcohol-dulled senses roaring to life. The scent of her shampoo teased his nose as the warmth of her cheek pressed against him reawakened his lust. It would be the work of a moment to have her undressed. "No—"

She pulled back, holding up a hand to cut him off.

"I'll respect your masculine need to keep your pride. Please just promise you'll call afterward."

"Absolutely." He reached for the remote control, anxious for a distraction. "What say we watch a couple comedies? I think we could both use a laugh."

Mia returned to her side of the sofa, curling her legs beneath her. "Sure. That'd be great." Her lack of inflection belied her words.

Fifteen minutes into *Mrs. Doubtfire*, Hank let out a snort. "Holy crap, this guy never gets old." He propped his feet up on the coffee table. Robin Williams and tequila had loosened the knot in his gut. He stretched his arm over the back of the sofa, brushing Mia's shoulders. "How many times do you think we've seen this movie?" When she didn't respond, he cut his eyes at her. She fixed her gaze on the flat screen, but clearly wasn't taking in the movie.

He'd give his left nut to be able to coax a smile out of her, to ease her sorrow over what she'd lost. Maybe it wouldn't take such a drastic measure. A solution worked its way from the depths of his memory. He trailed his hand and lightly dug his fingertip into her ribs. "I bet I can get a smile out of you."

She twitched, batting away at his hand. "Stop. You know I hate that." A smile played at her lips, indicating otherwise.

Hank pounced, capturing her ankles and dragging her down on the sofa. "I remember things a bit differently." He tickled first her neck, her underarms, and then back to her ribs.

Mia squirmed and thrashed. "You're going to make me wet my pants," she said between giggles. Then she retaliated, going for his knees, a spot she'd discovered many years ago when they'd regularly engaged in this method of torture.

As he dodged her fingers and she bowed up her back, he fell forward. He threw out a hand at the last second, keeping his weight off her. Her lips parted in a gasp that had him iron-hard. He pulled back, determined to keep his thoughts where they needed to be. Gazing into her eyes and finding them dilated in lust wasn't helping things. "I'll stop tickling, if you'll do one thing."

"What's that?"

"Tell me you believe everything's going to be okay for us. No more worries about things we can't control. No more glass half empty."

She leaned closer, cupping his cheek. "I will, if you promise there'll be no more secrets between us. No more going it alone."

Looking into eyes the color of spring, how could he refuse? "Promise," he said in a voice rough with lust. Sitting them upright, he dragged her into his lap and brought his mouth down to hers. One brush of their lips and reason fled. He cupped the back of her head, knowing he was about to ruin everything. Her lips were soft and tantalizingly responsive. He ate at her mouth until she opened and let him inside. Their tongues danced together as he deepened the kiss. He banded her waist, setting her fully into his hips. She ground her core against his erection, driving him toward madness.

When he finally broke the kiss, they were both panting for breath. Her green eyes had dilated to the point only a sliver of color ringed the dark pupil. He might have had the strength to resist until she tugged her tank top over her head.

His gaze shot to her gentle swells. "Sweet baby Jesus, you're beautiful," he said, thumbing her through her bra. He unfastened the front closure then brought his mouth to down to suckle her breasts. Her nipples budded in tight peaks as he stroked her.

"Yes," she said, in a throaty voice that had him nearly coming in his pants. "More, please. That feels so good."

He was hers to beckon and command. After laying her down on the sofa, Hank trailed kisses down the flat plane of her stomach toward his ultimate goal. He tugged at the waistband of the tiny shorts she wore, drawing them and her panties over her slim hips. In fluid movements, he dropped to the floor and drew her hips down until she lay flat. Then he hooked a leg over his shoulder and lowered his mouth to her core.

She gasped at the first swipe of his tongue. Her encouragement spurred him on. He buried deeper into her feminine folds, reveling in each of the tiny sounds she made. He could have feasted on her for hours, losing himself in her as her natural scent wound its way to his brain. Who needed sight when they had four perfectly good senses to cement this moment in his memory?

As she neared climax, Hank narrowed his focus to the bundle of nerves at the top of her cleft. Alternating between swipes of his tongue and drawing her clit between his lips, he drove her over the edge. She arched and bucked, riding her orgasm with passion he never guessed she had.

When the tremors and aftershocks ended, Mia tugged him onto the sofa to lie atop her. Her soft expression and the unfocused gaze made his rock hard erection worthwhile. She wrapped her legs around his hips, drawing him to the exact spot he needed to be. "Let me ease you. Even if it only for a little while."

Her words washed over him like February rain. Neither of them would be satisfied with a one-off moment. He'd never be happy anywhere else, and she'd start imagining a future where the two of them could be together. He'd never give her false hope or saddle her with a blind man when she had her own disability to work through.

She tilted her hips, rubbing her wet heat against the thin layer of his shorts. He shuttered his eyelids as an orgasm boiled inside him. A few millimeters of fabric were all that separated him from his own little slice of heaven. "I need you, Hank," she said in a sex kitten drawl.

He pulled back, every muscle in his body screaming in protest as he did. She did need him. She needed him to be her friend, her support system in this dark part of her life—not as a lover. He sat back on his haunches. "I can't do this to you, Mia. To either of us."

"What do you mean?" She sat up. Confusion, pain, and anger washed over her face. "This is what I want, for us to be together. I know it's what you want as well."

He wrestled with his own emotions. Desire and love warred with need for self-preservation. "Being together might be a quick fix, but in the long run it's not going to work out." The hurt that washed over her face cut him to the core. Instead of easing her worries, he added to it. "While you're in LaGrange tomorrow, I think it would be a good idea if you looked for another place to live," he said, before turning on his heels and fleeing the room. Perhaps with a little time and distance they could get back to where they'd once been. From there, he'd find a way to be the man she truly needed.

Chapter Fourteen

Mia worked conditioner into her hair then squirted a dollop of body wash onto a shower puff. After a quick head-to-toe rinse, she cut off the water. She'd overslept and was running behind. Her friend, Veronica, would be by to pick her up in less than half an hour. What should have been a pleasant day of errands and shopping lost its appeal thanks to the events from the night before. Regardless of her lack of enthusiasm, she had a life to get on with, and that meant keeping her appointments.

She reached beyond the shower curtain, fumbling for a towel but found nothing. She let out a growl of frustration. In her rush, she'd failed to snag one of Hank's bath sheets from the linen closet. She stepped out of the tub, dripping water as she padded across the tile floor. Her hand had just reached the doorknob when the door from the hallway opened with a bang, blocking her access.

Mia let out a squeak of surprised that must not have penetrated Hank's groggy state. She looked to the sink behind her for anything to cover herself with. The hand towel she spotted would do her little good. He stumbled forward, his eyes finally opening when he bumped into her.

His gaze raked over her naked body then narrowed. "Fuck," he growled through a clenched jaw. "Why don't you cover up, for Christ's sake?"

Seriously? She planted her fists on her bare hips, giving her temper free rein. "You're the one who barged in on me. Don't you know how to knock?" She refused to cover her body.

He opened the linen closet, yanking a towel off the shelf. "I thought you'd gone already." He kept his eyes averted as he passed it to her.

"I'm doing the best I can to get out of your hair." She wrapped the cotton sheet around her body, pushed passed him, and bolted for her room.

Mia dressed in a rush, amazed she'd yet to reach the pinnacle of the crap fate kept heaping on her. "I must have been a real bitch in a previous life," she muttered as she shimmied into her jeans. After tugging on a T-shirt, she combed her still-wet hair. She'd just have to leave without styling her two-inch locks. One of her appointments that morning was with a hairdresser, so what did it matter anyway.

She tied her sneakers, mentally adding apartment hunting to her to-do list. While she'd spent a tearful night reliving every moment of the night before and wishing for a different outcome, she also realized Hank had a point. She swallowed the emotions churning her insides. It was time for her to start the next stage of her life, and as much as it grieved her, it appeared she'd be doing so on her own. His words echoed in her head. Hank was many things, but she'd never known him to say something he didn't mean. "I can do this." She slapped her thighs with finality.

Mia drew in a deep breath. As she reached the living room, a knock came on the front door. "Just coming," she called to Veronica as she snagged her purse from the sofa.

Hank stepped out of the kitchen, blocking her path. His gaze darted to her then lowered. "Listen, I'm sorry about being an asshole earlier."

She shrugged. "No problem. I'm getting used to you being that way." She wasn't quite ready to let him off the hook.

Pain contorted his handsome features. "I deserve that." He shoved his hands inside the pockets of his jeans. "Well, anyway, I am sorry I embarrassed you like that."

Mia shook her head. Was he that clueless? It wasn't that he'd seen her naked. Hell, until a few minutes ago, she'd wanted nothing more than for him to see her bare body. What had her hurting like she'd been sucker punched was the rejection behind the steely-eyed look he'd given her. She could do without a repeat of that experience.

Yet, even with the hurt she nursed and her righteous anger, she longed to reach for him. It wasn't like his life was easy either. She couldn't imagine losing her sight, much less doing so on her own, as he seemed determined to do. Even with Veronica waiting on the other side of the door, if he asked, she'd cancel her plans. One look at his dark expression told her that scenario was about as likely as biking the Coastal Comet Trail again.

"Be sure…"

He arched an eyebrow.

The reminder of his promise to call after his doctor's appointment died on her lips. "Never mind."

He caught her hand as she passed. "What time do you think you'll be home?"

Mia jerked from his grasp. "I have no idea. I have a lot to do in LaGrange." He couldn't treat her like he had and expect her to tolerate his big-brother routine.

He nodded, backing out of her way. "So I'll see you later then."

After stepping over the threshold, she looked back over her shoulder. "I'll let you know if my plans change, but don't wait up." The door closed on his response, and she plastered a smile for Veronica. "Sorry about that. I had to get a few things straight with my roomie."

The curvy brunette flashed a smile. "No problem. You ready to go?"

"Absolutely." She shoved aside her anger and angst as they headed toward her friend's car.

The two of them struck up a friendship when Mia joined the district attorney's office. Veronica was a few years older than her, athletic, and happily single. Before the attack, they'd shared lunch almost daily and gone shopping on evenings when work kept Tripp at the office. She'd even asked her to be a bridesmaid.

"Let's get the yucky part over so we can do some shopping."

As Mia climbed inside the tiny import, the low-slung car reminded her to talk to her neurologist about getting cleared to drive. She pulled her notebook from her purse, adding it to the reminder to ask about job retraining. Excitement over the day's plans bubbled inside her, which seemed silly considering her to-do list included resigning from her job, collecting the final report on the fire at her condo, and leasing an apartment. Since the attack, she'd focused almost exclusively on putting one foot in front of the other.

The furthest she'd looked was the completion of daily therapy at the end of next week. Making long-range plans felt liberating, even if they weren't exactly the ones she hoped or included the person she loved most. Regret flared in her chest. If only she could find a way to make him open up to her, she could face any future if it included Hank.

"Did I hear wrong a minute ago? I thought you were living with your brother." She backed into the parking lot.

Mia closed the notebook and stowed it in her purse. The emotions of the past couple days threatened to suffocate her seedling joy. "He's not actually my brother, but yeah, Hank took me in after the fire," she explained, wondering if she'd made a mistake accepting his offer. Perhaps she'd have been better off if she'd stayed at Milestones.

"I'm so sorry about the fire. It must have happened right after I'd been there to drop those meals because everything looked normal while I was there." She patted Mia's knee. "You've had more crap rain down on you than anyone should have to deal with." Shooting Mia a quick smile, she added, "Girl, the universe owes you a break, like winning the lottery or finding Mr. Right."

"Amen to that." She chuckled. "But I'd settle for finding the guy who twice tried to kill me."

"What did you say?" Veronica turned her attention from the highway that would lead them from Hank's place in Wilmington north to LaGrange. "What else happened?"

"The fire was deliberately set, and the detective handling my assault believes the arsonist is the same person who attacked me on the trail."

Veronica's eyes widened. "Holy crap, girl, I thought the attack was random. Do the police have any leads on who did this?"

Anxiety bloomed in Mia's stomach as they neared LaGrange. She hadn't realized how secure she felt living with Hank until that moment. He'd been her constant companion over the past couple months. Her gaze traveled to the downtown streets. Perhaps she should consider moving to another town instead of simply relocating to another place where her attacker could easily find her. That prospect stole some of her anticipation for the future. Other than college, LaGrange had been her home for her whole life. She swallowed past a lump in her throat to answer Veronica's questions. "The detective is going on the theory it's either someone I prosecuted or their family. I'm going to touch base with him while we're in town to see if he's been able to narrow down the list."

Veronica shook her head as she turned onto the town's main thoroughfare. "Unfortunately, that makes sense. All of us at the DA's office have received threats from a defendant, but to act on it is another thing altogether. You'll let me know if I can help."

"I will," Mia said. "The boss turned over a list of my cases to the detective weeks ago."

By that time, they'd pulled into LaGrange General where Dr. Cowboy kept an office. She studied the people coming in and out of the building, suddenly feeling vulnerable. *I'm being silly. No one's going to attack me with dozens of people around.* She drew in a steadying breath then turned to her friend. "I'll probably be an hour or so in here. You're welcome to drop me off. I know you've got better things to do with your time than sit in a waiting room."

Veronica shook her head. "I don't mind. If I set foot inside my office, I'll get sucked into some crisis or another." She patted her purse. "I brought my tablet, so I can use the time to go through my emails."

The two of then exited the car. "Okay, if you're sure," Mia said, redirecting her thoughts. Looking over her shoulder or waiting for the other shoe to drop was no way to live. They entered the hospital through the main doors, crossing the lobby to a bank of elevators. "I really appreciate you doing this." She pushed the button for the second floor. "I have an idea. While I'm getting my hair cut, you should get a manicure. My treat."

"Sounds like a plan," Veronica said as the elevator jolted and began its assent.

****

"You look like a million bucks." Veronica blew gently over freshly polished nails. "You're going to be the prettiest woman at this wedding tomorrow."

"Thanks." Although given Hank's frame of mind, she'd bet that million dollars he'd try to back out of his friends' nuptials. She was on the fence as well despite buying the cutest dress and finding a killer pair of heels on sale at her favorite boutique. Perhaps she should stop trying to force Hank into situations he didn't want.

The stylist spun Mia around, giving her a first glimpse of the new haircut. After having her head shaved during the craniotomy, Mia had few style options to choose from. She fingered the pixie cut. "You're a miracle worker," she told Jamie, the woman who'd been doing her hair at Curl Up and Dye for the past five years. She turned her head, searching for the scar that arched from just above her left ear to her nape. Subtle highlights and the product Jamie worked into the strands hid the scar. "Somehow you managed to make me look like something other than a twelve-year-old boy."

"I'm pleased you like it." The woman smiled widely. "We can keep it in that style if you find you like it, or let it grow out."

Mia pulled a handful of bills from her wallet. "How much do I owe you?"

Jamie pushed the twenties away. "There's no charge, sweetie. When I heard about your attack, I cried my eyes out for days. I'm just so delighted to see you getting better."

"I can't let you do that." Gratitude warmed her insides.

"Yes, you can." She whipped the plastic drape off Mia's shoulders. "Seeing your smiling face in here is payment enough today."

Mia hugged the woman, slipping the bills into her smock as she did. As much as she appreciated the gesture, as a self-employed single parent, Jamie needed every dollar she earned.

"Wow," she said to Veronica once they'd left the shop. "For a day that started off rough, it's made a fabulous recovery."

Her friend smiled. "Glad to hear it. Like I said before, you're due a break," she said as they left the salon. "We got sidetracked and I forgot to ask how your checkup went."

"Nothing but good news." Mia let euphoria wash all her problems away for the moment. "I've been cleared to drive, and the doctor put me in contact with an agency that helps retrain folks with brain injuries for new jobs."

"Excellent." Veronica squeezed her hand.

Mia had confided the results of the neuropsych to her friend. As Hank had done, Veronica offered words of encouragement, but agreed returning to her job was unlikely. Not having her decision brushed off meant as much to Mia as the woman's encouragement.

"Want some lunch before we head to the courthouse?" Veronica pointed to one of their favorite eateries.

Mia patted her stomach. "Let's wait a bit. I'm still full from the muffin you made me eat."

Veronica laughed. "What did you expect me to do after seeing that dress on you? A stiff wind would carry you away."

"Not hardly," she laughed, although she'd lost nearly ten pounds of muscle while in the hospital. She was just now beginning to regain her strength and stamina thanks to the physical terrorist at Milestones who worked her into a sweat five days a week.

They soon reached the hundred-year-old structure that took up the east side of the square. The three-story Greek Revival building housed courtrooms, the district attorney's offices, and several other county government agencies. Stepping into the lobby with its twenty-foot ceilings, wainscoted walls, and heart-of-pine floors, a wave of longing hit her hard. Practicing law had been her only career aspiration, and now she was here to end that chapter of her life.

She breathed in the vaguely musty scent on her way up the stairs to the DA's office on the third floor. As Veronica chattered by her side, Mia couldn't help but look at the dozens of people around her. Was the person who'd attacked her and burned her home watching her from close by waiting for another opportunity? Had he or she been arrested for another crime and was awaiting arrangement in one of the courtroom on the second floor?

She couldn't ignore those possibilities any more than she could live looking over her shoulder. After she finished with her boss, she'd head down to the fire marshal's first-floor office to collect her copy of the arson investigator's report. After that, she'd walk over to the police station and have a word with Detective Price. She had to put the person who'd attacked her behind bars if she had any chance of moving forward.

"Come find me when you're ready to leave," Veronica said when they reached the landing.

"Will do." Mia turned in the opposite direction. She tugged on the wire-embedded glass outer door, stepping into the small reception area. The young woman on the other side of the glass window buzzed her through. She waved hello then made her way to Jim Connelly's office.

Her boss genuinely had an open door policy, only closing it when confidentiality demanded. She rapped on the doorframe. "You ready for me, boss?" she asked, having called the day before to schedule a few minutes with him.

He looked up from the file he was reading and smiled. "Sure thing, Mia." He came around his desk, taking her hand. "You're looking good, much better than when I saw you back in the ICU. When will you be finished with therapy?" He motioned for her to take a seat then leaned against the front edge of his desk and crossed his legs at the ankles.

Mia lowered into one of the wingback chairs, her stomach twisting. She'd rehearsed what she wanted to say, but now the moment was at hand, her thoughts tangled in a knot of anxiety and regret. Putting into practice the techniques taught to her by her speech therapist, she narrowed her attention to the question at hand. "Next week."

He nodded. "Does that mean you're ready to come back to work?"

She let out a breath. "That's why I wanted to see you." Could she actually slam the door on the only job she'd ever wanted? What alternative did she have? Building cases, interviewing witnesses demanded a strong mind, to say nothing of the verbal skills she needed to possess to try a case.

"I'm—" Mia began. She tried to say more, but found she couldn't. Most of the time she did well getting her thoughts from her brain and out her mouth, especially if it was a casual conversation or when she was talking to Hank. The myriad of emotions she'd experienced just during that morning alone was enough to have her stammering. Her cheeks flushed with shame as she tried and failed to recall the words she'd written out and practiced. She closed her eyes, imagining each word. "My doctors and I have reached the conclusion it's in my best interest to pursue another career."

His eyes widened. "What does that mean? You're not coming back?"

She met his gaze, putting it to him straight. "I still have too much brain damage, Mr. Connelly. It might be years before I could try a case or work full-time, and maybe not even then."

Pity washed over his face. "Christ." He combed his fingers through his graying hair. "I hate to hear that. The criminals in this county didn't have a chance when they came up against you."

She warmed in the praise, even if his words no longer rang true. "It means a lot to me to hear that."

"So what are you going to do with yourself?"

Wasn't that just the question of the day? "I have an appointment with some folks who'll be helping me with that decision," she said, knowing no matter which job she chose it would never bring her the same satisfaction as defending her hometown against criminals.

He stood and extended his hand. "I really hope this office gets the opportunity to prosecute the person who did this to you," he said through tight lips.

Mia couldn't resist a chuckle. She wasn't the only bulldog in the room. Connelly believed in the country's system of justice, but he also took extra pleasure in putting the bad guys behind bars. "Thanks, me too."

"If you need anything, Mia, I'm a phone call away." He escorted her to the door. "Anything at all. I mean that."

She widened her eyes to keep pooling tears from spilling down her cheeks. She'd expected resigning her job to be difficult, but she hadn't counted on it being this tough. "It's good to know that." She gestured over her shoulder. "I'm going to head over to my office. You know, pack up my things."

"I can get one of the paralegals to help with that if you like."

Mia shook her head. "I'd rather take care of it myself, but thanks."

Arriving at her office, she flipped on the light,

scanning the room that looked exactly the same as when she left it back in the early spring. Having grown up with so little in the way of possessions, she'd never gotten in the habit of collecting tchotchkes or other decorations. "This should take all of about five minutes."

It took ten because after she emptied her desk, she'd gotten distracted by a set of small reference books Tripp had given to her as a present. Mia eyed the leather-bound volumes she'd placed on the corner of her desk. She'd used them regularly while writing briefs, but what use would they be to her now? Mia grabbed the thesaurus, ready to toss it away but stopped. Why couldn't she let it go? "This is stupid." She let it fall from her hand into the bin at the side of her desk. "What do I want with his crap?" Thanks to the fire in her condo, she hadn't had to face the decision what to do with the gifts from her former fiancé. Yet, unease niggled at the back of her mind. Her gaze swung from the remaining books to the one in the bin. A tiny voice nagged at the recesses of her brain. "Oh, all right," she muttered aloud, fishing the book from the bin. She added the set to her box along with a calendar, a file of personal correspondence, and a flash drive she recalled buying back at the first of the year.

"I can always throw them away later." She pulled the door closed behind her and walked quickly out of the office before any of her former coworkers could waylay her.

****

Perched on the ophthalmologist's chair, Hank gripped the armrest like it was a lifeline. With each passing moment, the urge to bolt grew stronger. He'd give the doctor another five minutes and then he was out of there. "Keep me waiting a fucking hour." His screaming hangover and a sleepless night added to his already taut nerves. His heart rate ticked skyward as his imagination drew a bleak and dark future.

Don't go there. Though he held out little hope for a change in his diagnosis, giving free rein to his thoughts served no purpose. He channeled his ruminations to happier topics. In the past when depression sank its claws into him, he visualized the two joys of his life—flying and Mia. Fresh pain pierced his heart. Neither of these would ever again bring him the peace they once had.

Hank let out a breath and leaned his head back.

Big.

Mistake.

Behind his eyelids, the sight of Mia spread out for him bloomed to life. He could still hear her soft sighs and taste her sweet essence on his lips.

"I'm done."

He sprang from the seat at the same moment the doctor finally entered.

"I apologize for keeping you waiting," said Dr. Blount, a man in his late sixties who'd treated Hank on his two previous visits. "I got called into a consult for another patient."

Hank forced a smile to his lips. "No worries."

The doctor extended his hand. "Give me a moment to pull up your chart then we'll get started."

Anxiety danced up his spine. All those years waiting for an aircraft carrier's catapult to launch him across the deck had nothing on the gut-tightening anticipation he endured while the good doc tapped on the key board.

"Any changes in your vision since your last visit?"

Hank cracked his knuckles. "Not that I noticed. I do all right during the day or where there's plenty of light."

More typing. "That's good. And night, how's that?"

"Not great." He shrugged, wanting to downplay the truth—that he couldn't see three feet ahead after twilight. "I wouldn't want to be caught behind the wheel."

Dr. Blount nodded. "I think that's wise."

"What about during the day? I really need to keep driving as long as possible." Though after virtually kicking Mia to the curb last night, he doubted that would be an issue for much longer. Regret and self-loathing slithered in his gut like twin vipers. Did he have to be such an asshole to her?

"We'll cross that bridge when we get to it." Dr. Blount switched on the light strapped to his head and reached for a large reflective lens. "Lean back and let me take a look."

Searing pain stole his breath as the doctor shone the light in his eyes. "Jesus." Even without the hangover the beam would have felt like a laser cutting through to the back of his head.

"Sorry about that. Just let me get a good look at your retina, and I'll be done."

When the doctor pried open Hank's eyelid and trained the beam of light toward him, he had to grit his teeth. Perspiration dotted his brow as he rode the waves of pain during the interminable exam.

"You can lean back now."

Hank let his head drop to the headrest and prayed for the pain to subside. While the doctor typed on the keyboard, Hank's supplication shifted to a different type of mercy. *If only...*

"I have some good news and some not quite so good."

"Don't beat around the bush."

Pity creased the doctor's already-lined face. "I'm sorry. I wish it could be better news, but it's retinitis pigmentosa. No doubt about it."

The words rang in Hank's ears. Though he'd prepared himself for the worse, hearing it uttered with unwavering certainty struck him like a punch to the solar plexus. He worked at keeping emotion from his face. This wasn't the first blow life dealt him and likely wouldn't be the last. "You said"—he cleared his throat—"you said you had some good news."

"I do. I don't see where any more of the cells have coagulated since I examined you a month ago."

He clutched at hope like a starving man does a grain of rice. "Does that mean it won't get any worse?" He could live with things the way they were.

Dr. Blount shook his head. "I can't say for certain how quickly the disease will progress. Quite frankly, I'm surprised it waited this long to show itself. With luck, it might take a decade for you to completely lose your sight."

Ten years. That would give him plenty of time to see Mia back on her feet. Though not nearly enough days and weeks to soak in her beauty. Desperation made him greedy. "Is there any way to predict how fast the disease will progress or if I might keep some of my vision?"

"Not really, although family history might be some indication."

"I don't know my birth family." Though not strictly the truth, he'd be damned if he'd go to them for anything.

"Then my suggestion is to continue taking the vitamin A palmitate, use sun glasses when you're outside, and hope for the best."

Hank stifled the rueful laugh burning its way up his throat. It wasn't like he and hope were on a first name basis.

****

After returning to the building's first floor, Mia made her way through the labyrinth of hallways to the fire marshal's office. While she waited, she used her phone to Google apartments in Sope Creek, a town twenty miles north of LaGrange. Staying in her hometown wasn't an option despite the fact she'd be close to her doctors and therapist. That choice would also put her in proximity to the person who'd twice tried to kill her. She rejected the idea of finding a place in Wilmington. Hank made his feelings abundantly clear. As much as she loved him, she'd put herself out there as much as her wounded heart would allow.

Yet—the thought of him had her checking her messages. How had his doctor's appointment gone? Had he been granted a reprieve? Was he handling a dire diagnosis with his usual stoic resignation? The lack of news did nothing to ease her anxiety.

"Ms. Jones."

A uniformed man stepped into the tiny lobby, drawing her attention to her own situation. "I'm David Puckett." He extended his hand. "I have your copy of the investigator's report if you'd like to step this way."

A short while later Mia exited the fire marshal's office. Once again, no news wasn't good news. Despite a thorough search of the site, the arson investigator hadn't uncovered any forensic evidence that would lead them to the person who'd torched her home. Texting Veronica she was ready to head up to Sope Creek, Mia rounded a corner on her way toward courthouse lobby. Distracted by the remaining tasks on her to-do list, she bumped into someone. "Excuse me," she said, without looking up from her phone.

"Mia?" a familiar voice questioned as a hand on her arm stilled her.

Damn.

She resisted the urge to wrench herself from Tripp's grasp. The last thing she needed on this already emotional day was another dramatic scene. Instead, she fixed a smile on her face. Perhaps if she played along, he'd go away faster. "Hello there. What brings you here?" His practice as a corporate attorney rarely called for court appearances.

He held up a folder. "Filling some papers." His gaze poured over her, narrowing to the box in her arms. "And you?"

Plastering on a smile, she shrugged. "Just collecting a few personal items from my office."

"Will you be returning to work soon?"

"In one capacity or another." She felt no guilt over lying to him. "How're your mother and sister doing?"

"Dianne's great." A shadow crossed his perfect face. "Mother has been unwell. She's undergoing a battery of tests this week to determine the cause."

Mia's last conversation with Mrs. Brooks flooded

her brain. *Ungrateful little minx. I never did understand what my boy saw in you.* Despite Pamela Brooks turning on her, she bore the woman no ill will. "I'm sorry to hear that. I'll keep her in my prayers."

His gaze lowered. "That's very kind of you considering the way we left things."

Mia waved away the apology. She had too much grief on her plate to hold onto things that should have never been. "All water under the bridge." She made her move toward the lobby.

Tripp caught her by the elbow before she could get away. "One more thing. What did the arson investigator determine caused the fire?"

Her eyes widened. Both the police and fire departments agreed it was in her best interest to keep that information under wraps, hoping to lull the culprit into a false sense of security.

"How did you know?"

The corner of his mouth upturned. "You know how it is in LaGrange. My secretary's husband was one of the firefighters who put out the fire."

If Tripp knew, who else was privy to that information? And why did he look so pleased to share the inside track? Fear danced across her skin. "The inspector determined the fire started in my bedroom and the arsonist used kerosene as an accelerant, but other than that, there's been no evidence to lead them to anyone."

"I'm sorry to hear that. You've been through more than anyone deserves." He tucked a strand behind her ear.

"I've got to go." Her stomach tightened. "Veronica's waiting to take me home."

"Tell Hank I said hello," he drawled. His smile made her wonder if he knew what his touch did to her.

Her eyes narrowed. "I will when I see him."

"Oh, aren't you living with him?"

"How did you know that?" Her senses screamed. Perhaps Sope Creek wasn't far enough. Maybe she needed to disappear altogether. She knew of an attorney in Raleigh who could make that happen.

"Just because we're no longer together doesn't mean I've stopped caring about you."

Her blood chilled in her veins. The urge to tell him off grew stronger by the second. The guy needed to understand in no uncertain terms her life was none of his concern. As the rebuff formed on her tongue, a small voice warned not to antagonize him. Beneath the cool, laidback exterior, Tripp possessed a fiery temper.

Mia forced a smile to her lips as she searched for an escape. "That's very kind of you."

"Ready to go?" Veronica called.

Relief spread through her body. "Just coming."

"I'll tell Mother you said hello," Tripp called to her. "I'll see you around, Mia, dear."

****

"Mia," Hank called out the second his foot hit the foyer. God, he needed her in the worst possible way. Needed to hold onto her, draw strength from her steadiness. Silence mixed with the failing light to form a specter. He chucked the pharmacy bag in the general direction of the kitchen counter and fumbled his way to the liquor cabinet. He held it together as long as he could. Just one to take off the edge, he promised taking a deep draw from the bottle. Just one to make his hellish reality bearable.

Where the hell was she? Bringing the bottle with him, he settled on the sofa, only to be reminded of the events which took place on that spot the night before. He let darkness wash over him, hiding his shame. She obviously took him at his word. Perhaps she'd already found a new place to live and would return here only to collect her belongings. He drew the bottle to his lips, emptying it. No reason not to. Even if he wasn't shitfaced, it wasn't like he could go after her. Helpless. Blind. Impotent. And too stupid to cling to a good thing when he had it.

His self-flagellations rewound to his teens. Stubbornness had been his friend back then, helping him endure his foster father's beatings. All for the sake of the other kids at the Gilbert home. For Mia.

Tequila warmth spread throughout his body. Hank allowed his eyes to shutter close. Exhaustion pulled him down, giving him a break from reality. Anything for Mia. Except for the one thing she wanted most. But in his dreams he was able to answer her plea, to make love to her. All the things he couldn't risk doing when he was awake.

The sound of the front door snapped him out of that little bit of heaven.

He levered upright. "Where the hell have you been?"

Mia eased next to him on the sofa. "I didn't mean to make you worry. Things took longer than I expected." She leaned her head against his shoulder. "What are you doing sitting in the dark?"

"Practicing."

Mia laced her fingers with his. "Okay, then I'll practice with you."

The warmth of her body provided a balm he couldn't resist. Maybe if he begged hard enough, she'd agree to stay. As she brushed his knuckles with her delicate touch, his breath steadied.

"I'm so sorry. I'm here for you." Her words drifted toward him barely above a whisper.

Hell, no. Her misplaced sense of loyalty would have her putting his needs ahead of her own. "I'm fine." He bolted from the sofa, knocking over the bottle. "I don't need your pity." He pointed to her room. "Go to bed."

"I'm leaving you to sort through your shit."

Her brittle voice conveyed all the pain his failing vision hid in the low light. Standing, she gathered her shopping bags. "Don't think we're not going to have a hard conversation about your drinking in the morning."

Chapter Fifteen

An explosion of shattering glass jolted Mia from an uneasy sleep. She stumbled toward the kitchen where the smell of tequila permeated the morning air. "Are you all right?" she asked Hank who stood bare-foot and surrounded by large shards. Still dressed in the clothes from yesterday and with his dark-blond hair standing at odd angles, it was clear he'd spent the night where she left him.

"Stay right there," he barked, holding up one hand to ward her off while he held a broom in the other. "I broke a bottle."

Ignoring him, she worked her way around the edge of the breakfast area. "Let me help." She took the dustpan off the counter and squatting held it while he swept up the shards.

He shook his head. "What a goat fuck."

"Don't worry about it." She added the broken bottle to the others in the kitchen pail. "I think we got it all."

His gaze caught hers. Dark shadows accentuated bloodshot eyes. "Sorry about waking you up."

"I needed to get up anyway."

Not that she'd had a restful sleep. After the state she found Hank in last night, she wavered on the decision to move out. She'd spent most the time weighing the pros and cons, even making a list. In the end, she'd made the hard and heartbreaking choice, one which would best serve them both. She'd keep the one bedroom apartment she rented yesterday.

Relocating to Sope Creek wasn't the only way she was moving on. No more trying to persuade Hank that changing their relationship wouldn't put it in jeopardy.

"What were you doing?" She surveyed the liquor bottles lining the counters.

"Hoping to avoid the ass-chewing I deserve by getting rid of the booze. Can't even manage not to fuck up getting sober."

Right decision, wrong reason. Perhaps her persistence was why he'd slid from social drinker to functioning alcoholic. God, no wonder he wanted her gone. She really didn't know when to let up. The man learned he was going blind and all she could do was ride him about his coping mechanism. "You're in luck. I'm not up to bitching you out."

He arched a brow.

"Too tired." She lowered her gaze. "Anyway, what's on your agenda this morning?"

"Looking up AA meetings, finding guide dogs, you know, getting real. You?"

Mia swallowed the emotion bubbling inside her. "Packing."

Pain flashed across his face.

"I found a place in Sope Creek."

His jaw ticked. "Why so far?"

She toyed with telling him about her run-in with Tripp, sharing the unease their conversation instilled in her. Moving on meant handling her own problems. "Starting fresh seemed like a good idea."

He clenched his fists before raking his fingers

through his hair. "When do you leave?" he asked through taut lips.

Tears pricked the backs of her eyes. No matter what she did, she couldn't seem to avoid hurting him. "Monday. Veronica is coming to help me move."

Which still left a long two days together. That much time put too great a burden on her resolve. Searching for a reprieve, her gaze landed on the ivory cardstock hanging from the refrigerator. "What time should we leave for wedding?"

"Not going."

Mia rolled her eyes. "No way. You're a groomsman."

He shook his head. "They'll never miss one guy."

"Believe me, they will," she countered, remembering how carefully she and Tripp chose their wedding party. "Besides, we both need some socialization. It's been so long since I have had a conversation with someone that didn't concern either my accident or recovery, I might have forgotten how to make small talk."

Hank's harsh expression softened. "I just thought you wouldn't want to be reminded of…"

"Thanks for thinking of me, but I'm good." She suspected there were other reasons for wanting to skip his friends' nuptials. "I've made peace with my relationship with Tripp." But would she ever be able to do the same with Hank?

"We'll need to leave by eleven."

"It's a date." She smiled. For once a battle won didn't cause her guilt. He needed to reconnect with his friends, now that she wouldn't be there to look after him. "Can't wait to see you in your tux." She scurried to her room before he changed his mind.

Sitting atop her desk, the box she'd used to collect her office belongings sidetracked her thoughts from Avery and Connor's wedding. She'd meant to sort through everything last night, but that plan had been supplanted by more pressing events. Drawing in a deep breath, she tugged off the lid. Unpacking the last vestiges of her legal career wouldn't take long, leaving plenty of time to get ready for the wedding. Immediately, the set of small reference books given to her by Tripp caught her attention. After the unnerving run-in yesterday, those definitely belonged right there with Hank's liquor bottles. Their practicality be damned. Scooped up the lot and dropped them into the wastebasket at the end of the desk. All but one landed in the bottom with a satisfying thud. One, however, bounced off the rim and flipped open to a spot bookmarked by a square of paper.

"Never was good at basketball." She stooped to tug the paper from the book, tossing it on her desk.

She caught a glimpse of writing bleeding through the folded paper. "When did I do that?" Her memory had so many holes, more like Swiss cheese than gray matter. Though filling them all in was futile, she fought to reclaim each lost event. She unfolded it. Instead of finding a note to pick up her dry cleaning or another outdated reminder, three names written in all caps jumped off the page.

DILLON O'RILEY
PATRICK BUTLER
KATIE BUTLER

Mia had underlined the woman's name with three broad slashes. Was this woman responsible for her attack and the fire in her home? If so, what role did the men play?

A myriad of other questions swirled in her head as she switched on the laptop she purchased to replace the one she'd lost in the fire. Her heart raced as she scanned the page-long list of defendants. Finding even one name would mean the first solid break in a case gone cold.

Nothing.

Her hope deflated. "I don't understand it." Surely, she'd had a reason for emphatically writing the names but also secreting them away. Perhaps during the prosecution of one defendant, she'd stumbled onto information related to other criminal activity.

A soul-deep impulse had her bolting from her seat. Hank would help her sort through her tangled thoughts. He'd listen even if he thought her findings meant nothing to the case. Her hand stilled on the door knob. Despite her desperate need for help taming the beasts wreaking havoc in her life—not his monkeys, not his circus.

Solving her mystery on her own wasn't much of an option either. Too much was at stake for her to rely on her faulty brain. Who could she rely on to take her seriously when she had so little to go on? Only one name came to mind, and he likely would dismiss her findings as another dead end. Frustration tensed her muscles as she tapped in Detective Price's number. Her instincts were certain even if her brain wasn't—those names unlocked the mystery of why she'd been attacked.

After leaving a message with the detective, she moved to the bathroom to get ready for the wedding. Between the chasm of unfulfilled desire separating her and Hank and her recent findings harrying her thoughts, much of the anticipation for the event bled away. Once she fixed her hair and applied makeup, she returned to her bedroom to dress. If only she still had access to the DA's databases, she could really get the lowdown on these people. For the time being, she'd have to settle for good ole Google.

An hour later, she learned the three owned businesses in town, but not ones she would have used. Why couldn't she make her brain retrieve a seemingly vital piece of information when so many other events surrounding the attack had returned?

A light tap on the door brought her back to the here and now. "You about ready to go?"

Willing to break her vow of independence, Mia opened her door. "I have something I want—"

Only the sight of Hank in a tux could sidetrack her thoughts. Mia's core heated as she took in his slicked-back hair, freshly shaven jaw, and cautious smile. God help the female population at the wedding. Actually, it was she who needed help. The fevered impulse to rip off the suit had her clenching her fists by her side. Would she ever again be able to look at him without wanting him so badly her breathing stopped?

"You were saying?"

She shook her head. "Nothing."

His eyes narrowed. "Something wrong?"

Nothing time, distance or a cold shower wouldn't make better. "No." She grabbed her purse and stepped quickly into hallway. "If you're waiting on me, you're backing up."

****

"There's the base chapel," Hank said, stating the

obvious since he'd parking in front of a white clapboard building sporting stained glass windows and a steeple with a cross on top. Thirty minutes of heavy silence was enough to have him talking to himself. When Mia didn't answer, he crossed to the truck's passenger door, opening it for her. "We're here."

Man, was she up in her head, and going by her pinched expression, she wasn't exactly reliving a trip to Disney World. He should have fought harder to skip this, even if it meant leaving his friends in a bind. A wedding was sure to have her thinking about her ex-fiancé—the seersucker-wearing bastard. Unfortunately, it was too late to back out now. He waved to Titan who pointed to a large oak where Opie stood with the wedding photographer. "On my way."

He touched her arm. "Mia."

She jolted. "Sorry. Were you talking to me?"

He lifted his sunglasses to his head. "What's wrong?" he asked not for the first time that day.

"It's nothing. I'm just lost in my own little world." Her gaze combed the length of him, boring heat into his chest.

"Do I look all right?" He glanced down at his shirt, expecting to find the source of her assessing stare. "Did I miss a button?"

"You're fine." She climbed out of the cab and began walking toward the chapel's front door. "You clean up good."

He caught up to her, dying to know what had her so distracted. The unsolved cases, her ongoing recovery, the move to Sope Creek—she had her pick of issues complicated enough to make anyone broody.

Once inside, Mia stepped to a corner of the empty

181

vestibule. "I'll hang out here until the wedding starts. Which side should I sit on, bride or groom?"

"Either is fine." He tucked a curl behind her ear and indulged in a little staring of his own. Her amber-hued silk dress hugged her delicate curves from shoulders to thighs and brought out the magnolia-perfection of her skin. "I hate leaving you, but Titan needs me for pictures."

She lifted her face to him and smiled for the first time in days. "Go do your groomsmen stuff. Don't worry about me."

Her tongue darted over her full lips, hardening his cock. The imperative to kiss her crushed the breath out of him. *Just one.* A quick brush of his mouth against hers. *No!* He was supposed to be letting her go, not drawing her closer. With the restraint of a saint, he reined in his lust.

"Wait to let me escort you down the aisle," he said, listening to his inner caveman.

A small smile played at her lips. "I wouldn't have it any other way."

As Hank headed outdoors, desire still had its claws in him. If only having what he wanted was best for her as well. A bark of laughter broke from his throat as he remembered what his foster father had been fond of saying. *If a frog had wings, he wouldn't bump his ass.*

Then sunlight blinded him, killing his dark bit of humor. "Jeez." His breath came out in a hiss, and he lowered his sunglasses in place. The rays also offered a fresh reminder of why he needed to let her go. He stalked toward the guys he'd known for years, slapping on a happy face. "I'm here now. Let the festivities begin."

After posing for pictures and sneaking a quick word of congratulations to Avery, Hank took his place in the church's entryway. He and Opie took turns escorting guests to their seats. Two elderly ladies dressed in colorful hats and a former shipmate later, Mia stepped forward.

"I think I'll sit on the bride's side since I've actually met her." She took his arm.

"That makes sense. I feel guilty for dragging you to this."

"Don't. Any excuse to buy a new dress."

What a dress it was. The neckline suggested modesty. The rearview gave an entirely different impression. It plunged to the small of her back, showing off her perfect neck and shoulders. Male heads turned as Mia passed, and Hank walked a little taller, meeting a number of envious stares. If only she were truly his.

"I spent a lot of time dreaming about you escorting me up a church aisle."

His thoughts were instantly above his beltline. "You did?"

She nodded, slipping into an empty pew. "I wanted you to give me away, but Tripp asked you to be his best man first."

His heart ached imagining Mia in white. She'd be ethereal in yards of tulle and satin. "It would have been my pleasure, angel," he said, even if it killed him to give her to a man unworthy of her love and devotion.

She stood on tiptoe to kiss him on the cheek. "It means a lot for you to say that."

He swallowed past the lump in his throat. "I'll catch up with you at the reception," he said making a quick departure.

After seating females from twelve to eighty, he finally caught a moment to think. Why did it sound like Mia was telling him goodbye? He rubbed at the heaviness in his chest.

Because she was.

Even if they continued to keep in touch, things would never be the same between them. Thanks to his lack of self-control, he'd ruined a once-wonderful relationship.

The organ music changed. "That's our cue," Opie said.

Hank reached the door first, drawing on his sunglasses before he opened it. They'd have to make their way around the outside of the building in order meet Titan and the chaplain at the altar. Sebastian Baron stood on the other side, breathing hard like he'd been running. "Going to be late for your own funeral," Hank chided his friend and former shipmate.

"Probably." A broad grin creased Bash's face. "Looking good, man." He clasped Hank on the back as he passed. "Save some of the ladies for me."

An idea sprang to life—one that would alleviate his guilt over dragging Mia to a wedding where she barely knew a soul. Despite the player persona Bash liked to project, he was really one of the straightest arrows Hank ever met. And trustworthy enough to see to it none of the riffraff honed in on her. Plus, he could talk the ears off a jackass. "I'll catch you up in a second," he told Opie. He turned his attention on Bash. "Will you do something for me?"

The guy cocked an eyebrow. "What do you need?"

Hank stepped inside the chapel. "See that girl

sitting by herself."

He shook his head. "I don't see any girl."

"There, the one with short hair," he said pointing.

"You mean that one in the backless dress?"

Hank gritted his teeth. "That's the one."

"Man, that's not a girl, in case you hadn't noticed."

Hank suppressed a growl. Maybe this was a bad idea after all. "She's my—" Certainly not sister. Date didn't fit either. "That's Mia, and I'd appreciate you sitting with her during the ceremony."

The corner of Bash's lip curled. "No problem whatsoever, my man." He took a few steps then turned to look over his shoulder. "If you like, I can keep her company all evening."

Hank let out a breath. Why did even his best intentions turn to crap?

Chapter Sixteen

"Why do you do these things to yourself?" Mia muttered under her breath. A kiss—even one on the cheek—served only to intensify the agony of separating from Hank. His clean, masculine scent still filled her senses and sharpened the ache in her chest. She could add this impulsive act to her long list of regrets. "Embrace the future," she said, quoting a plaque she'd seen in a coffee shop. No more looking back. No more wishing her life was different. She shuttered her eyes, letting Pachelbel's Canon in D emanating from the organ at front of the church take her to a future free from looking over her shoulder.

"May I join you?" a masculine voice drawled.

Mia's gaze darted up, finding a guy who looked like he'd just walked off the pages of an Armani ad.

"Is this seat taken?"

"No." She failed to keep the surprise from her voice. Neither were at least a dozen other spots in the chapel. She scooted over to make room for the stranger with dark hair that brushed the collar of his bespoke suit.

"Sebastian Baron." He extended his hand. "My friends call me Bash."

"Mia Jones." She accepted his handshake then returned to her wandering thoughts.

Had Detective Price received her message? She

resisted the urge to check her phone, instead, focusing on the list of household items she needed to purchase for her apartment. She also had to get her car out of storage and follow up on the job retraining—all steps forward. Unlike beating her head against the brick wall that was Hank Taggart.

"How do you know the bride?" Bash studied the program everyone received as they entered the chapel.

Why the twenty questions? She started to ignore him, but southern manners trumped her mild annoyance. "I don't really. I'm one of the groomsmen's plus one."

"Lucky guy."

Her eyes widened. "Excuse me?" Was he flirting?

Casting her a sideways glance, he said, "You're very lovely, if you don't mind me saying." He shot her a lopsided grin. "You might outshine the bride."

Heat bloomed on her cheeks. He was definitely flirting—with her. Jeez, it had been ages since she'd received this type of attention. She smoothed her hand over her skirt. "Thank you." She was nowhere near ready to try dating again, but what woman didn't enjoy a little male appreciation?

Bash turned in his seat, facing her. "Can I be honest?"

She arched an eyebrow. "Were you being dishonest before?"

He barked a laugh. "I like you. You're a straight shooter." He rested an arm against the back of the pew so his fingertips brushed her shoulder. "Everything I've said so far is the God's honest truth, but I haven't told you everything."

"Let me guess. You're one of those wedding

crashers."

"Nope." He shook his head. "I've known the bride and groom for years." His megawatt smile dimmed. "Hank sent me over to keep you company."

"Oh." She turned her face to dab tears pooling at the corner of her eyes. Hank was so anxious to get rid of her that he was foisting her off on his buddy. God, wouldn't it be lovely to simply redirect her feelings as he supposed she could.

"That seems to bother you."

"Why should it?" She met his gaze, noting the electric-blue color. "He was only being polite."

Bash studied his hands. "I know, if you were my date, I'd be for damn sure no other guy got anywhere near you."

"We're not involved in that way," she insisted. "Hank and I grew up in foster care together."

"Excellent." He held up a hand. "Not the foster care part. I mean that you and Hank aren't a thing."

Any reply she might have managed was cut off when the door by the altar opened. First the chaplain entered, followed by Connor, Opie, and Hank.

He stood ramrod straight, looking as if he were facing a firing squad rather than standing up for a friend. *Smile.* She willed him to look at her. When he finally did, his glower only intensified. She lowered her eyes, his censorious glare hurt too much to endure. *You only have to put up with me for a few more hours.*

Thankfully, the ceremony began, offering Mia a reprieve from her dark thoughts. The first notes of "The Wedding March" rang out then the bride entered on the arm of an older gentleman dressed in a naval uniform. Avery beamed as she walked toward Connor.

If only all stories ended in happily ever after. When the bride passed Mia's pew, a slight bump beneath the ivory silk gown caught her attention. God, how wonderful would it be to have a family of her own. An ugly, green-eyed emotion bubbled inside her. She quickly uprooted the choking vine of jealousy. *I have my health. I have enough money to support myself. I have people who care about me.*

Mia watched transfixed as the couple exchanged the time-honored vows. She clung to the rituals, especially the ring ceremony that outwardly bound their lives. Promises—whether until-death-do-us-part or a pledge made between alone-in-the-world children—meant something to her. More than something, they were everything. She'd tried to keep up her end. Her gaze slipped up to Hank, while he seemed determined to make that impossible. She shoved her pain into a far corner of her mind, locking the door on the pain. Sometimes the heroine ended up wearing the torn gown and sitting atop a pumpkin at the end of the fairy tale.

Bash turned to her after Avery and Connor processed up the aisle. "Shall we head to the reception?" He winked. "I don't know about you, but all this romance made me thirsty."

Mia took his proffered arm, laughing despite her woe-is-me mood. Wallowing in self-pity wasn't part of her moving forward plan. "Thank you. I think a glass of champagne is exactly what I need," she said, deciding to fake happiness in the hopes eventually her heart would fall in line.

The two of them followed the other guests a few yards to the Officers' Club which had been decorated in ivory and deep blue. She searched the room for Hank before remembering he would likely be posing for pictures.

Bash snagged two champagne flutes from a passing waiter. "What do you do for a living?"

She took a moment to savor the bubbles as well as the last moment of being treated like a regular woman. In her experience, once people learned about her traumatic brain injury, they either treated her like she was addled or a child. "I used to be an assistant district attorney in Polk County."

"Impressive." He once again fixed his full attention on her. She squirmed under the stare that probably dampened most women's panties. "But you're not in that position anymore."

"No. I was…"

Bash arched an eyebrow as she toyed with whether to offer him the whole truth or the edited version. "I'm making a career change." She indulged in his appreciative stare.

His smile brightened. "Me too. You share your story, and I'll tell mine." He pointed toward a cluster of empty tables on the far side of the room. Once they crossed the expanse, he held the chair for her then signaled for a waiter who replaced their empty glasses.

"You first," she said, buying time while she decided how much of her story to share.

He leaned across the table, a lopsided grin playing at his lips. "I typically don't like talking about myself. It's a sordid tale for the most part."

"Those are the best kind." The rare feeling of mischief spread her lips in a smile.

Bash narrowed his eyes. "Why is it that you and Hank aren't together?"

She let out a breath. "We just aren't."

Okay." He cocked his head, studying her again like if he stared hard enough he'd figure her out. "So you want to hear a tale of misspent youth and unexpected windfall."

"Who wouldn't?"

"I left the navy when Fairchild Productions bought the movie rights for one of my books. My agent negotiated for me to write the screenplay, and I'll be the onset technical advisor when filming begins in a couple months."

"Wow," she said when he finished telling her how he began writing military dramas to alleviate the long hours spent aboard ship, and his surprise that his novels garnered a multi-book publishing contract as well as a loyal following. "My life seems dull in comparison."

He brushed the back of her hand. "Nothing about you is dull."

Her heart raced. What began as innocent flirting was running away with her. "Oh, look." She redirected his attention. "The bride and groom are getting ready to make their grand entrance."

The moment Hank entered the room, Mia excused herself and made a beeline for him "Ready to go?"

He rolled his eyes and nodded toward the other groomsman. "Opie says I've got to stay for the dinner and then help him decorate the getaway car."

Mia glanced behind her, finding Bash chatting with a very attractive woman wearing a dress that made hers look like a nun's habit. The tension eased from her shoulders as she joined Hank at the table set aside for the wedding party. "Far be it from me to prevent you from doing your duty," she said, trying for levity.

Bash's *joie de vive* lightened her mood. Perhaps she could pass it on.

"That's me, duty first." He snatched a napkin off the plate and laid it on his lap.

Her bubble of optimism burst. Why she insisted they come? Surely a weekend spent hiding in her room was preferable to enduring this. Mirroring his action, she waited for the dinner to begin, praying it would be served with military speed and efficiency.

"There you are, Mia. I was afraid you'd left without saying goodbye." Bash squeezed her shoulder before taking the seat to her right. He nodded toward Hank. "Any time you want me to keep Mia company, just let me know. The two of us got along like a house on fire."

Mia's jaw dropped. Why was he baiting Hank? The heavy atmosphere gave new meaning to the phrase, silent killer. She wished Opie would send the signal it was time for whatever decoration he had planned for the groom's car, but he and his wife seemed determined to spend the evening on the dance floor.

The band beat out the beginning notes of "Treasure" by Bruno Mars, one of her favorites from her clubbing days. Beneath the tablecloth, her feet danced, and she couldn't help moving to the beat. Asking Hank to join her, poised at the end of her tongue. He played like he couldn't dance, but the guy had moves. She didn't even need to look in his direction for his answer. The ever-present tension radiating from him held her request in check.

"Come on, Mia, let's show these stiffs how it's done," Bash requested instead.

Her gaze cut to Hank. Would he object? Or better

yet, take the hint and ask her himself. She'd never been a wallflower who waited for a man's invitation or the vixen who pitted two men against each other. Still, a spark of protectiveness from him would have been lovely—any sign that she still meant something to him

He shrugged. "Go ahead. I know you're jonesing to get out there. Have fun."

"If you don't mind." Mia eased out of her chair in case he changed his mind.

Bash took her by the hand, leading her to the parquet floor. He moved like his joints were oiled and pop music ran in his veins. One song bled into the next, this time "Come Away With Me". He took her in his arms with practiced ease that tripped a few of her warning sirens. However, his hands stayed at the small of her back, and she soon relaxed.

"You're making someone jealous," he said just as they neared the bar.

Hank leaned against one of the highboy tables, a drink in his hand. Her stomach twisted. She'd had hopes his vow to stop drinking was one he could stick to. "I doubt that. He's just ready to go."

"Trust me. I'm right. Your boy over there would like to tear me away from you. Maybe even rip off an arm or two while he's at it."

"It's not like that between us."

"So you keep saying."

"It's your turn to trust me. I know what I'm talking about."

The corner of Bash's mouth turned up. "That's not all you know. You're making me look good out here."

Mia blushed under his praise. "Thanks for asking me to dance. I don't know when I've had this much fun.

It's been a rough year for me."

He did a couple quick steps and a spin that kept her on her toes. "You never did tell me what led you to leave the DA's office."

"It's nothing as exciting as your story."

"I'd still like to hear it. You might even spark an idea for my next book."

"Only if you switch to unsolved crime."

Without meaning to, she ended up giving him the mini version of the past several months. She found him to be a great listener, who while shocked at all she'd been through, didn't show the least indication that he pitied her.

Maybe Hank was right. She should give Bash a chance. Mia focused on the bold blue of his eyes, the feel of his firm bicep under her palm, and his carefree smile. A relationship with him would be gloriously uncomplicated. She pictured him holding her hand, perhaps drawing her into a shadowy corner for a kiss.

No fireworks ignited at her imagination's urging. Not even a spark. He was handsome, charming, polite, and if the way he danced was any indication, he'd be a skilled lover. Resignation mixed with sadness and guilt. How could she even look at another man, much less expect her libido to rise to the occasion. There wasn't room for another man. Hank commanded every inch of her heart.

An old standard began, "At Last", made famous by Etta James. The wedding singer did justice to the song.

"Another perhaps?" Bash asked.

She stilled in his arms as a long ago memory flooded. Before Hank's last deployment, he'd taken her out dancing. They'd capped off the evening with this song. As they'd swayed to the music inside their private bubble, he'd promised one day the two of them would at last find the love they both sought.

"Can we sit this one out?"

"Certainly." He led her away from the crowded dance floor. "We can slip out on the balcony if you'd like some air."

Her aching heart managed to skip a beat. She couldn't let the charade go any longer. It wasn't fair to either of them to pretend she was interested. "I need to excuse myself. Thank you for dancing with me."

"The pleasure's all mine." He brought her hand to his lips. "Hurry back. I have something I want to ask you."

****

As Bash held Mia, every nerve in Hank's body screamed to bust up their little dance party. He tightened his grip on the highball glass in his hand instead of sending it sailing across the room. Mr. Charisma was definitely putting the moves on her. He recognized the tactic Bash used on sharper women who couldn't be wooed with big talk and a flash of cash. They'd even given it a name—Sincere Sebastian—and it had a ninety-five percent success rate. Surely, she could see through his act.

Bash seemed to hang on Mia's every word, though, and his hands stayed where they belonged. Mia tilted back her head and laughed at something Bash said. This was right, good. Hank did the right thing sending Bash her way.

Try telling that to his inner caveman.

"Thank fuck." He growled when she finally extricated herself from his former friend's grasp. Then the guy kissed her hand, sending Hank's mood into the shitter. Just because he'd done the right thing didn't make it easy to watch.

He downed the rest of his cola in one, wishing like hell it was something stronger. The monkey on his back screamed for the fix that would allow him to endure this living-color nightmare. With any luck, Mia would soon be ready to head home. He moved closer to the exit, hoping for a quick getaway. Instead, Bash strolled his way.

He clasped Hank by the shoulder. "What are you doing in the corner, Tank? You should be out on the dance floor having fun. I can introduce you to a couple ladies if you're interested."

Hank ground his molars. "I'm having fun right where I am."

"You seem like it," he said with a chuff.

"What's your deal? What do you care what I'm doing?"

The guy's lip curled in a smirk. "Just want to repay the favor. Thanks for hooking me up with Mia."

Hank bit the inside of his cheek to keep from telling the guy to go fuck himself.

"So what's the deal with you two? I get a sense there's more than she's telling me."

"We grew up in foster care together."

"Anything else going on?"

"No!" Perhaps if he said the lie with enough force, he'd come to believe it himself.

Bash held up his hands in surrender. "I hear you, my man. I'm just getting the lay of the land before I take the next step." He latched on to Hank's gaze. "Before you tell me I'm not good enough for her, or threaten me with bodily harm, I'll be a perfect gentleman. Mia's something special."

"I'm glad you see that." But Bash needed to hear the whole story, even if it wasn't his to share. "Listen." Mia would hate him for what he was about to say. "There're some things about her you need to know." He let out a breath. "She was attacked a few months back."

"I know." Bash nodded. "She told me all about it. I'm bowled over by her courage, and I swear I'll be good to her."

"Here's the thing." He ran his fingers though his hair. "She's suffered a lot of brain damage during the attack. She's... She has trouble talking, thinking, and remembering."

Bash cocked his head. "Really? She was holding her own with me. We had a riveting conversation about the Irish mob moving down from Boston. While you were skulking in the corner, she told me how they're taking over construction, trucking, and other small business in this part of North Carolina." He narrowed his gaze. "Listen, I came over here as a courtesy, check in with you since you're her date. Both of you claim there's nothing romantic between the two of you, so I'm going to ask her out." He lifted his chin. "Mia deserves someone who'll show her a good time. Dote on her and treat her like a princess. Not glare at her from across the room."

Every cell in his being wanted to be the one to do all those things for her. His angel deserved Prince Charming, Superman, and Mr. Darcy, not Heathcliff with Hulk tendencies.

"You got a problem with that?"

"No, go ahead." His jaw clenched. "No reason you

shouldn't."

Bash gripped him on the shoulder. "Great, thanks. I'm going to call her next week once she gets settled in her new place." He turned, and then looked over his shoulder. "By the way, you're a bigger fool than I thought."

No doubt about it. But what was the alternative— Mia caring for a blind man the rest of her life? Like Bash said, she deserved better. And he couldn't afford to lose what little of her he still had.

He tensed when she sidled up to him, wrapping an arm around his waist. "Are you ready to go?"

Does a marine want to fuck his weapon? But why would she want to leave? Perspiration misted her forehead and her cheeks were bright pink. "Are you running a fever? Is your head hurting?"

"No. I've been having a great time, but you seem miserable."

"I'm fine. We can stay as long as you like. I know you're enjoying Bash's company."

She chuckled. "He's okay if you don't mind the charm running over the tops of your shoes."

"The guy's definitely got that gift in spades." He led them to the O Club's exit. Opie could handle decorating Connor's car on his own. If his angel wanted to leave, he certainly wasn't going to argue. Besides, his temper had withstood all the challenge it could take.

"He wants to ask me out."

The image of Bash kissing her flashed in his mind. Hank paused by his truck, a wave of fresh hell hitting him squarely in the chest. He swallowed the bile in his throat. "Oh, good, you should definitely go. He'd be perfect for you."

"I'm going to tell him 'no.'"

"Why would you do that?"

She caught his gaze, her lovely green eyes boring into him. "He's not the man I want."

"Angel," he groaned, dragging his fingers through his hair. "I can't—"

She held up her hand. "Just don't, okay. I get it. You don't want me." Her breath escaped in a sigh that spoke of defeat and resignation. "Could we go?"

"Sure." He reached for the truck's door handle, but the late afternoon sun reflecting off the side mirror stopped him. "Could you drive? I don't trust my eyes to get us home this late."

Mia shot him a sympathetic smile. "Glad to."

Traveling down the highway, the slow boil churning his insides threatened to blow the lid on his self-control. Another silent car ride wasn't doing anything for his mood either. Too bad he wasn't limber enough to kick his own ass. The way he'd behaved had him nauseated like he'd hammered bacon grease instead of cola. Bash had been an upstanding guy, and all he'd gotten for his efforts were eat-shit-and-die looks and barbed comebacks. His friend wasn't the only one he owed an apology to. Would Mia even listen? If she didn't, he had no one but himself to blame.

Finally, they pulled in front of his apartment. Mia killed the engine but didn't make a move to head inside.

"What's wrong?" He cut his eyes at her. "You look like you're in pain." Had she overdone it? She was still so fragile.

"I am actually." Tears glistened. "I know you don't feel the same as I do, but you don't have to make it so obvious you don't want me."

Hank dropped his head to his chest. "It's not that." He wanted her more than the air he breathed—more than he wanted to retain his sight. "You're confused. It's been a hellish year for you, and that's bound to mess with your head."

Mia hammered the steering wheel with her fist. "Shut up." Her breath came in pants. "I might not remember the attack or be able to practice law anymore, but I know what and who I want." She crossed her arms over her chest. "I'm in love with *you*, Hank Taggart, and there's not a damn thing either of us can do about it." She reached for the door handle. "I'm going to bed. I've had all of this day I can stand."

After so much strain, the chain broke on his discipline. Hank was out of the truck and on her before she'd gotten two steps away. Tugging her to a stop, he said, "I don't know what to say."

She grabbed the front of his jacket, pulling him so close he could see the flecks of gold in her eyes. "Tell me that you love me."

He bracketed her face with his hands. She needed to know the truth. He owed her that much. "More than you know." He had every intention of explaining himself—finally make her see reason. Then she licked her lips and he was lost. His mouth angled over hers, in a kiss laced with desire and need. His tongue swiped over her lips and she opened at its beckoning, letting him slip into her mouth.

His pulse soared as his arms banded her, drawing her into the cradle of his hips. His erection brushed against her belly, reawakening a need that had been ignited weeks earlier.

"You've pushed me to the breaking point—this

dress, the way you dance"—he buried his face in the crook of her neck, inhaling the delicate citrus scent—"your perfume." He kissed the spot behind her ear, tasting salty perspiration dried on her skin. "We both know how much I love to drink. I love the burn as the tequila slips down my throat, and when the alcohol sweeps through my system, dulling the pain, it's a little slice of heaven." He met her eyes. "None of that has the draw you do. It's all I can do to resist. Every minute of every day, I want you so badly it feels like I'll die if I don't have you."

"But why resist if it's what we both want?"

The excuses he'd used—her attack, his blindness, protecting their friendship—dissipated like fog burned away by sunshine. For the first time in months, years maybe, he could see clearly. He'd used them all to protect his heart from the one person who had the power to hurt him most. Yet, who else could he trust to never betray him as Tiffany had or abandon him like his birth parents? "I don't know anymore. It used to make sense to keep you at arms' length."

"Then will you make love to me?"

Her plea pierced him to the core. "Yes." He groaned. "It's all I've thought about for months."

Hank crushed her body to his. Raked his fingers through her hair. Brought his mouth down to hers. After denying his lust for so long, he wanted to devour her. He licked at her lips, begging entrance. She opened to him, moaning into his mouth. God, he was a hair's breadth from coming in his pants.

When Hank finally broke the kiss, they were both breathless. "Let's get inside. What I'm about to do isn't fit for public observation." He scooped her into his arms and stormed up the pathway. The process of entering the apartment proved more difficult since he had no intention of setting her down and couldn't keep his mouth off her. He trailed kisses across her shoulder then drifted south to her breast.

"Hold up," she said with a low chuckle that further hardened his cock. "I can't get this open with you doing that."

"Not possible." He nibbled her earlobe. "You taste too good."

He couldn't wait to go down on her again, having relived that time on the sofa every night since. "I'm laying you out on the first flat surface we come to."

She kissed him, squirmed out of his hold, and had the door open while he was still anticipating her essence. "While that's an appealing idea." She tugged him inside. "Carpet burns aren't my idea of fun."

Hank eyed the sofa with desperation. She'd be comfortable there, and if he shoved the coffee table out of the way, he'd have plenty of room to maneuver. He tugged her in that direction.

"No." She dug in her heals and redirected their path. "Your bed," she murmured between kisses. "You need to be comfortable for what I want to do."

"I like the way you think, angel."

She stalled just inside the room. "Why have you always called me that?"

His heart ached with the need to express what she'd meant to him all these years. How did a guy who barely had a handle on his feelings find words rich enough? "Because, angel mine," he began once he could finally speak. "For so long, you've been the only good and pure thing in my life."

"I feel the same about you." She smiled up at him. "This won't change a thing. I swear it."

Tears suddenly pricked his eyes. *Please let that be true.* He shook himself loose from the fear. Like hell he was going to mess this up by getting a case of the weepies. He wrapped his arms around her from behind, kissing down the long column of her neck. "This dress has been driving me crazy all day."

She ground her ass into his crotch. "What? You don't like it?"

"I love it." He cupped her breasts. "I'm going to love it even more once it's off you."

Mia made a show out of unzipping the dress and sliding it off her slender body. Then as she stood nearly bare before him, he was speechless with a different type of emotion. He eyed the scraps of ivory lace that made up her panty and bra set. "I think I'm going to have to find a new name to call you. Definitely not an angel." She was a temptress—he, her willing quarry.

He backed her to the bed, lowering her with infinite care. His breath came in ragged pants with the effort of restraining his lust. Beginning at her trach scar in the hallow of her throat, he kissed down her body. He paid particular attention to each scar, honoring all she'd survived. Finally, he settled at the apex of her thighs. Burying his nose in her mound, he breathed in her natural scent.

"Please." She sucked in a breath. "You're killing me."

Hank chuckled darkly. "Payback, baby, for the torture you put me through today," he said, hooking his fingers under her panties and drawing them down her slender hips.

Mia opened herself to him—a gift he was unworthy to accept given how hard he'd made the last few days. Yet, there she was ready to accept him into her heart as well as her body. He tongued her, sucked at the bundle of nerves at the top of her sex like a man on a mission. He'd give her enough pleasure to wipe the memory of his many fuckups.

Her juices coated his tongue and slid down the back of his throat. He could have spent hours, days even, tasting her. Mia gripped his head, directing his mouth where she wanted it. God, what a fucking turn on, to have her that wanton and needful. Her orgasm crested and she bucked and rocked against him. Gently, he held her in place and slipped a finger into her wet channel to draw out her pleasure.

While she recovered, he shucked out of his clothes then stalked up her body. She wrapped her legs around his hips, fitting his cock at her entrance. He searched her eyes, suddenly terrified. "What if—"

Mia touched a finger to his lips. "It won't, because we won't let it." Her smile danced with mischief. "Now, no more talking." She raked her fingernails down his back. "No more thinking for a while." Then she gripped his ass at the same time she tilted her hips upward. "Just feel." She let out the breath she'd been holding as he slid into her heat.

Wet and achingly tight, her core gripped him like a velvet vice. Answering his cock's insistence, he plunged deeper with each thrust. He wanted to savor the experience, take his time to learn what made her moan and writhe with passion. His dick had other ideas. An orgasm poised for release, but he'd waited too long and dreamed of this night too often to have it over in seconds. Besides, he wasn't done giving his Mia pleasure. He could live to be a hundred and never grow tired of watching her come undone. He brought his mouth down to her breast, drawing the tight bud into his mouth.

"More." She groaned. "So good."

"You like that, do you?" He fingered her clit. "What about that?"

Her eyes fluttered closed and she orgasmed again. Mia's pleasure ignited his, and he came on a roar. Pumping into her, he filled her with his seed. Then, he collapsed on top her, utterly spent.

She tucked her face in the crook of his neck and held tightly to him as if to fuse their bodies. "Oh, my," she managed between breaths.

"I must be crushing the life out of you," he said when he finally found the energy to move. As he withdrew from her, their impulsivity hit him. "Shit."

"What's wrong?" Her lust-glazed eyes narrowed.

"We didn't use protection."

She stretched lazily. "I'm on the pill to control my periods."

"Thank God."

She froze then turned to him, biting her bottom lip. "Would you hate it that much if we made a baby together?"

Hank let out a breath. Less than a minute after making love to Mia, and he'd already fucked things up. He brushed a sweat-soaked tendril from her face. "Nothing would make me prouder than to see you grow ripe with my child." He trailed a hand along the flat plane of her stomach. "But I wouldn't pass along my fucked up genes to a kid of mine for all the world."

She nodded. "Then we'll adopt from the foster care system when the time comes, give a kid the opportunity neither of us had."

The corner of his mouth turned up. "Just like that, we're planning a family."

She placed a whisper-soft kiss on his lips. "Hank, baby, don't you realize we've always been family. We'll just be adding to it."

Would she feel the same in a few years when she'd have to care for not only a child but a blind man? His heart beat out a tattoo. The room spun.

Mia tangled her fingers in his hair, using it to lever his gaze up to hers. "Get out of your head. We can table the adoption discussion until we're ready. Right now, let's enjoy this moment of bliss."

Hank lay next to his miracle, drawing her tight against his body. "I can do that." Because making love to Mia had been like coming home.

His old man's curse could wait until later.

Chapter Seventeen

Morning light touched Mia's eyelids. With a groan she rolled over, clinging to remnants of the sweetest dream—her and Hank together, friends and lovers, the best of both worlds. As she woke, traces of his evergreen scent teased her sleepy senses. Instinctually, she hugged the pillow closer. The coarse sheets weren't hers, but they weren't unfamiliar either.

Last night hadn't been a dream.

They had made love.

Suddenly, greeting the day didn't seem so distasteful. Mia reached for Hank.

What she found chased away her momentary joy as quickly as sunlight had her dreams. Her hands touched only long-cold sheets where he should have been. "Noooo." She hated the thoughts of having to face a regretful man when she'd fallen asleep with a contented lover. She tugged the pillow over her head, willing away reality.

The door opened with a snick that rang as loudly as a scream. Maybe if she pretended to be asleep, he'd leave her alone.

"Rise and shine, angel."

She cracked an eyelid. His expression mirrored her own—tentative, anxious. "I'm awake." She sat up.

On the baking sheet he held in his hands, he'd placed a cup of coffee, a bowl of cut fruit and a pair of granola bars. "I made you breakfast in bed."

Her heart warmed at his thoughtfulness even as dread crawled up her spine. What if he was softening the blow?

He sat on the edge of the bed. "About last night."

Oh, God, here it came—the back pedaling. "Before you begin, I want it noted for the record, that I regret nothing. I would do everything," she cocked a meaningful eyebrow, "I mean everything, again."

He sagged on a breath. "Oh, good." He crawled into bed with her. "I've been awake all night worrying you'd regret us making love."

"How could you think that?" She took a sip of coffee. "By the way, I'm not moving out either."

He kissed her quickly. "That's another conversation I can cross off my list."

Her mood lifted, and with it her desire sprang to life. She ran her tongue around a piece of fruit, toying with it like she wanted to toy him. "Talking isn't what I had in mind."

His hand edged across her shoulder and down to her breast. "Exactly what did you have in mind?"

From the living room, her phone rang. She slumped. Once again, the real world barged in on their bliss. If only they could stay in their bubble a little longer. "Hold that thought." She scooted out of bed.

"That better not be Bash," he called behind her. "If it is, he's a dead man."

Mia chuckled, enjoying his possessiveness. "I'll handle him, don't worry." Seeing the caller ID, her stomach twisted. "Detective Price."

"Good morning, Ms. Jones. I'm following up on your message. I apologize for the delay, but I wanted to check out the information you gave me first."

Her heart thundered in her chest. "Please tell me those names mean something."

"What names?" Hank asked as he eased his arms around her.

"Shh." She put the call on speaker. His kisses gave her hope her life was finally moving forward in all areas. If the police could find the person who'd attacked her and then burned her home and get him or her behind bars, she and Hank could truly put the past behind them.

"Here's what we discovered. Katie Butler operates a home health care business in LaGrange. She pays her taxes on time and hasn't had so much as a parking ticket. She's also Dillon O'Riley's sister and Butler's wife."

"I see. I'd underlined her name, so I was hoping she was somehow significant to my attack or the arson."

"Not as far as I can tell. Dillon O'Riley doesn't have a criminal record, but Butler has a couple of misdemeanors for minor in possession and a DUI."

"I checked my list. I never prosecuted him," she interjected.

"True. There is, however, a small connection to your attack. The two men co-own a lawn care business, Shamrock Landscapes, that backs up to the Coastal Comet Trail and isn't far from where you were attacked. I had one of my men drop by the place. O'Riley remembers reading about your attack in the paper. According to an invoice he provided, he was in Norfolk that day buying a new piece of machinery. Butler's whereabouts also check out. He was in town but working a job at the time."

Her heart fell to her feet. "Thanks for letting me know."

"I'm sorry I didn't have more good news to give you."

Embarrassment joined frustration in a knot that twisted her stomach. "No, it's me who's sorry I sent you on a wild goose chase. I thought for certain those names were significant."

"I understand your desperation to have your case solved, however…"

She squeezed her eyelids closed, anticipating where the conversation was headed. Only Hank's tight hold kept her from sliding to the floor in a puddle.

"Without any solid leads to go on, the captain ordered me to move my resources to more active cases."

"I appreciate your efforts," she said in a voice tight with emotion. "Once again, I'm sorry for wasting the department's time."

"One more thing. With your attacker still at large, I want you to be cautious."

"I am," she said as Hank's embrace strengthened. "I'm very safe where I am."

"Good to know. I'll be in touch if anything develops."

Tears flowed down her cheeks. She'd pinned so much on those names and now she felt a fool for raising the alarm. For all she knew, the lawn care business could have been one she and Tripp planned to employ once they bought a house. The woman still bothered her, though. To her soul, she knew Katie Butler played a role in her life. Was she the one Tripp had been having the affair with?

Hank turned her in his arms. His narrowed gaze bored into her. "You want to tell me what this is all about?"

"It would be easier to show you." She retrieved the slip of paper from her bedroom. "I found this tucked in one of the books I kept in my office."

Hank took the folded sheet from her, studying the names. "What made you think this was important?"

She shrugged. "Hope, gut instinct, desperation—I don't know. I thought perhaps I'd been on to some type of criminal activity and that was why I'd been attacked." She gripped the sides of her head, pressing hard against her temples as if she could force the memory to the surface. "I wish to God I could remember those last few days."

He led them to the sofa where he took her hands in his. "I know you do, angel. I want that as well, but the shitty truth is that may never happen. There's another subject Detective Price mentioned, and I want to discuss something with you." He tilted her chin. "Hear me out before you go jumping to conclusions."

She flashed him a smile. "I have a tendency to do that."

"I said earlier I wanted you to stay, but I've changed my mind. You should keep the apartment in Sope Creek."

Panic gripped her chest. "But—"

He touched her lips. "It's only because I'm worried about your safety."

She tightened her grip on his hand. Now that they'd finally closed the emotional chasm, the last thing she wanted was to put physical distance between them.

She pictured the small third-story apartment she'd rented Friday. Tucked, at the back of a quiet complex, its anonymity had appeal. So did the town where no one knew her. "I'll do it, but only if you'll come with me."

"It's a deal." He smiled like he'd expected her to put up more of an argument. "I've got no ties to this place. I can have us packed up in a few hours."

She crawled into his lap. "Can we go back to bed now?" The steady beating of his heart soothed her battered soul. "I want to ignore the world for a while."

He kissed the top of her head. "Later, angel, we need to talk about one more thing first."

She kissed his jaw. "Can't it wait?"

He moved her from his lap, which sent her anxiety skyrocketing. "As tempting as that is..." His gaze drifted to the kitchen. "There's also something else that's calling my name." He licked his lips. "There's one bottle I didn't get rid of yesterday. Any time I'm not focused on you, it's all I can do not to pour myself just one more drink."

His admission sent fear dancing along her spine even as it shifted her focus. He'd stood by her through every moment of her recovery. She could do no less for him. Taking his hands in her, she said, "You can do this, baby. I know you can."

"Not by myself, I can't." He squared his shoulders. "There's an AA meeting at the Methodist church around the corner that starts in half an hour."

Happy tears pooled in her eyes. She'd attend every meeting with him, go to AL-ANON, anything to support his sobriety. "I'm so proud of you. Give me five minutes to dress, and I'll be ready."

He tugged her back down to the sofa. "No."

"Please let me go with you. I want to be there for you the way you've always done for me." She wanted to shake some sense into him. Why couldn't he let her carry some of the burden?

He stroked her shoulder. "When it comes to the RP shit, I will." His voice lowered to a whisper. "Right now, you still have some respect for me. I'd like to keep it that way. If you knew how bad the drinking's gotten, all that would disappear."

His lack of faith in her cut deeply. She bit her lip, trying to keep the pain bottled inside. Even as the emotions burned inside her, another truth took root. She should be whatever he needed, not what made her feel good. She let out a breath. "I don't like it, but I understand."

He wrapped her in his arms again and the two of them clung to each other for several long minutes. In the silence, the sound of light rain made her long to return to his bed where they could pull the covers up and hide from the world.

Hank kissed her temple. "Now let me up so I can change. The sooner I leave, the sooner I can get back. We still didn't get to finish what we started."

A few minutes later, he emerged from his bedroom. "I'm not sure how long I'll be," he said, snagging his phone and wallet from the breakfast bar.

Mia followed him out to his truck. "Don't worry about me." She stood on tiptoe, planting a kiss on his lips. "I'll be fine." She watched him leave, hoping he'd change his mind about her accompanying him to the AA meeting. When his tail lights disappeared around the corner, she finally went back inside. Heeding Detective Price's warning, she shot the deadbolt and latched the chain.

She'd just changed into shorts and a T-shirt when someone knocked. Her lips spread in a smile and she was at the door in a pair of seconds. "I'm so glad you came back."

Except it wasn't Hank on the other side. "Tripp." She noted his untucked button-down, wrinkled trousers as well as the dark circles underneath his eyes. "Why are you here?"

He shifted from foot to foot. "I'm sorry. I know I shouldn't have come, but I didn't know who else to turn to."

"What's wrong?"

His gaze darted to meet hers. "Can I come in? It's raining."

Mia hesitated. While she wanted nothing more to do with him, it was obvious he was in distress. "I guess it's all right." She motioned him to the sofa while she took a seat on Hank's recliner.

He chewed on his thumb, something she'd never seen him do before. "You look good, Mia. Except for the trachea scar, you'd never know you'd been hurt."

She wanted to scream for him to just spit it out. Instead, she banked her frustration. "Thank you," she said, internally rolling her eyes at his backhanded compliment. A dozen questions swirled in her head. Instead of giving voice to those queries she stuck to the one that would have him on his way soonest. "Why are you here, Tripp?"

"I've missed you."

She held up a hand. "If that's all you came here to tell me, you can leave now."

"I screwed up. I admit that. I'm sorry."

"Thank you for the apology." She stood. "You can move on with your life with a clear conscience."

"But—"

"Hank and I are together now. We plan to marry soon." Though they hadn't actually discussed making their relationship formal, she wanted to make it abundantly clear Tripp didn't have a hope in hell getting her back.

His face contorted in disgust that sent her temper ablaze.

"I don't owe you or anyone else an explanation. Please leave."

Tripp clenched his fist. "Mother has breast cancer. It has metastasized. The doctors say she has weeks to live," he said in a burst of words that stunned her.

Her hand flew to her mouth. "I'm so sorry." Whatever her feelings for Tripp, his mother had always been kind, or at least *had been* until Mia broke off the engagement. Regardless, she wished no ill for Mrs. Brooks.

"Thank you. It's been hard." He scrubbed his face. "I wanted you to know in case you'd like to visit."

"I don't think she'd appreciate that."

He shook his head. "She's been asking for you. Mother loved you. She really took our breakup hard."

Mia swallowed against the knot of emotion. Having never known a mother's love, she'd reveled in Mrs. Brooks' doting attention. Shopping trips before the attack, help with the wedding plans, bouquets of flowers that filled her hospital room—those meant a great deal to her. The least she could do was repay her kindness in some small way. "Is she at LaGrange General?"

A single tear made its way down his face. "She wants to be at home during her final days."

Pity softened her heart. She couldn't deny the woman the opportunity to make peace with people she would soon leave behind. "Please tell her I'll come by to see her this week."

"God bless you." His voice broke. "That would mean the world to her."

Tripp stood then made like he planned to hug her, but she held him at arm's length. She wouldn't give him an opportunity to confuse pity with affection. He'd slammed that door closed well and good. "I'll call the house before I come to make sure she feels up to visitors," she said, leading him to the door.

Mia shut the door on Tripp, her mind a jumble of emotions. Suspicion warred with the sadness weighting her heart over Mrs. Brooks' illness. Surely he wouldn't use that as a ploy to worm his way back into Mia's life. She recalled his appearance at her condo right after the fire and the coincidental meeting the day she'd been to the courthouse. In retrospect, his behavior both times was uncharacteristically desperate—to the point of being needy. He certainly wasn't the confident and charming man she'd once been in love with. Part of her wondered what caused the fundamental personality change, the other part wanted to keep that time of her life firmly where it belonged.

Vowing to only visit Mrs. Brooks if she could be certain Tripp was away from the house, she redirected her efforts to packing and her mind to sending Hank positive energy as he attended his meeting.

****

Scared, amped, and jonesing for a drink, Hank

didn't so much drive away from the AA meeting as he flew out of the church parking lot on two wheels. The last couple hours had been as real as shit got, short of ditching his plane in the Atlantic. At least now he had a couple tricks in his toolbox when thirst threatened to get the better of him. He breathed through the desire to drink until the urge leveled off then refocused his thoughts on the one bright spot in his life—Mia. The promise of the homecoming he'd receive propelled him out of the danger zone, and on to the one errand to complete first.

Pulling his truck into the rundown strip mall, he hit the front door of B.J.'s Bottle Shop like he had countless times. He took a moment to let his eyes adjust to the low light then headed to the counter.

"Tank, my man," the owner said. "You're timing is spot-on as always. I got a shipment of Herradura Silver in yesterday. Do you want one case or two?"

My drink of choice, fuck yeah.

Hank skidded to a halt as if he'd trapping a wire aboard an aircraft carrier. His throat suddenly got dry like he'd been sucking on cotton. Resolve wavered. He could taste the spicy bite and smooth finish as clearly as he could feel the store's AC blowing across his skin. Swallowing hard, he gripped the coin in his pocket his sponsor gave him. "Not today. I was coming to see if you had any boxes I could have."

Bill cocked an eyebrow. "The navy moving you?"

"Something like that," he replied, not wanting to take the time to clarify. He had no business driving by the place much less coming inside. Using a liquor store for boxes came as mindlessly as pulling into Kroger for groceries.

The guy thumbed over his shoulder. "I got plenty out back."

Hank followed him through the store to the alley. "Have at it." The guy offered his hand. "You take care now and stay out of trouble."

If only it was that easy. "You bet." He eyed the dumpster. The stench of fermenting trash set his stomach off. Was he trying to prove he could poke the bear and get away before it bit his hand off? If so, not only was he an alcoholic, he was a masochist to boot.

He grabbed an armload of cardboard bearing logos he knew as well as his own name. As he filled the truck bed, irony slapped him upside the head—he was using the shells of old and dear friends to transport Mia and him to their new life. He guessed it really was impossible to completely leave the past behind.

Moving at warp speed, he filled the truck bed and booked it out of there. The perspiration trickling down his back had nothing to do with Indian summer. Fear clawed at him the five blocks home. By the time he made it to his apartment, he was shaking. He gripped the steering wheel, unable to move from the cab. Damn, that had been a near thing. With a promise not to test his limits any time soon, he walked to the door and put the key in the lock.

The chain lock blocked his progress. "Mia, baby, let me in."

"Sorry," she called. Her eyes widened as she let him inside. "What's wrong? Was it that bad?"

He couldn't face telling her how stupidly he'd behaved. Instead, he shifted the focus to a more comfortable area. "What's with the locks? Did something happen?"

She folded her arms across her chest and looked at the floor. "I got a little nervous,"

He could follow that, but there was more than anxiety at play here. He wanted to push the subject, but like he could call her on diversion tactics when he was doing the same. "No, that was the right call. You should listen to your fear. It's your instincts overriding all that polite southern lady shit you've got going on." He narrowed his focus, trying to decipher what had her moving around the room and evading his gaze. "What did you do while I was gone?"

"Nothing much." She waved her hand dismissively. "Enough about me. Tell me about the meeting."

"It was okay. I did more listening than talking, and I met up with a guy who agreed to sponsor me." He moved to the sofa and patted the cushion next to him. "He's retired navy, so that works out well. All in all, it wasn't as bad as I expected."

After joining him, she cocked an eyebrow. "Then why do you look like hell?"

The near miss churned inside him until the words practically exploded from his lips. "I stopped by the liquor store."

Mia's hand flew to her mouth "Oh, Hank."

He held up his hands. "No. No. It wasn't like that. I went to get boxes."

"What the hell were you thinking?" she asked, her voice climbing several octaves.

"I wasn't—obviously."

"How are you doing now?"

He held out a hand that shook. "I feel like I've been ridden hard and put up wet. Can I just hold you for a while?"

She crawled into his lap and tucked her head under his chin. "For as long as you want."

He lost track of how long they sat together, but even as her presence lent him a measure of peace, he couldn't move past the fact Mia was keeping something from him—something that frightened her enough to make her latch the door chain. But why would she confide in him if he wasn't willing to do the same? "Can I tell you something?"

"Of course. Anything."

He let out a breath. "I'm scared I won't be able to face losing my sight sober. The booze numbed me enough that I could avoid dealing with the disease. Now I've got nothing to help me cope."

"That's not true. You've got me," she said nuzzling into his chest.

Hank voiced his deepest fear, the one that had him waking in a cold sweat at night. His own mother hadn't been willing to put up with him, what made him think anyone else would? "What if you decide I'm more trouble than I'm worth?"

Mia threw an arm, catching him in the gut. "Thanks for the vote of confidence, jerk face."

Air rushed out of his lungs. Of all her reactions he could have predicted, this wasn't even on the list. And damn if it didn't make him love her all the more. She was exactly the kick in the ass he needed. "Oww, jeez. That hurt. You've got boney elbows."

She kissed him then leaned back against his chest. "You deserve it. If your behavior over the last few months wasn't enough to drive me away, don't you realize by now I'm in it for the long haul?"

A raw laugh left his throat. "I get it; you love me and aren't going anywhere." Another urge replaced the need for a drink, one he could indulge in. "If I stop being an idiot, will you let me make love to you?"

****

With Hank's words, Mia's anger bled away. She molded herself to his body. "Absolutely, yes." She teased his lips with tiny nips till he opened to her. Their tongues tangled in slow strokes. She might have begun the seduction, but he took over, driving their kisses into a frenzy of lips, tongues, and teeth. Her breath leapt from her lungs in a gasp as he scooped her into his arms and stalked to his bedroom. He crawled across the mattress, laying her gently in the middle.

His frank stare heated her blood, and her hands went for the hem of her T-shirt, wanting to lay herself bare before him. Before she could get it over her head, he stilled her hands. "No, let me. You're like Christmas and my birthday all rolled into one, and I want to take my time unwrapping you."

Before when they'd made love, they'd been at each other in a hectic frenzy. The promise of leisurely-paced sex sent a rush of desire through her veins. She lay back against the pillows with a smile she couldn't suppress even if she'd wanted to. "This time don't tear the wrapping paper," she said, giving him a hard time about ripping her favorite panties yesterday.

His gaze took on a feral glare as he worked her shorts down her hips. "Don't play like you didn't love that."

Boy, had she ever. She couldn't get enough of him, especially as his kisses trailed down her belly to the apex of her thighs. She practically purred as he went down on her. He stroked her with this tongue, lighting a fire in her core. She tried controlling the orgasm barreling down on her but failed miserably. Far too soon, her pleasure peaked in a crest that had her calling out his name.

Afterward, Hanks licked his lips. "You taste mighty fine, angel. I'm going to love doing that for the next hundred years or so."

Her pulse soared into triple digits. Since the attack, she'd looked no further than the next doctor appointment or the completion of therapy. Even when she'd looked ahead to the future, all she'd seen were bleakness and struggle.

Hank entered her in a single thrust that ripped a moan from her throat and narrowed her thoughts. "Feel me." He stroked her core. "Feel me inside you, Mia baby. That's where I'm going to be as much as you'll let me."

She wrapped her legs around his narrow hips, drawing him more deeply inside her. With every piston, he drove away fear and uncertainty. His expression contorted in a beautiful mask of erotic torture. "Come for me," he coaxed.

They exploded together, her orgasm taking her higher and higher until everything else disappeared and there was only the two of them, protected a cocooned in a bubble of their own making. Inside there no one or nothing could get to them.

He collapsed atop her and buried his face in the crook of her neck. Then with utter grace, he rolled them without losing their connection so that she was on top. "Next time, I want you like this. I want to watch your beautiful face as you ride me."

Next time. What a beautiful phrase, one that held such promise it made her heart ache.

Despite her efforts and his mad sexual skill, the outside world began making inroads. Beyond the details of packing, Hank's near miss at the liquor store, and even her sadness over Mrs. Brook's illness, Tripp's odd behavior eroded her peace of mind. A sixth sense whispered there was more to his showing up than he'd admitted. Had he been keeping tabs on her and if so why?

"What ya thinking?" Hank asked as he stroked his hand down her back.

"This and that."

"You worried I want a drink?"

She bit her lip. "Among other things."

He stroked her hair. "I do but being like this makes it manageable." He pistoned his hips, driving himself deep inside her. "In fact, I think I might be getting addicted to making love to you."

Mia chuckled. "I don't think I should be laughing at that."

"I have an idea."

"I like your ideas," she said a satisfied smile turning up her lips.

"Let's wait until tomorrow to start packing."

"Okay, I can go with that."

"Your turn. A penny for your thoughts."

"You really want to know?"

"Didn't we agree to be straight with each other?"

"I was thinking about Tripp."

"Jesus, seriously. You say his name while I'm still inside you?"

Mia cringed. "Sorry. I wasn't comparing." She

flashed a grin. "Well, actually I was."

Hank quirked an eyebrow. "And?"

"You blow me away."

"Good to know. Now why were you thinking about that jerk?"

"He came by earlier when you were at your meeting."

"What the fuck? He came here?"

"His mother is dying. She has cancer."

"I'm sorry to hear that. She's a classy lady."

"Tripp is a mess. I feel sorry for him and Dianne."

"Let's talk about something else. Let's get up first thing in the morning and start packing. If we get to it, we can be out of here by late afternoon."

"I need to do one thing first. I promised Tripp I'd go and see Mrs. Brooks."

"That's got bad idea written all over it."

"I understand where you're coming from. Right after he left, I called the Brooks' home and talked to his sister. It's as bad as Tripp said."

"I still smell a set up."

"I thought the same. I came right out and told Diane I didn't want to come if Tripp was there. She assured me he would be in court all day. The only person who'll be there is the nurse."

"Now tell me what's got you acting like hell hounds are after you."

"I'm beginning to think Sope Creek isn't far enough away." Hank's jaw ticked.

"They're not pulling me back in. I swear it. I need this closure so I can move on."

"Okay. Anything for you. We're almost there, angel. I can taste the freedom. I can't wait to start writing on our clean slate."

****

Mia zeroed in on the only thing that stood between her and a completed to-do list. Her thirty-pound lockbox taunted her from the corner of Hank's desk. She could wait until Hank returned from his AA meeting, but that would put them off their moving schedule—not a good thing when they would be racing against darkness. If she got a good grip on it and bent at the knees, she could wrestle the thing to the floor and then begin disassembling the desk. She wrapped her arms around the oversized safe and got a couple inches from the desktop before her fingers lost purchase. The box hit the floor—just barely missing her foot—with a thud that rattled her teeth. Thanks to an unsecured lid, papers littered the floor.

She lowered herself to pick them up and as she did, her gaze landed on her birth certificate. In an instant, she was sucked into the past. *Unknown* typed where her parents' names should have been opened the old wound. She shuttered her eyes as the pain washed over her. Perhaps that mystery lay at the root of her determination to regain her lost memories. With such an enormous gap in her identity, the events taken from her by her attacker seemed intolerable. She replaced the document, along with the other papers, in the safe. As she did, her hand brushed against the mementoes she also kept there.

Mia brought her favorite of Hank's gifts, a tattered blue rabbit, to her chest and found herself recalling her first recollection of Hank—the first memory she claimed as her own and not something repeated to her. She was three years old when she'd wandered from their foster parents' house and been caught in a thunderstorm. He'd been the one to find her hiding in a drainage pipe in the neighborhood park. As his seven-year-old self hauled her out, lightning struck a nearby oak tree, lighting up the night sky and giving her the lifelong terror.

"Mia?"

She jumped with a yelp. "You're back." She turned to find Hank giving her a pensive stare.

He crossed the room bending to touch her cheek. "Where were you just now?"

A melancholy smile formed on her lips. "A long time ago."

He eyed the safe. "Something you need to tell me?"

She waved away his concern. "Nothing important. I just got sidetracked. Were you telling me something?"

"Titan and Mad will be here at three to help us load the van."

"I can't believe they didn't take a honeymoon."

Hank shrugged. "I guess they have other priorities right now." He pointed to the rabbit Hank had given her the night she'd gotten lost. "Is that the one I gave you? Man, that thing is a mess."

She stroked the worn fur. "Don't hate on Peter. He's gotten me through a lot of rough times. I don't know what I would have done if he'd been lost in the fire."

He tilted her chin to meet his gaze. "I'd have bought you another."

She offered her lips to him in silent thanks for his ever-present support. Of all that was unknowable in her life, his love was the one thing she'd never doubted—

even when he'd been fighting to keep them apart. "He does look a little rough for wear." She poked a small hole in the toy's back, her finger meeting with something hard. "What in the world?" She dug deeper and extracted a flash drive.

"Did you do that?"

Wasn't that the questions of the hour? She had no mental image of even buying the external memory much less secreting it away. "I have no idea. What do you think is on it?"

"Only one way to find out."

Her stomach tightened as she teetered on the edge of decision. "I'm not sure I want to know. What if it's evidence of Tripp's infidelity? I don't want to be reminded of that." Especially now that it held no bearing on her life.

"The decision's yours, but what's your gut saying?"

Mia closed her eyes as if she could avoid the truth. "I wouldn't have gone to the trouble to hide the thing if it wasn't really important." Her heart thudded. "You look for me." She offered it to him. She turned away as he inserted the flash drive into his computer. With every tap of his fingers against the keyboard, her anxiety ratcheted up a notch.

"What the hell?"

She chanced a glance, seeing lines of scrambled script. It had been weeks since she'd had trouble reading and she squinted to make sense of what her eyes saw. "Read it to me," she said when the random letters refused to coalesce into words.

"I can't. It's encrypted."

She pointed to another icon, anticipation making

her skin hum. "Check this one." More of the same. One file after another, all unreadable. "What do you think's in those?"

Hank shook his head. "I have no idea." He closed out the pages and handed the memory stick to her. "Why don't you give it to Detective Price and let him sort it out?"

"No way." She held her hands up. "Not after that list of names I gave him turned out to be nothing." The memory of her embarrassment heated her cheeks. She'd been foolishly optimistic to think her case could be solved with a simple slip of paper, and she wasn't anxious to make the same mistake again. "He did everything short of tell me not to bother him with any more of my 'leads.'"

Hank's jaw clenched. "It's his fucking job to follow up leads whether he wants to or not."

"Perhaps so," she conceded. "But that doesn't mean he had the manpower to do it. I want to see what's on this before I give it to him." But who could she get to do that? She toyed with her lip trying to think of someone who she could call on for help. "Do you know how to decipher this?"

He took her into his arms. "I have another suggestion. Let's move away. Forget Tripp, the attack, this whole year. Just walk away from all of this." Kissing his way down her jaw, he continued, "I talked to Bash earlier. He said we could use his boat. We could literally sail off into the sunset."

Everything in her screamed in protest. She'd never been one to walk away from a fight. "Why do you want us to run away?"

He strengthened his hold on her. "Truth?"

"Of course."

"I think you were onto some illegal activity and that's why you were attacked. Right now, as long as you don't remember what's on those files, I think you're relatively safe. But if you get someone to decrypt them, you're going to be in danger again."

Reluctantly, she nodded. "You're right." She swallowed against the knot in her throat. "But I need to know, Hank."

"I'm scared I could lose you. I can deal with never taking another drink or losing my sight. I can't face a life with those things in it if I don't have you. It wouldn't be worth it. Let's do it, just drop everything and leave."

"It's tempting." A vision of the two of them alone on Bash's boat formed in her mind. She could smell the salty sea air and feel his sun-warmed skin against hers as he made love to her. She stroked his arm. "You're tempting." Could she sail away knowing a criminal walked free, even if she was the victim instead of another citizen? Not many days before she'd vowed to stop pushing, to recognize when it was time to back off.

Yet... Her voice trembled as she spoke, "I can't let someone get away with a crime just because it's easier to pretend it didn't happen."

Hank pulled back to meet her gaze. "We could start fresh, angel. Don't you see? Be completely different people. It would be perfect."

"No, it wouldn't," she countered. "Not knowing would hang over me, and I'd always wonder if my attacker was doing the same to someone else." She brushed a thumb across his whiskered jaw. "I need closure, babe, or at least to know I gave it my best shot."

His lips compressed to form a straight line, and several tense moments passed as he seemed to struggle with a decision. She hated her selfishness. They had enough troubles for two lifetimes without her hunting for more. Her stomach twisted as if she'd eaten week-old sushi, and she was ready to change her mind when he broke the silence.

He clenched his eyes. "You're right. After everything you've lost, you deserve justice."

Mia gripped him in a hug so tight she knocked the breath out of him. "Thank you." Gratitude had tears welling in her eyes.

"Anything for you, angel." He sealed the promise with a kiss.

He called her his angel, but it was she who felt protected. Blessed. After taking a moment to send up a prayer of thanks, her thoughts turned practical. "Now we just need to find someone who can decipher the gibberish."

Tension radiated from Hank.

"What is it?" she asked. "I swear, if this turns out to be another dead end, I'll move on."

"That's not it." His heartbeat pounded against her cheek. "I know someone who might be able to help us."

She drew back to stare up at him. "Who? Someone in the navy?"

"No, my brothers."

Chapter Eighteen

The next morning Hank's ears still rang with his own words. *Impulse strikes again.* He shook his head, recalling how the offer left his lips milliseconds after forming in his head. Gazing at Mia asleep next to him, he couldn't muster a microbe of regret. His finger traced where his eyes had been, lightly touching the contours of her slender neck, soft shoulders, and bare breasts.

The first time he'd visited her ICU room, he'd never have been able to predict they'd end up here. Nor could he have envisioned the host of life-changing events that had taken place in that time.

His angel deserved every opportunity to put her attacker behind bars, even if it meant utilizing people he didn't want to lay eyes on much less interact with. He just had to keep Mia from turning today into a family reunion. Jason and Cameron Dowell were respected businessmen in LaGrange, and therefore appropriate tools for the job—nothing more.

Mia's eyelids fluttered, but he continued memorizing her body with his fingertips—cheeks, collarbone, the divot at the base of her throat where her tracheotomy had been. Eventually, she smiled then yawned and stretched like a contented kitten rousing from a nap.

"How long have you been watching me?" she

asked, her voice low and sensual from sleep.

His cock woke with her and he drew her in for a kiss. "Not nearly long enough." He relished the feel of her warm body draped over his.

"Today's the day I get to meet your brothers."

"Half-brothers," he reminded her. Not even that in his book. Sharing a common father made them blood, not family.

"Don't be like that," she cooed, trailing her hand along his arm. "This is a great opportunity to finally connect with them."

He drew her across his body. "You're the only family I need." He let his hands roam over her back and buttocks.

Mia pushed his hand away. "Not that again. You're not distracting me with sex like you did last night. I have questions you haven't answered."

Letting out a breath, he resigned himself to cross-examination. "All right, what do you want to know?"

"When did you find out about them?"

"As you know, I looked up my old man when I turned eighteen."

Her eyes softened. "Yeah, and he didn't want to acknowledge you."

Hank rolled his eyes. "That's putting it mildly." His old man practically kicked him out of his office.

"His loss." She propped her head up on her palm. "Go on. When did you meet your brothers?"

"When I got stationed at New River, I got really drunk one night and rode over to confront the sperm donor only to find he'd died about six months before. I had a buddy in intelligence do a little investigating and found out they own Dowell Computers. Most of their business is devoted to repair and installation, but they also do forensic data recovery for a few businesses in the region."

"So what are they like?"

"Jason is in his late thirties. Cameron is a few years younger."

"That's not what I mean," she said shaking her head. "Are they nice? What do they think about having a half-brother? Do they have RP?"

Hank shrugged. "Don't know. Never met them."

Mia combed her fingers through his hair. "We're about to remedy that. It almost makes going through all this worth it for you to connect with your family. You can get some idea how the disease affects them." Her voice rose in pitch as her words picked up speed. "I have a good feeling about this. I bet they're going to be so excited to meet you. Even though they might be shocked to find a long lost brother, I know they're going to want you in their lives."

He stilled her with a touch. "You're getting ahead of yourself. I have no intention of telling them who I am." When she opened her mouth to object, he touched a finger to her lips. "You're not going to tell them either."

Disappointment shone in her eyes, but on this he wasn't willing to budge. Gently, he shifted her off him, not wanting her to feel rejected. "It's going to take us half an hour to get over there, so we need to get going if we're going to make our appointment."

On the drive over, Mia sat silently beside him— plotting, if the way she vibrated was any indication.

As Hank pulled up in front of a nondescript office building in a revitalized part of LaGrange, Mia reached for the truck's door handle. "Just a second." He held up the flash drive. "Are you sure you want to play Nancy Drew? We can still ditch and run."

Mia let out a breath. "Not the detective part. I'm scared to death what I'll find. What if it's something stupid like old wedding plans or evidence of Tripp's infidelity?"

"You can change your mind at any time. I'll support you whatever decision you choose."

She squeezed his hand then reached for the door again.

"Let me do that."

"I'm perfectly capable of climbing out of the pickup myself. Been doing it for years," she said over her shoulder.

"I want to take care of you while I can. There'll be a time when I won't be able to do that."

In a rush, she closed the distance of the cab and crawled into his lap. "You take care of me in ways you don't even know." Her kiss made him forget they were in public. "Let's go before your brothers call the cops on us."

His heart hammered in his chest as they reached the front door. "You promised, no dropping hints, no leading questions. None of that lawyer stuff. We're here because they're good with technology, nothing more."

Mia folded her arms across her chest. "I wasn't."

"Yes, you were. You forget that I know you." He tapped a finger to her nose. "You like to push."

She let out a huff. "You're the most stubborn man I know."

"Then we're a matched pair," he countered, opening the glass front door for her.

Two feet inside the storefront, Hank's feet stalled. The guy behind the low counter sat hunched over a disemboweled laptop, a bright lamp illuminating his work. A familiar shade of dark blond hair stood out at artfully arranged angles on his head. Cameron—he guessed, recalling the newspaper advertisement dating back to when the brothers opened their computer repair shop.

He'd never wanted to meet the two men with whom he shared a common sperm donor, but not because of a lack of curiosity. Hank wasn't interested in enduring rejection 2.0. Beads of perspiration dotted his forehead and trickled down his back.

"How can I help you?" Cameron asked, pushing a magnifying headset out of his field of vision.

Hank tugged his ball cap lower on his brow and let Mia take the lead. "I have an appointment with Mr. Dowell."

"I'm he." A broad smile creased the guy's face. "One of them anyway." He stood and extended his hand across the counter to Mia. "I'm Cam Dowell."

"Mia Jones." She took his hand.

Cam glanced at a computer screen and clicked through a couple screens until he reached a calendar, the font of which he could read from several feet away. "It looks like you made the appointment with my brother. He was called away unexpectedly, but I'd be glad to help."

The magnifying headset, bright lights, and enlarged text answered Hank's most pressing question. At least one of his brothers suffered from retinitis pigmentosa. The knowledge did nothing to the heaviness on his chest. One query down, a thousand more to go. A wave of emotion hit Hank squarely in the chest. What had the brothers' growing up been like? Were they close? Did they know Hank even existed?

Mia dug the flash drive out of her purse, pulling his thoughts to the present. "There are encrypted files I need on this, and we were hoping you could open them."

Mia's inclusion of him in the request had him taking a step backward. Maybe he should wait in the truck. Pride steeled his spine and kept him in place. He'd promised to be there for her just as she'd promised not to reveal his identity. Nonetheless, if Cameron bothered to look closely, he'd certainly notice their similar appearance.

Thank God, Cam seemed more interested in the device in Mia's hand than the subtle drama playing out on the other side of the counter. His eyes narrowed, and all his jovialness evaporated. "I'm not sure what my brother told you—"

"It's mine." Her voice climbed several octaves. "I promise I'm not up to anything hinky."

"How did you acquire these files?" He folded his arms across his chest.

Mia squeezed Hank's hand. Her desperation radiated from her palm to his. "That's the tricky part. I found this in my safe, but I don't know why I have it." She tapped her temple. "I was attacked on the Coastal Comet Trail earlier in the year and suffered a brain injury. I've lost some of my memories. I'm hoping this will lead me to the person who attacked me."

His eyes widened. "I remember hearing about your attack," he said, taking the external memory from her hand. "I'm glad you're doing well."

"Thank you." Mia gestured over her shoulder to Hank. "My boyfriend's been a huge help in my recovery, but getting some closure would go a long way toward helping me move on."

Hank braced himself for a sudden dawning of recognition to flash in Cameron's eyes as he looked in his direction or for Mia to give him away. Instead, the guy seemed more focused on the task at hand.

"I'll do my best. Give me some time. I'll call you tomorrow and let you know where I am with unlocking the files."

With the hand-off made, Hank practically dragged Mia out of the shop. He told himself he wanted to keep the focus where it needed to be—on Mia's needs. The kernel of truth he could barely acknowledge kept his feet moving across the asphalt.

"What did you think of him?" she asked, struggling to keep up.

"He said he'd try, so all we can do is hope he's as good as his reputation."

She threw an arm, catching him in the side. "That's not what I meant, and you know it."

Smiling at the tenacious desire to make his world whole, he halted his steps and tugged her into his embrace. "He seemed nice, I guess."

"We can go back inside if you want." She batted her eyelashes at him.

He barked a laugh despite the lingering tension coursing through his veins. His girl did not know when to stop pushing. It simply wasn't in her makeup. "Still haven't changed my mind, but good effort."

Mia's pout tempted him.

"I know. I'm the most stubborn man you know.

That's why were perfect for each other." He took her in a hard kiss that left them both breathless.

Chapter Nineteen

"I wish you'd wait until after my meeting when I can go with you," Hank said, the next morning as he escorted her to her car.

"It's better this way." Mia plastered a smile on her face even as her stomach somersaulted. "If she's asking for me, she probably has something specific she wants to say. I imagine it has to do with the way we left things after I broke up with Tripp. Perhaps she wants to apologize."

His jaw ticked. "You're sure he won't be there?"

Mia touched his forearm. "When I talked to Dianne the other day, she said he's in the middle of a trial," she said, equally anxious as Hank not to run in to Tripp. Something about their last meeting still rang off key. "Only Mrs. Brooks' nurse will be there."

"I'm still not crazy about you going over there." His green eyes darkened to the color of the sea after a storm. "What if she's not done raking you over the coals?"

"I don't think that's the case. I think she wants closure." Mia cupped his face. "I need it too. If your brothers call, head over there and I'll join you when I'm done."

"Half-brothers," he said, then touched a finger to her nose. "And before you start needling me about telling them who I am, it's not happening."

She held up her hands in surrender. "You've already heard my arguments. If that's what you want, then I'll have to accept your decision. Let's find out what they've got to say about the flash drive, then we'll move on from there."

Hank tugged her close. "Together." He kissed her. "The two of us, just like it's always been."

"I'll meet you back here," she said before he closed her inside her car. "I love you." She'd said those words to him hundreds of times over the years. While they'd been true, they seemed so much truer now.

"Me too, angel."

Mia gripped the steering wheel as she aimed her car for the highway, the cars buzzing past making her nervous. She'd been cleared to drive in the last couple weeks, and she'd timed her visit for early afternoon to miss both rush hours. She'd been dependent on others for months, and the heady sensation of freedom elevated the sad task ahead.

Exiting the highway, she resisted the urge to turn toward her condo. The rebuilding was nearly complete, but her life was now taking her in a different direction. She made a mental note to contact a realtor about putting the place on the market.

Her stomach twisted as she drove past the courthouse that sat on the east side of the town square. Coming to terms with the certainty she'd never again practice law was a work in progress. Having decided it was her life's purpose at such an early age, she'd never considered other options. In her mind's eye, she could see herself in the courtroom, at her desk writing out her arguments or looking at evidence. Unfortunately, her imagination didn't match reality. She hoped in time, she'd find another passion that worked with her limitations.

She headed inland, toward the affluent part of town. After pulling in the circular driveway, she turned off the car. Mia exited, noting rose petals littering the ground. Mrs. Brooks would have a fit if she saw that. She wondered what had become of the family's longtime gardener, who'd lovingly tended the estate for decades. Just as she placed a foot on the first step, a uniformed man came around the corner.

"Hello," she said, calling to him. "What happened to Mr. Rodrigues?"

The man leaned the rake against his shoulder. "I ain't got no idea, lady. Mr. Brooks hired me back in the summer."

Mia noted the logo stitched on his shirt, Shamrock Landscapes, as well as the man's name. Patrick. The name leapt off his shirt—the same as one she'd written on her list. So that was the reason for the name. Tripp must have been making arrangements back in the spring to replace the family's gardener.

She crossed the deep porch and rang the bell. A mid-twenties woman dressed in scrubs answered. "Can I help you?" Traveler darted out the opening and scurried over to her. His tail thumped against the porch.

"Hi there, boy." Mia bent to scratch behind the dog's ears. "Did you miss me?" With a final pat on the head, she then addressed the woman still blocking the doorway. "I'm Mia Jones. Mrs. Brooks is expecting me."

The woman moved aside, leaving a small space for Mia to squeeze past. "Come in, please. Can I take your coat and purse?"

Mia hesitated, wavering between the desire not to seem rude and the need to make a quick retreat if necessary. "I'm still a little chilly, so I'll hang on to it for a while."

"Mrs. Brooks is upstairs in her room." She pointed with nails painted a bright red. "I'll take you to her."

"No need." Why Tripp was employing such low quality staff? Had his mother's illness drained the family's finances? "I know the way." As she passed the nurse, the woman's perfume assaulted her. Cloying and sweet, it seemed to burrow into her nostrils. None of the medical professionals who'd cared for her wore perfume.

Mia knocked at Mrs. Brooks' door, her stomach plummeting when a weak answer followed. "Hi." She wrestled with her emotions at the sight of a very sick woman propped up on pillows. Her skin was yellow and tight. Yet, some evidence to the woman's pride remained. She wore a pink quilted bed jacket with a matching scarf around her head.

The woman patted the bed. "Come sit here, dear. I'm so glad to see you again."

She eased down on the edge of the bed. "It's my pleasure, Mrs. Brooks."

"Call me Mother, will you? Once more like you used to."

Mia swallowed past the lump in her throat. The first time Tripp's mom made the offer had been one of the happiest days of her life. "I don't think that would be right, considering."

She closed her eyes as she lowered her head to the pillow. "I suppose you're right. So many regrets, especially how I handled things in the end."

"Tripp is your son," she said, justifying the woman's handling of the breakup.

"He is. He is indeed." Mrs. Brooks took her hand. "Are you doing okay? Have the police made any progress in your case?"

"I'm doing fine," Mia said, deciding to keep her answers superficial. "There's been no progress on the case, and I'm coming to terms with the fact my attacker may never be found."

"That's probably for the best. Life doesn't always take us in directions we hoped." She let out a breath. "I guess Tripp told you I'm dying."

"He said the cancer has spread, and you are refusing more treatments."

"I didn't see the point in dragging things out, but I couldn't meet my Maker with this unfinished business."

Mia brushed away her tears. "All is forgiven. Just concentrate on the happy times we spent together. I know I will. They were some of the best I've ever had," she said, letting go of drops of bitterness. "You made me welcome in your home when many wouldn't."

"You're kind to say so, dear."

"Why don't you rest? I can come again another day. All you have to do is ask." Then as she pressed a kiss to her forehead, Mia offered a prayer for Mrs. Brooks. "I'll be going now," she whispered when the woman's eyes shuttered closed.

At the bottom of the stairs, Mia looked around the empty foyer for the nurse. "Hello," she called to a seemingly empty house. Anxiety prickled her scalp. How would Mrs. Brooks receive the care she might need with no one within hearing? Mia crossed through the formal living room, Tripp's study, and the ballroom-size dining room on the way to the kitchen. At least it was being kept to Mrs. Brooks' exacting standards, unlike the garden. "Traveler," she called, wanting to say goodbye to the pet she'd grown so attached to. "Maybe the nurse is taking him for a potty break."

Finally, when her excuses for lingering dried up, she retraced her steps to the front door. Mia let out a breath, silently saying goodbye to the house and the people inside.

"No looking back." As Mia reached for the large brass handle to the front door, hands closed around her throat from behind. She scraped at the door while someone slowly cut off her air. She pulled at long finger nailed hands and kicked backward as she fought for her life.

Traveler's growl was the last thing she heard before darkness took her.

****

Hank shifted from foot to foot, keeping his eyes on Mia's car until all he could see was taillights. She shouldn't be going to the Brooks' estate, regardless of the old dame's need for absolution. Guilt twisted inside him. He should have done more to stop her—forbade her from going until he could accompany her. He rolled his eyes at the idiocy. "Hell, who am I kidding," he said, turning back to the apartment.

No one kept Mia from doing anything she set her mind to—most of the time, anyway. She hadn't let the bastard-brother secret out of the bag while they were at the Dowell's store despite a desire so great it radiated off her body.

For a moment, he'd considered doing the deed

himself. Witnessing how his half-brother coped with the RP had him jonesing for answers about how the man managed so well. Hank dared not stoke the flame of optimism. Cameron and Jason were oblivious to his existence and would likely want to stay that way. They wouldn't welcome him into the fold any more than their old man had.

Back inside, he tackled the few remaining boxes to be packed. He wanted the two of them ready to leave the moment Mia returned. As he shoved balls of newspaper into voids and then taped lids shut, his mind churned over Mrs. Brooks' hidden agenda. His gut told him it was more than making amends before she died. The only thing that made it tolerable to let Mia go was knowing Tripp wouldn't be there.

The trill of his phone brought him out of his musing. "Taggart here."

"This is Cameron at Dowell Computers."

Hanks pulse ticked up. "Have you been able to crack those files?"

He cleared his throat. "My brother is still working on it. He should be finished by the time you get here."

"You want us?" Hank asked finding it odd they wanted him to come by before the work was finished. "What did Mia say?"

"She didn't answer her phone. But the real reason I called was to talk to you. Would you mind coming to our office? I'd rather discuss this in person if you don't mind. You'll excuse my paranoia. Occupational hazard, I'm afraid."

He couldn't stop the chuckle that escaped his throat. Perhaps it wasn't so much an occupational hazard as a family trait. "I'll be there in forty-five minutes," he said, glad for an excuse to shorten the distance between him and Mia.

After grabbing his wallet, he flew over to LaGrange like he had rockets strapped to his truck. He entered the store to find Cameron and Jason crowded behind the counter. Their heads turned in unison, reactions to his presence equal and opposite.

"That was fast." Cameron came over to the counter and extended his hand. Hank took what was offered, his attention on the older brother whose assessing stare continued to pierce Hank.

Anxiety prickled his scalp. Hank had been so focused on finding out the contents of Mia's memory stick he'd forgotten to worry about being recognized. "What you got for me, guys?" he asked, struggling to hold a gaze so much like his own.

Jason joined his brother, leaning his forearms on the counter. "I'm going to come right out with it." He thumbed in Cameron's direction. "Unlike my brother here, I don't have the patience for beating around the bush."

Hank swallowed hard. "You're starting to make me nervous here, guys. Mia's visiting a sick friend. Should I call her?"

"See. I told you." Cameron punched his brother in the arm. "You always get people's back up. I'm sorry to worry you. What we wanted to discuss is of a personal nature."

"We know who you are," Jason said.

Hank folded his arms over his chest to hide the shock zinging through his body. "Oh, really? Do you make a habit of running background checks on all your clients? You might find that's bad for business."

"Didn't have to do that." He met Hank's gaze. "We already knew about you from our father."

Cameron turned to his brother. "You can't imagine how surprised we were when you called us. We thought you were finally reaching out to us."

A dozen questions tangled on the way to his lips. He grew light-headed and had to reach for the counter for support. "You knew?" he finally managed. "How long?"

Jason shoved his hands into his pockets and glared at the floor. "Our dad told us a couple days before his death."

"Another death bed confessional."

Cameron arched an eyebrow. "Excuse me."

"I suspect the woman Mia's visiting is doing the same."

"Speaking of Mia." Cameron grinned. "We like her. How long have you two been together? It can't be long. I remember the news mentioning a fiancé."

Jason cuffed his brother's head. "Let's stick to the topic at hand."

"Right," Cameron said. "Eight months ago, dear old Dad dropped this bombshell on us. He told us you'd contacted him many years ago." He looked down at the floor. "He said he didn't handle things well."

Jason's jaw ticked. "What my brother means is that he wanted to keep you a secret from our mother."

"That about sums it up," Hank said, recalling the painful scene. "If it weren't for Mia, I wouldn't have contacted you now," he added in case either man wondered his intentions. "I don't want—"

"Don't jump to conclusions," Jason bit out. He let out a breath. "Two days after his announcement, he dropped dead of a heart attack. We even contacted a private investigator to locate you."

"Well, now you've found me." Bitterness burned his gut. "You can go back to your life as usual. If you'll let me know when you get those files opened I appreciate it." He turned to leave, pissed as hell about the whole situation.

"Has it started yet?" Cam called from behind.

Hank stopped in his tracks. He toyed with the idea of ignoring the question. The need to know won the battle with his pride. "About six months ago. I ditched my F-18 in the drink. It ended my career."

Cam made a sympathetic noise. "That sucks ass, man. I started losing my sight in high school."

"I was in my early twenties when mine started," Jason added.

He could no longer resist the tide of questions rushing to his lips. Turning back to the two men, he asked. "How bad is it going to get?"

Jason shrugged. "Hard to say. There are a lot of variables. I have some central vision, as long as there's plenty of light."

"I'm a little worse, but it's been stable for the past few years," Cameron said.

Hank let out a breath, bitterness coloring what could have been—if not a happy meeting, at least a productive one. "Of all the things our father could pass on to us."

"It stops with me, as far as my wife and I are concerned. We've decided to adopt rather than risk passing this on to the next generation."

"My boyfriend and I don't plan to have kids," Cameron added.

Hank recalled the conversation he'd had with Mia not long ago. "Having grown up in foster care, Mia and I plan to go the adoption route when the time comes."

Jason reached across the counter to grip his shoulder. "I know we've dropped a lot on you. We can take this a slowly as you want, man."

The simple touch eased the knot of grief and bitterness inside him. While it didn't erase their father's rejection, it was a start. A good start. Both he and Mia yearned for a family that extended beyond the two of them. "God, I wish Mia was here to see this." No doubt she'd already have them sharing Thanksgiving.

Cam winked. "Speaking of the lovely lady, I shotgun the best man job."

Hank couldn't resist the smile playing at his lips. "I'll run that by her as well."

A chime came from Jason's computer. "Let's see what we've got."

Hank leaned closer to the computer screen. "Those look like financial statements."

Jason nodded. "They're records for a high-end clothing store, a home healthcare business, and a landscape company—all businesses that tend to lose a great deal of money. Look, this one processed five hundred thousand last year and still managed to lose money. This one's never shown a profit."

"Who owns these companies?" Hank asked.

"I'm on it." Cameron sat in front of another computer and a few clicks later he said, "They're owned by a company called Traveler Holdings, LLC."

The name tickled a memory Hank couldn't quite recall. "I've heard that name somewhere."

More key strokes from Cam. "Know a guy called

Charles Phillip Brooks III?"

A string of obscenities left Hank's lips before he could rein them in. "That's Tripp, Mia's asshole ex-fiancé."

"If I had to make a guess, I'd bet this guy was laundering money for someone." Jason said.

"Holy fuck." He leapt to his feet. "I've got to get Mia out of there."

"I thought you said she was at a friend's house."

His heart raced as fast as his mind. "Yeah—Tripp's mother. I gotta go—"

"Go to your girl. We've got all the time in the world to talk."

Hank called Mia as he raced to his truck. It immediately went to voice mail. "Call me back as soon as you get this." Thirty seconds later, he dialed her again. "Never mind the first message. I want you back at the apartment. I don't care what you have to say to Mrs. Brooks, I want you home now."

Hank counted his heartbeats on the tortuous drive over there, but as he pulled up the drive of the Brooks' mansion and didn't see Mia's car some of the tension left his body. "Thank God." He dialed Mia's number again, hoping the reason she wasn't answering was because she was driving. He hoofed it up the walkway to the front door.

"Can I help you?" a woman dressed in nurse's scrubs asked.

"My friend was visiting Mrs. Brooks."

She nodded "Yes, she was here, but left quite a while ago."

Relief washed through him. "Did she say where she was going?" he asked before the woman could close the door on him.

****

Sometime later, Mia groaned as she swam up from unconsciousness. *Wow, what a nightmare she'd had.* No more ice cream before bed if they caused this type of dream. She tried stretching her stiff arms and legs and found she couldn't. A cold sweat instantly misted her skin. She struggled against the duct tape binding her wrists at the small of her back. A wet tongue swiped the side of her face. "Traveler," she breathed. "What happened?"

Light peeked around the edges of window blinds and allowed her a dimmed view of *her* bedroom, the one Mrs. Brooks had offered for use while Mia recovered from her injuries. Thinking of the woman on the floor above, Mia called, "Mother Brooks, help."

The door opened and a hunched figure limped in. "Scream all you want, dearie," the ailing woman said. "There's no one here to come to your rescue this time."

Sickening truth washed over her. "It was Tripp who attacked me."

"Hardly." Mrs. Brooks inched closer. "My boy doesn't have the stomach for violence."

Icy shock flashed through her body. "It was you?"

Mrs. Brooks barked a laugh that set off a coughing fit. "Not me personally. The only time I enjoy hands-on activity is in the garden. I supervised, though." She pushed past Traveler whose whine morphed into a low growl. "You were barely breathing, and your pulse was so weak when I had Dillon and Patrick leave you on the trail. I thought for sure you'd die."

"You attacked me because I found out Tripp was having an affair?"

"Hardly." Mrs. Brooks brushed Mia's hair from her face, the gesture sending ripples of terror across her skin. "All men cheat. It's a fact of life, and if I did away with every woman who discovered my boy couldn't keep his thing in his pants, I'd have a lot of dead girlfriends on my hands."

The woman's calmness scared Mia more than displays of anger could. "Then why?"

The sound of the doorbell cut off her answer. Mia screamed, only to have her calls for help drowned out by Traveler's barks.

"Shut up, both of you." The woman produced a small gun out of her housecoat pocket to back up her order.

Terror raced through her veins. Mia clamped her lips together, and thank God, the dog did as well. Then the woman extracted a cotton handkerchief from the same pocket and shoved it in Mia's mouth. She shuffled to the door and opened it a crack.

Hank's low timbre drifted from the foyer, escalating Mia's desperation. Her hands and feet still bound, she rolled off the bed in hopes of making enough commotion to draw his attention. Her body thudded against the deep carpet, but only succeeded in knocking the breath from her lungs. The muffled exchanged between Hank and the nurse continued without interruption.

Mrs. Brooks shot a glare in Mia's direction. "Serves you right, stupid girl." Then the old woman shook a bony finger in her direction. "Now don't go anywhere. I'll be right back," she said, slipping out the door.

Chapter Twenty

An elderly woman slipped around the nurse. "Mr. Taggart, what can I do for you?" The woman tottered a few steps onto the porch and motioned for the other woman to close the door. It took a second for Hank to recognize the hunched-over woman wearing a pink scarf around her head. Tripp's mother had aged a hundred years since he'd last seen the proud, lively woman. "I'm looking for Mia, ma'am."

She coughed into a lace handkerchief. "I'm sorry I can't help you. She left some time ago."

His gaze shot past her to bore into the door behind her, desperate to determine if Tripp was holding Mia inside. A gnawing certainty rooted him to the wooden planks, but he could hardly push past a dying woman to get inside. At least not until he had proof she was lying. "If you hear from Mia, please tell her to call me right away."

Mrs. Brooks smiled up at him. "I'll be sure to do that. Good day."

Not until she moved back inside and the latch thudded into place could he force himself off the porch. Returning to his truck, he drove down the long drive to the main road, his mind racing with scenarios to get inside the Brooks' mansion. The sense of impotency roiled in his gut. At the end of the neighborhood, he pulled over on the side of the road to call Detective

Price.

"Mr. Taggart, how are you and Mia doing?"

His growing fear burst from his lips. "I can't find Mia. She went to visit Mrs. Brooks a couple hours ago. I drove over to the house, and they say she's not there, nor is she answering her phone. I need you to get over here now."

"Hold up a moment," Detective Price began, using soothing tones. "I can't send a car over for that. Besides, she's probably running an errand and can't hear her phone. Just relax, Mr. Taggart. Give it another couple hours."

"It'll be too late." Hank tightened his grip on the phone, the desire to rail at the cop gnawing at him. What would it take for the cops to see what he'd suspected all along—the Brooks family wasn't as upstanding as they appeared? "That natty bastard has her."

"How do you know this? Did you see or hear something?"

A lie poised on Hank's lips. He'd gladly accept the consequences if it turned out he was wrong, but if the detective had two brain cells to rub together, the facts should prompt him to act. "No, I didn't, but here's what makes me think Tripp is holding Mia against her will. Yesterday she found a flash drive among her things. When she tried to read the files stored there, she discovered they were encrypted. After taking the memory stick to a computer expert, I learned they contained Tripp Brooks' financial records. It appears he was laundering money for someone." If that wasn't enough to get the cop to act, tear gas and a battering ram were his next options.

A pair of heartbeats passed in silence before Detective Price responded. "Where are you now?"

"Down the road from the Brooks' house." But not for long. If the detective wouldn't take action, Hank would.

"I've got units rolling now. Do not go back to that house."

"I'll stay put," he said, ending the call and chunking the phone onto the seat. "Yeah, right," he growled to himself. After the crap it took to get the detective to act, Hank wasn't willing to stand back and hope for the best. He moved his truck to one of the subdivision's quieter cul-de-sacs and hoofed it through wooded lots and around fenced backyards to the large estate. He eased around the back of the house, hoping to find a window to peer into. His insides churned like he was at sea in a hurricane. Why had he allowed her to go? For once, it was Mia's tender heart getting her into trouble, instead of her hard head.

Ancient magnolias lined the perimeter of the Brooks' home. Their low branches provided ample cover so he was able advance to within a few yards of a bank of windows overlooking a bricked patio. He drew closer to the house, moving with excruciatingly slow steps.

"Stop right there," came a voice emerging from the same trees that offered him cover. "What do you think you're doing?"

Hank eased around to face a man dressed in a Shamrock Landscaping uniform. His attention brushed over the man's nondescript features to the gun he held in his hand.

****

The moment Mrs. Brooks left, Mia rolled on her side and began working to get her hands around front. She drew her knees to her chest and with a lot of wiggling, managed to loop her arms over her feet. Her wrists were still bound, but after extracting the handkerchief from her mouth, she could gnaw her way free. She bit into the duct tape, tearing at the rough edge that cut into her lip. When that proved slow-going, she tried twisting her wrists. Between that effort and the rolling around she'd done earlier, she'd exhausted herself. Perspiration ran into eyes already burning with tears.

Damn. Damn. Damn. What else could she do to free herself? Unable to stand, she scanned the corners and under the bed for a left-behind object she could use to cut the tape or defend herself and Traveler. She couldn't find so much as a nail file. Frustration mixed with fear to form a swirling, bitter cocktail. Tears streamed down her face, knowing without outside intervention she'd never escape. Traveler lay next to her and licked her face as if he too understood the direness of her situation.

"Not looking too good, is it boy?"

The door clicked open. Mia quickly stuck the handkerchief back in her mouth and lowered her arms. A low growl escaped from the dog's throat. "Shut up," Mrs. Brooks bit out. She stepped to the far side of the room where Mia had rolled underneath the only window. "I'm back," she said in a singsong way as if she were returning to a party. She lowered onto a slipper chair and leaned over to examine Mia. "I sent your lover on his merry way."

Hank left her behind. Despair tightened its grip on

her.

"Where was I?" Mrs. Brooks tapped her finger to her lips then brightened as if finally remembering the punchline of a joke. "Oh yes. We were discussing all the problems you've caused." She plucked the handkerchief from Mia's mouth. "I might as well let you ask all those questions I know are swimming around in that brilliant brain of yours." She eyed Mia who was lying on her side straining to look up at the woman. "You are still smart, right?"

Shock danced along her spine. When had madness taken hold of the once gentle lady? Mia appealed to the ghost of sanity she hoped remained in the insane woman's mind. "Please let me go. I thought you cared about me."

Mrs. Brooks waggled a boney finger at Mia. "It's all your fault I have to kill you. You know that right?"

Fresh fear raced through Mia's veins. "You're right. It was my fault," she said, placating the woman. "Don't tell me anything," she pleaded, willing to say anything to buy her freedom "We can forget this all happened. I swear I don't remember anything before the accident, and I won't say a thing about this."

A lightning-quick hand slapped her face. "Stupid girl."

The effort of striking Mia set off a coughing fit. When she finally could breathe again, she leaned in close. "You were perfect for my son—pretty enough for social engagements, eager to please, and sitting on inside information from the district attorney's pending investigations—but you had to go and ruin it." She let out an exasperated huff. "Then it fell to me to make things right. My boy couldn't even manage that much—the fool." She clenched her fist. "I've been fixing his messes his whole life. I suppose that will be my legacy to this family."

Would the woman add Hank to her list of victims when she was done with her? "Hank and I are moving away. If you let me go, we'll be out of the state in two hours."

Mrs. Brooks cocked her head, her small, dark eyes glinting as she stared. "If only I could believe you, but I can't risk it any more than I can wait to let the cancer take me. I wish things could be different. If only you'd left well enough alone." She tsked at Mia. "Always so inquisitive. And scrupulous, too. A deadly combination, don't you think?" The woman let out a breath. "If only Tripp hadn't gotten involved with those Yankees from Boston. Whitey's Boys, I think he calls them."

Mia sucked in a breath. In the past couple months, a reporter with the *LaGrange Daily Journal* had been writing exposés on a small offshoot of the Boston mafia that made their way south, seeing coastal North Carolina as fresh territory. The group stuck to the classics, drugs and prostitution with a little extortion on the side.

While she remembered those facts learned long before her attack, details of her former fiancé's involvement eluded her. What had tipped her off to his illegal activities? Were financial records what she'd stored in the flash drive?

With Mrs. Brooks pointing a gun at Mia, it was unlikely she'd ever learn the answer to those questions, or any of a dozen other queries. She did give voice to the most pressing concern of the moment. "What are you going to do with me?" She hoped to keep the woman talking as long as possible while she figured out what to do.

The woman pressed the gun to Mia's temple. "I considered shooting you," she began, speaking as calmly as if they were discussing where to go for lunch. "However, that leaves me with your body to dispose of—again."

She fell silent, cocking her head, before nodding to herself. "Tell me what you think of this story. A nurse, seeing her ailing patient's wealth, began stealing from her—little bits here and there, not enough to immediately be detected by any but the most observant visitor." She used the gun to gesture toward Mia. "You, being the do-gooder you are, realized the woman's nefarious deeds and confronted her. Katie ties you up, forces me to send Hank away, and then sets fire to the house to cover her tracks."

Horror at the woman's descent into insanity and depravity washed over Mia. "You're willing to kill yourself to cover up for Tripp?"

Mrs. Brooks smirked. "Haven't you figured out by now there's nothing I won't do for my boy? But I have my own selfish reasons as well." She drew in several heavy breaths. "I've been in so much pain in the past few days, and it's only going to get worse." She pressed her free hand to her chest. "I've never been very good at suffering."

Her gaze shot to Mia's. "On the other hand, you, my dear, are a pro."

****

Hank eased his hands above his shoulders. "It's all cool. I'm just looking for my girlfriend, buddy. She was here earlier. Have you seen her?"

"She's gone. I heard Mrs. Brooks tell you that a few minutes ago." He brandished the gun at Hank. "Head toward the back door. I'm taking you inside until we can figure out what to do with you."

With deliberate movements, Hank complied with the orders as the landscaper cursed someone called Katie.

A muffled thud behind Hank halted his steps. He spun. Two officers had tackled the man to the ground. *Finally.* Hank's attention shifted between the action on the ground and the rear of the house. Every nerve screamed for him to storm the French doors that led into the home's library, but he had to be smart about how he did it. He studied the numerous windows, praying none of the home's occupants were watching. Heart thundering away, he inched his way toward the house until from the corner of his eye he spotted Detective Price approaching from the other side.

The officer paid no heed to the two uniformed cops or the now handcuffed landscaper. Instead, his narrowed gaze was trained on him. Hank nodded toward the magnolias where he met the officer under the branches' cover.

"I thought I told you to stay where you were," Price began. "I ought to…"

Hank cut off the man's threat. "Arrest me later. Hell, I'll even crawl in the back seat of the cruiser, but get my girl out of there first."

The cop reached for Hank, and for a second he figured he was following through with his threat. Instead, he patted Hank's arm. "I know you want us to go in there guns blazing, but we've got to be smart about this if we want Mia out alive." He nodded over his shoulder to the pair of patrol cars which had managed to creep along the driveway. "Get over there and let us do our job."

If they'd been doing their job in the first place... Hank kept that to himself and started toward the cruisers. Dread settled on his shoulders and weighted his steps. Without a miracle, he'd never see Mia again. *His eyes.* He'd gladly trade his sight to save her.

A shot rang out. Hank jolted as if the bullet struck him. *Mia.*

****

Anger surged inside Mia. All the suffering she handled with such supposed grace came at the hand of this family. Mia struggled against her bindings. There was no way she could passively stand by—or lay awkwardly on the floor as was the case—while this woman enacted her plans. Still hogtied, she lunged at Mrs. Brooks.

Traveler followed her example, helping Mia knock the woman off the chair. He caught Mrs. Brooks' arm in his mouth as she raised the gun. The crack of gunshot echoed off the walls but did nothing to deter the dog's attack.

Mia rolled out of the way as Traveler went for Mrs. Brooks' throat. She turned away from the brutal fight, but while she could prevent herself from seeing the gore, nothing could block out the sound of teeth meeting bone. Mia too made good use of her mouth, ripping frantically at the duct tape until it finally gave way. Then she went to work on her ankles. Once she was free, she scrambled to her feet.

Mia burst through the French door leading outside. She rounded the side of the house, ready to bulldoze the gardener if he blocked her escape. The cops, their weapons drawn, met her on the way out. She drew up short for a split second before Hank came into her sightline.

He caught her as she threw herself into his arms. "Thank God," he groaned, scooping her into his arms and racing toward an ambulance's open doors. He lowered her to the waiting gurney, only to envelope her in an embrace so strong it squeezed the breath from her lungs. "My sweet angel." He buried his face in her hair.

"Sir, we need to look her over."

Hank pulled back, anxious eyes combing over her.

She held up wrists rubbed raw from the tape. "I'm fine. Nothing some ointment and a couple bandages won't fix."

The paramedics stepped back, and Hank crawled on the gurney next to her and pulled her into his lap, rocking as he chanted her name. Finally safe, she released the cap on her emotions. Tears flowed, until they dissolved into hiccups and she had drenched his shirt. She survived. Somehow, from a tangle of arms, paws, legs, and a gun, she'd managed to escape.

"You came back for me," she murmured when she could finally speak. Of all she'd been through in the past couple hours, she'd reached her lowest point hearing Hank left her.

He tilted her chin. "I never left, angel. Never. I knew Tripp had you in there. I just had to find a way to get you out."

"Not him," she said, still perplexed how Pamela Brooks' slide into insanity had gone undetected by her family.

Hank's brow knotted. "Say that again."

"Mrs. Brooks, not Tripp."

"That tiny, frail woman?"

Mia nodded. "She had help, but it was her all along—the attack and the fire."

"Not the other stuff, though." Detective Price approached the couple as Hank added, "Tripp was up to his eyeballs with the Irish Mafia."

"I want to hear everything you know, Mr. Taggart, but right now I need to hear from Miss Jones what happened inside."

Hank shot the detective a glare. "Leave her alone. Why don't you do your own police work and figure at least one thing out for yourself."

Price's jaw ticked. "My men are going through the house as we speak, but I need to know who all was involved in holding Miss Jones captive."

Mia patted Hank's arm, letting her hand slide down to twine through his. "It's okay. He needs to know this." She turned to Price. "The gardener, Mrs. Brooks, and her nurse are the only people I saw—and Tripp's dog, Traveler. He attacked Mrs. Brooks which was how I was able to bite through the duct tape."

"Start from the beginning." Price flipped open the cover of a tablet.

"Your questions can wait, Detective." Hank motioned for the paramedics. "I want these guys to take her to the hospital first." He cut his eyes at Mia. "No arguments from you. At the very least you're dehydrated, and I think that's a knot I see popping up on your forehead."

Mia touched the bump, her thoughts turning to the possible side effects of a seemingly small knock to the head. "Good idea." She leaned back and let the medics give her the once over as the day caught up with her. A short time later, with an IV in her hand, she was being transported to LaGrange General. "Find out what's happening to Traveler," she called to Hank who would follow the ambulance in his truck.

****

Two bags of IV fluids, an MRI, and many hours later, Mia dropped her head to the gurney's stiff mattress. Much to Hank's displeasure, Detective Price had been asking her questions between nurses coming into the ER cubical and trips to radiology. Mia insisted the cop get his questions out of the way. "From what Mrs. Brooks told me, she played no role in Tripp's money laundering, but it was she who had a couple low-level thugs try to kill me."

Detective Price flipped the cover closed on his electronic pad. "I guess that's how her alibi checked out. She had someone else do her dirty work for her, and the landscape guys from your list had other members of their mob cover for them. Without the information you saved on that flash drive, I doubt we'd ever have connected the Brooks to Whitey's Boys. I think you've given us enough to bring down the lot of them."

Mia's heart warmed. The TBI prevented her from trying another case, but she still had the satisfaction of knowing she'd put a few more criminals behind bars. "I'm pretty pleased with myself even if it took me months to figure out I had the clues to solving my own case all along."

He stared at the ground for a moment before lifting his gaze to hers. "Miss Jones, I wish I could have done better by you, but I'm damned if I know how I would

264

have done it."

She tightened her grip on Hank's hand, who at the detective's words had tensed beside her. "I don't blame you. They were all good at covering their tracks, especially Mrs. Brooks."

Price stood and extended his hand to her. "You're a resilient woman, and I wish you all the best."

"Thank you." Fatigue settled into her bones. Yet, things were hardly finished. "I guess I'll be seeing you at the trials."

During the detective's questions, they'd gotten word a warrant had been issued for Tripp as well as the gardener's partner. Mrs. Brooks would escape earthly justice having died on the way to the hospital. "One more thing before you go," she said to the detective as he turned to leave. "Explain to Animal Control about Traveler. He's a good dog, never even growled at the mailman before today."

He nodded. "Will do. I'm sure they'll be able to release him to family once his quarantine period is over."

Once the cop left the cubicle, Mia closed her eyes and reached for Hank's hand. "Take me home."

"Your neurologist may want to keep you overnight."

She cracked an eyelid. "No. I don't care what Dr. Cowboy has to say. I'll never spend another night in a hospital."

"Okay, if you say so." Hank pressed his lips to her palm. "We still have one problem. I packed everything up. It's all in a U-Haul sitting in front of the apartment."

"Even better. Let's just start driving, find

somewhere to sleep along the way."

"I have another suggestion. What if—"

Her pulse ticked up. "Go ahead," she prompted, the first rays of optimism peeking out from beneath the blanked of grief.

"I talked to Cam and Jason."

The corner of her mouth lifted. "Like, really talked?"

He squeezed her hand. "I'd like to get to know them better if you're willing to stay close by."

"Absolutely." Her energy made a rebound. "We could buy a house with the money from my condo, one with room for a dog."

"And a couple kiddos when you're ready," he added, saying words she never imagined coming from his lips.

Pure joy whelmed her soul, bubbling over in tears that streaked down her cheeks. Was it wrong to plan their future while other's lives imploded? Her chin dropped to her chest. Poor Dianne, even if she'd played no role in her family's scheme, her life now lay in shambles.

"Stop it." He tilted her chin.

"I feel guilty for planning our life while someone else's is falling apart."

"You have no reason to. We need to look to the future. Plan all you want—Thanksgiving, a wedding, whatever your heart desires. It won't be perfect, but we have earned our forever."

Mia clung to Hank—friend, lover, family—her everything. "I'm—" She choked on the words, as she would likely always do when her thoughts stumbled over each other.

Happy failed to express the right sentiment, for it relied too heavily on circumstances that could shift without warning. Lucky, content, a dozen adjectives came to mind that didn't live up to the surge of emotion inside her.

With Hank at her side and the future before them, the losses she endured seemed worth the price. Mia crawled into his lap, thankful for the journey that led her to this moment.

"I'm blessed."

A word about the author...

Melissa Klein writes contemporary romance. You can visit Melissa's website at
www.melissakleinromance.com